WITH SHUDDERING FALL

Joyce Carol Oates
author of *By the North Gate*

WITH SHUDDERING FALL

THE VANGUARD PRESS, INC., NEW YORK

for DONALD A. DIKE

What is done out of love always takes place beyond good and evil.

NIETZSCHE

CONTENTS

SPRING

1

One morning in early spring a man and his daughter made their way along the country lane that led back from their house. The man walked ahead, stepping easily over the frozen ruts. The girl, hugging a paper bag, walked clumsily—she wore old shoes of her father's, great cracked shoes hardened with mud but suited well for this trip; she did not want to ruin her own shoes. Karen had not wanted to come with her father to visit the sick man—the crazy hermit, everyone called him—but her older sister, Celine, had gotten out of it somehow, and her father would not go alone carrying food; that was woman's work. Karen muttered silently to herself arguments she might have used. Sickness—she had a stomachache. Fear of the old man—she had been afraid of him all her life. Or she might have simply refused to go. But before her father's words all defenses vanished and there she had stood, sulking, cleaning out a canning jar while the soup warmed on the stove. Celine had rattled pots around, trying to look busy. Finally she cried with vexation: "You needn't look so put upon! He loves you best, you shouldn't mind going back with him!"

Karen had stared around at her sister. Celine was twenty-six now, but looked older. She had always seemed old to Karen, who was nine years younger, but this morning her thin little eyebrows, her small, moist eyes, her flat cheeks seemed those of a woman who had never known youth. I will never look like that, Karen thought clearly. Karen and Celine were the last of the children at home: their three brothers and two sisters had all gone off or married or both. Their closeness in the last several years had never developed into intimacy, but Celine, interpreting Karen's look as a reproach to her own rudeness, said, "Albert's taking me for a drive this afternoon. Would you like to come along?" Albert was Celine's fiancé of sorts—a teacher at the town high school. "Would you? I know Albert wouldn't mind."

The thought of going for a ride that afternoon ought to have pleased Karen, or at least made her indifferently curious, but in the face of the visit to the old man it was impossible to care about anything. They were nearing his cabin now, having left the lane, and were following a path toward the creek. Karen walked along doggedly. Her eyes were still stale from sleep. Down at the creek swift brown water rushed against the ice, cutting a channel through it. Every day the channel grew wider, the ice was broken away an inch at a time. Thick muddy water in the rapids churned with uprooted bushes, propelling sticks and trunks and parts of boats before it. As they neared old Rule's cabin Karen stared through the dead weeds to the water: it was alive and moving, squirming, the only real movement in this chill morning. Only a few weeks ago she had walked out onto the snow-covered ice, and now the creek had changed entirely—it looked luring and sinister, and the rapids gurgled as if they gloated over its violent metamorphosis. Karen pressed the paper bag against her and felt the vague warmth of the jar of soup.

Then they were at old Rule's cabin. An eyesore, a disgrace: tar-paper shanty with old rusty pieces of tin nailed up any which way. Plyboard hanging out of one broken window like an arm waving them off, and, around the shanty, piles of junk. Scrap metal and parts of crates and soaked, limp cardboard lashed together with twine. Boards with raw nails sticking out of them, short rusted rolls of chicken wire, barrel staves, junk washed up on the creek shore. Karen remembered a time years ago when Rule had tried to sort out his junk, putting boards and wooden material into one pile, metal into another, miscellaneous things like nails and cardboard into another. But apparently he had given up and all piles expanded outward, touched one another and dissolved into one great, insane pile of debris: to look at it was to invite a sensation of madness.

The inside was no different. Junk cluttered the front room, leaving just enough space for a passageway. Things were neater inside, lashed together with twine, but a strong, sweet, sickening odor eased out to Karen and her father and Karen felt again the impulse to refuse to go. "Pa," she whimpered. Her father did not look around. He raised one big hand and rapped at the door. The shanty seemed to tremble beneath his blow.

No answer. This almost pleased Karen's father. "We're com-

17

ing in," he announced. He opened the rickety door and went inside. "You awake, Rule?" he said. Karen held her breath. The stench of the cabin, contrasting so with the fresh morning air, made her feel nauseated; but she followed her father inside. "That boy of yours found his way home yet?" Karen's father said chattily, though he could not yet see Rule. He picked his way through the clutter at the doorway to the back room and, turning just a little, motioned for Karen to follow.

The old man lay in the tiny back room. He was in a bed of some kind, with dirty quilts piled up around him. Karen was surprised at how quiet it was—there was no sound except the rushing of the creek; and for an instant she had the foolish thought that dying here, in this little room, might not be so bad. "Well. No boy come back yet, huh?" Karen's father said, putting his hands on his hips in a grand gesture. "How you feeling this morning, Rule?"

The old man lay inside the quilts and looked up at the ceiling as if he had not noticed anyone at all. His eyes were soft and black and his hair, though he was supposed to be old, was also black, not touched with gray like Karen's father's. "I asked how you were this morning," Karen's father said. He took a deep breath. There was no sound except the churning of the water down in the creek. "She made some soup for you to eat," Karen's father said, and the "she" made Karen's heart jump a little. "It's to get your stomach warmed and make the blood move faster. She made it all specially for you."

Karen had eased over to the window. She was hardly able to breathe. A draft of cold air touched her face here and she pretended interest in the scene outside: colorless world, colorless morning sky. Light did not seem to come from the sky but pervaded everything—so sullen, so massive, it certainly gave no hint of spring. "We thought maybe your boy would be here

18

when we come," Karen's father said. "Most likely he'll be here any day now. Maybe today."

She saw that Rule was still staring up at the ceiling stubbornly. His face had hollows and jutting lines and looked like a mask. He licked his lips. He said, "Get out of here."

A smile flickered about Karen's father's face. "I s'posed you'd welcome us like this—always were one to keep folks away. Never knew a friend when you had one. Here, Karen," he said, "let's have that soup. Here. I brought you a spoon too."

"I don't want it," Rule said sullenly, as if he had been tricked into talking. "You two just get out of here."

Karen's father was opening the jar of soup. "A person must have someone to look after him in his last illness," he said ceremoniously. "A man like you, dying, seems he ought to have more charity toward the world." At this remark the old man's eyes narrowed and Karen thought that he did not look old at all, but as he had always looked when she and her brothers or sisters had come upon him down at the creek, sitting on his rock and fishing. He had always ignored them, even when they hid in the weeds and threw stones in the water to scare the fish away; but none of them had had the courage to sit on his rock, even when he wasn't around. "Your trouble is always been pride," Karen's father said, "but what need is there for pride now? Two neighbors come to help you. Or do you s'pose that son of yours will make it back in time—s'pose he'll have some soup to give you?"

Rule smiled contemptuously. "Do you s'pose so?" Karen's father said, warming to his argument. "A man-grown boy you ain't seen for a lifetime. Ha!" He dragged a wooden box over to the bed and sat on it and crossed his mighty legs. His leather boots gleamed sullenly in the poor light. "Always been the un-neighborly kind," he said expansively, as if he were addressing

19

a number of people. "Here you been down by the creek for so long, on the edge of my property, and never come over to see me except once to bring a little kid home—a long time ago—or help us with that fire once— I told her, one of them, it was because you never learned any better."

"Told who?" Rule said. He cleared his throat.

"One of them. They all thought the same, all women."

"Who was it?"

"It was her mother, Karen's," Karen's father said after a moment. He had married and outlived four wives. "The one with the hair like Karen's—almost pure white, hardly any color in it. Do you remember that one? Died ten years or so ago, maybe twelve. Now, a person with proper belief like myself," Karen's father said, changing the subject so easily that Karen was surprised and saw that even Rule looked puzzled, "he don't just let another one lay alone and die. It's against our belief. We got to come and help."

There was a joke in his last words that Rule was supposed to see, but if he did, he gave no sign of it. "Well, you'll come to us in the end. We got to do something with you—with your body. Do you refuse us the chance to be charitable?" Karen's father said. He sat with the jar of soup in his big hands, about to offer it to Rule. "We'll put you over with our family, the same place I'll be put when I die; how's that? Take care of you. A man gets all in a sweat, thinking there might be nobody to take care of him."

"My son—"

Rule stopped, as if tricked. His words hung in the air around them. Karen's father grinned. "Yes, yes, your son. Coming home, ain't he? Let the children see to their fathers' deaths— their fathers got them into the world, let them get their fathers out of it! Right, Karen?"

Karen lowered her eyes.

20

"She knows. Women know. My youngest girl there. I can remember her a baby like only yesterday, can't you, Rule? Some of these days now she looks just like her mother—a queer thing to see, at breakfast and such. Gives me a start. . . . Are you scairt of it, Rule?"

"I'm tired," said the old man.

"Ain't scairt?"

"An' cold too. I'm cold too," Rule said oddly.

"They say it starts in your little toe and spreads up—up your legs and all, till it gets your heart. A cold feeling."

Karen turned suddenly. She fumbled with the buttons of her sweater. "Where are you going?" her father said.

"Back home."

"You stay here."

She hesitated. Her eyes were blurred and stinging.

"You stay here," her father said.

"Pa—"

"I told you."

There was a silence. Karen stared at the doorway, her back to her father and Rule. She was looking at something there without seeing it—a word carved into the doorframe. SHERTON. She blinked back tears, staring at the word as if it would help her. That was the name of Rule's son. Sherton. Shar. "You don't need me here," she said with a courage she had not known she possessed.

"You knew Rule all your life," her father said, "and you ain't leaving him now. And don't you cry about it either."

She could feel when his attention shifted away. The box on which he sat creaked. "You take some of this warm soup," he said. "Before it gets cold."

Something happened then; there was a scuffling noise, then a crash. Karen turned to see the jar broken on the floor. The coarse dark soup ran hungrily between the floor boards. Karen's father wiped angrily at his legs. "Now look at that! Look what you done!" But when Rule did not reply, when his gaze shifted again to the ceiling, Karen's father relaxed strangely and smiled again. "A hard one to take care of, ain't you? Proud of it too, ain't you?"

He laughed and took out his pipe. It took a while to light. Finally Karen's father blew out a cloud of smoke, spat a little toward the floor, and said, "Think you'll know him when he comes?"

"Maybe," said Rule.

"Time changes them all." The box creaked again. "He looked like you, I thought, the older he got. He had the same look. . . . Remember the baby that got lost? That was Karen, wasn't it? I came back here and her mother with me, a passel of kids following, all excited and scairt. I asked you if you seen her and right then around the corner of the shanty we saw her running, a baby girl, running in the dirt, with that boy of yours, Shar, running slow after her, pretending he couldn't catch her. . . . You remember that? Then he saw us and never changed how he looked and took hold of her and swung her up into the air, her feet going like she was still running, he swung her up into the air and gave her to me. . . . Do you remember that?"

"Yes," said Rule.

"A big boy for his age, always dirty. He run away from home off and on, and the time he was sixteen he never come back. So that was that. . . . What's that underneath your bed there? Part of a trap, ain't it, a rusty trap chain?"

Rule leaned over and looked down. "Looks like," he said. He lay back and smiled a little, tightly and rather cruelly, his gaze spreading to Karen as well.

"Pa," Karen said.

"What?"

"I want to—"

"You want to go home again?" He looked right around at her, as if he could hardly believe it. "What the hell is got into you this morning? Can't you hear what your father says to you? A man here you might never see again—how can you be so quick to get rid of people that you knew all your life?"

"He isn't going to die!" Karen said angrily.

"What?"

"He isn't. He isn't. You let me go—"

Her father took her arm at the wrist. She began crying softly and passively, like a child. "A big girl like this!" her father said. "What are you crying for? For him or yourself?" He turned to look at Rule, maybe exchange a glance with him. "She's thinking how time fooled her, all along she thought it was a fog a person could walk in and out of, and here it turned into something that runs away from you. It goes on, it runs away from you. Look at Rule there, he doesn't feel sorry for himself. What is there to feel sorry about? It will be Rule first, and then me second, in a few years, and then you too—one thing you can be damn sure of."

Karen tried to pull away. "Please let me go," she said.

"Karen!"

She began to cough. "I can't breathe," she whimpered, "it's the air here, he's got something—some old stale food—something I can't—"

"You stand still, here!"

"I don't want to— Let me go, I don't want to stay here, I hate it here, I hate it! I hate it and I hate him, I hate everything here, I hate everything—I hate him—*him*—"

"Karen, don't you make me mad. Don't make me—"

"I do!" she cried wildly. "I hate him for what's happening, all of this, and you—and you too—"

He must have let her go, for the next instant she was running through the front room, tripping over junk, sobbing with fear and horror at what she had done. Everything seemed to have happened in a dream. And once outside in the cold air, once running back to the house, she could hardly tell the difference between the fresh air and the deathly air of Rule's cabin—it was as if the stench had permeated her and was carried with her, all the way along the path and the lane and into the warm house and up to her room.

2

Karen lay in her rumpled bed, staring at the ceiling, when her sister opened the door. "Karen," she said. Karen looked around. She felt the impulse to cry out at her sister, tell her to get away, not to come to her room any more, but speaking would have demanded too much effort; so she lay still and stared. "Albert just called and I told him you'd be along. He said that was fine and asked if he should bring his cousin along . . . you know . . . and I told him you'd like that. Is it all right?"

"What time is it?" Karen said.

"About twelve-thirty," Celine said. She waited, but Karen had nothing to say. "What's wrong with you? Are you sick?"

"Rule is sick," said Karen. She sat up and rubbed her eyes. Crying had exhausted her and left her oddly hollow and cold. "Is Pa downstairs?"

"No, he's out with the men. They're going to start adding onto the barn."

Karen looked toward her steamy window. If she stood at it she could probably see the men over on the hill where the barns were. "Did Pa say anything about me?"

"What's wrong with you? They were talking about the barn at lunch and Pa asked where you were, I think, but nothing else. Are you sick?"

"No," said Karen. She lay back down and closed her eyes. "You can leave me alone now," she said.

Seeing Albert's cousin Jack again had no effect at all on Karen, though everyone else seemed a little embarrassed. As they left the big house, making their way down the absurd stone steps Karen's great-grandmother had wanted, Jack smiled tightly and told Karen how glad he was to see her again. "Yes," said Karen.

On the opposite hill a few men stood about, talking. Karen could not distinguish her father from the hired men. "So many cows now," she murmured. "He gets up himself to make them run around at night to keep from freezing." Jack, staring down at the steps, nodded quickly as if he had meant to say something of the kind himself; in reality, Karen supposed, he had no idea of what she was talking about. With other people Jack was charming, bright, sometimes a little loud; he conversed easily and with a certain delight in himself and his words; with Karen he became vague, worried, groping after her meaning while the time for his reply passed. Even his habitual posture with her was stooped, making him look already old, at least tired and uncertain. Everyone remarked about it.

They had met at a church picnic when Karen was sixteen. Rather, they had met again: everyone in Pools Brook knew everyone else. Jack was too old for Karen to remember from school—he was about twenty-seven—though he claimed to remember her. He was tall, with a blond, heavy, handsome head, and that day he had worn a new-looking suit and tie, and the girl he was with was dressed in a soft, shiny, rich white outfit. Later it was the girl's outfit, especially her big straw hat, that Karen remembered. Jack and the girl had drifted by to look at the cattle judging and Jack, whose father was in gypsum, stopped to talk to Karen's father. Karen liked to hear other people talk to her father; she liked their tones of respect, their careful words, their repeated "Mr. Herz." Herz, Herz, Herz: it was like an incantation. It always surprised Karen to remember that it was her name too.

She and her father had only driven over for the judging, and so Karen was dressed in shorts and an old blouse. Oddly enough, the girl's Sunday clothes did not make Karen feel uncomfortable, but rather pleased her; she smiled and talked with the girl, something she ordinarily did not do, since the company of other girls—of most people—bored her. In talking she had noticed Jack's eyes easing from her father to her and back again. She sat beside her father on a bench, her arm through his in a parody of decorum, her bare legs stretched out, not yet tanned, measuring themselves against her father's; and she felt a delicious, curling sensation, as if she were seeing herself through the eyes of the girl Jack was with. Jack and her father talked about the gypsum plant; Mr. Herz, by tradition a farmer, made most of his money out of interests in gypsum mining. In the middle of a conversation about gypsum her father stopped abruptly and laughed: "Ain't my littlest girl here

27

getting big now!" His words surprised Jack and the girl—Karen could tell by their faces. But Karen laughed, squirming on the bench, squeezing her father's arm. In his company she was never more than eight or nine years old: she sensed rather than knew this, and it pleased her. She was his littlest girl. Afterward the memory of that meeting was so fine, her impression of Jack so good, that she was glad to see him again . . . though none of their dates had ever lived up to what she expected.

She and Jack got into the back of Albert's car. Albert drove carefully, like an old woman. He was a soft, morose man of over thirty, very serious, very quiet. He had been teaching at the town high school as long as Karen could remember and, almost as long as she could remember, he and Celine had been going together. By this time no one except Celine expected anything to come of their courtship. Karen hoped vaguely they would marry, for Celine's sake, but Albert's manner, his treatment of Celine—familiar without being interested, concerned without being warm—promised little.

They stopped at a country tavern, a nameless place set back from the road in a muddy lot. "You oughtn't to let your students see you here," Karen said to Albert, teasing. Albert frowned and did not reply. "I was only joking," Karen said.

Inside, a few men turned to look at them. The others had beer, Karen had a soft drink that she sipped at continuously, as if she were alone. Jack wore a coat Karen had not seen before; he looked coolly handsome, and when he spoke with the others he presented himself as a proud, superior young man. Certainly he was superior—Karen compared him to the country men sitting at the bar: big, coarse, clumsy hands, whiskery faces, muddy feet. But now, as he spoke of his father's plans to help him run for the legislature, Karen, as always, could not sense any vitality in their relationship, any feeling in her for him that went beyond a polite interest. Sometimes when he called her she had told him she was not interested in him, that she "didn't like him much." Just so would a child speak, she had thought coyly; a child would tell the truth. Not for Karen the intricate games of other girls. She would tell the truth.

"I suppose I oughtn't to have come," Karen said suddenly.

They looked at her. Jack said, "What do you mean?"

"I make things awkward for you," she said. What did she mean? She did not know exactly; she thought remotely that she ought to be somewhere else instead of here—that she had something to do. She could not think exactly what it might be. "I'm not much company."

Celine looked up, annoyed. Albert said, "You *are* company." He had soft, moist eyes, and Karen thought for the first time that he was a good man—a kind man. "Do you miss school?"

"Me?" said Karen. "Oh, I suppose so. Yes. I miss some of my friends."

"You might be taking a course from me this year," Albert said. Jack cleared his throat, uncrossed and crossed his legs under the table. "If you like math."

Karen sucked at her straw. "I always hated arithmetic," she said, conscious of Celine's irritation, conscious too of Albert's queer interest in her, which she was trying to block. She listened to herself talk. "There was one day in the country school when I was in eighth grade and I had one of my brother's old math books. The boy behind me, a Revere boy, used to punch my arms and back and squeeze my neck, pull my hair—you know—" she said inexplicably to Jack—"how boys do— And there I had Judd's old dirty book, numbers and signs to lull the mind away from itself, like a fog. A fog got between you and things. Nothing there was lost but that it was got back again, because of magic—you add a remainder to make a problem check, or look back to see your mistake." Jack had lit a cigarette

29

and watched her now as if she were making an important point. Celine picked at the peeling label on her bottle of beer and Albert frowned, staring at the table top. There was silence. Evidently they did not know she had finished. "So with a fog like that," Karen said, smiling, "you wouldn't know where the pain came from—a boy poking you in the back. All you would know is that you felt pain."

Albert smiled along with her. But there was nothing to say. He pretended to be interested in something written on the table.

"Did the boys bother you much?" said Jack.

"Sometimes," said Karen.

"My poor little sister," Celine said, smiling tightly, "had to walk home with her brothers. She had the idea that if she walked home alone something would get her."

Jack smiled and winked at Karen. "Is that so?"

"Yes," Karen said. "Yes."

"Country schools are disgraceful—terrible," Albert said. "My worst childhood memories have to do with what I endured at school in the country. Big farm boys, eighteen years old, in eighth grade—"

"Did they bother you too?" Karen said.

"My glasses. They didn't like my glasses for some reason."

Karen laughed. Albert looked perplexed. "Is that funny?" Celine said. She had a bright, blank smile.

"They still feel the same way," Karen said. "Only you can't tell it when you grow up. They do. They do," she said, lifting her chin to Jack in a slow, challenging gesture. "In grade school they did what they wanted—played running games and ripped your clothes half off, or rubbed your face with snow to make you cry, or took off your glasses and hid them. But now . . . now . . . no one does those things, but don't they all think about it? Don't they all want to?"

30

"My poor little sister," Celine said.

"They all want to," Karen said. "Don't tell me."

"Do you think I want to?" said Jack.

"Yes," said Karen. Albert's eyes dropped in confusion, Celine no longer tried to disguise her vexation. "You want to take Albert's glasses and hide them," Karen said.

Jack burst into laughter. Then he stopped. Karen sucked at her soft drink. In the moment of his laughter Karen was reminded of her father—it was so that he laughed, deeply, broadly, giving himself up to it, abandoning himself. At dinner that night he would be cold; Karen would glance at him, smile tentatively, say little during the meal. Afterward, in the parlor, she would approach him discreetly, she would ask him something—about the addition to the barn, about the cattle. Gradually his coldness would ebb; his gaze would accept her, she would be forgiven. There was nothing to be forgiven about, of course, since neither Karen nor her father for an instant believed Karen's words—"I hate you!"—but the ceremony of forgiveness, the ritualistic subjection and apology, were somehow pleasant.

"I'm sorry you did decide to quit school," Albert said. His bringing up of an old, dead subject caused even Celine to grimace secretly. "Of course you could return again next year."

"Why did you quit?" Jack asked.

Karen said nothing, though they looked at her. She was proud of her ability to withdraw from the presence of others so completely that her indifference was not even feigned. Celine understood and said, "I think we ought to be going now, Albert."

"Why, what time is it?" Albert said, a little startled. He looked at his watch as if he expected to see something alarming registered there. "It isn't late, is it? Has my watch stopped?"

"Do you want to leave, Karen?" Jack said.

"Yes," said Karen.

"Is something wrong?"

"What could be wrong?" Karen said. She had bent her straw so that it was no longer any good; now she poked it sullenly into the bottle. "Except that people always are attracted to people who don't care for them. Why is that? Why do they waste their time? It isn't as if their choices were made intelligently—their choices are made for them. They have nothing to do with it."

"What the hell do you mean by that?" said Jack. A dull red flush began to cross his face, moving up from his throat. Celine and Albert breathed sharply.

"Choices are made for them," Karen said sententiously. "A girl's legs somewhere pick a man to love them—or a man's voice, or the way he lights a cigarette. Isn't that so?"

"We really should be leaving," Celine said.

"It doesn't seem to me you would know much about it," Jack said, bending to Karen. "You haven't done a hell of a lot of living yet."

"I haven't done any living yet," Karen said. "But I see things. I can feel them. What do you care for in me, except—"

"Karen," Celine said. "Please, Karen."

"Except what?" Jack said.

Albert stood awkwardly, sliding out of the booth. Celine stared at her sister's blank face. "Please, Karen," she said, "haven't you had trouble enough for one day?"

"Trouble? What trouble?" A certain looseness in Jack's voice made Karen realize suddenly that he must have been drinking quite a bit; but she had not noticed. She looked at him curiously. "What kind of trouble are you in, little lady? My little Karen?" In spite of the horrified looks of Celine and Albert, Jack took hold of Karen's shoulders and kissed her. She did not move, not even to raise her arm from the table. "That's the way it is," Jack said savagely, pushing her back. "Look at her. Look." He grabbed Albert's arm. "Do you wonder at what's between us? All our relatives and all the gahdam gossipy old ladies? Well, this is what's between us—this right now. You think it's ever any different? Do you?"

"We'll be leaving now," Albert said, licking his lips.

Jack got unsteadily to his feet. Karen had the idea that he was exaggerating his intoxication. "What the trouble was at the Revere wedding was this—all the commotion—it was *me, me*. Not Karen. Everybody came out from the dancing to see me breaking up that chair in the hall. And Karen standing off a ways with her head down. But it was me that had the trouble —not her. She didn't care. She didn't. I'd tell it to her father himself if he asked. But she didn't care—just stood there. It was nothing to her. She knew that would be worse to a man than fighting, or throwing up all over him—God! With her looking at my forehead like she does!"

"Then leave her alone! Don't call her!" Celine said angrily.

"What the hell have you got to say about it?" Jack said.

"You heard what she said, what she just told you— Can't you understand that she means you—"

"Celine," Albert said, "we're leaving. We're leaving."

"Go on then," Karen said.

"Aren't you coming?"

"No. I want to walk home."

"All the way home? Alone?" Albert said.

"Go on and leave us," said Jack. "Go on. Thanks for the ride. Go on."

After they left, Karen rubbed her eyes. Jack still stood by the booth, watching her suspiciously. The men at the bar stared with interest; a woman had even appeared and stood with a rag crumpled in her hand, watching. "You got yourself any trouble, honey?" the woman called.

"No," said Karen. She looked up at Jack and smiled. "Should we walk back?"

Outside, they walked along the road. Karen stepped precariously on the ice in the ditch. "It's been frozen so long here," she said, "I can't remember warm weather."

Jack stood up on the road, waiting. His breath made angry little clouds about his face. Seeing him, Karen was struck by his firm, strong handsomeness, by the uncertain mixture of contempt and victimization she could read in his expression. She ran up to him and took his arm. "There's a man dying," she said.

"Dying? Where?"

"The old hermit. The crazy hermit," she said.

They stared at each other as if Karen's words made sense.

"The old man by the creek? Down by your pa's land?"

"Yes."

"Is he sick bad? What kind of sickness is it?"

"I don't know," said Karen. It surprised her to realize that no one had mentioned Rule's sickness. "Maybe old age. Or the weather. Something. Do you think he will die?"

Jack shrugged his shoulders. "Sure," he said. He grinned bitterly. "Is this another game you're playing?"

She swung his arm back and forth. "I feel so alive," she said softly. "I want to live. I want to love—I want to love," she said, pulling him along the road. "I feel so happy. Let's run. Do you want to run? Please—please—"

Jack walked heavily, resisting her. "You said some pretty bad things back there. About me."

Karen did not look around. "I wish we could run," she said. "I want to do so many things. That man there dying—he looked at me. He was there when I was born and can see my whole life when he looks at me; like my father. I don't think I would want someone who wasn't there when I was born."

34

"What do you mean by that?"

At the side of the road a dense thicket led back to the woods. There branches of small stunted trees and bushes locked and interlocked like lace: surprisingly delicate, clear. Winters here in the northwestern hills of Eden County were long and brutal and recovery from them always seemed to Karen a miracle. In the worst days the snow looked like an incredible sifting of earth and heaven, blotting out both earth and heaven, reducing them to an insane struggle of white that struck at human faces like knives. Summers reeked with heat, and heaven pressed downward so that the sun had to glare through skies of dust. Sometimes there would be holocausts of fire in the woods, churnings and twistings of white smoke rising into the white sky. The brutality of the land somehow evoked joy in Karen. She pulled at Jack's bare hand again. "Can't we run!" she whispered.

"If you don't want to see me again it's all right," Jack said. "I got what you meant back there, about people wasting their time. I got it."

"What if I got home and the old man was already dead?" Karen said. "He has a son coming. Maybe his son is here. Did you know him?"

"Who? Karen, look at me. Just a minute, just for a minute. Is there something wrong with you? You've been acting so strange today. It isn't me—is it? It's something else. What was that trouble Celine mentioned? Tell me about it."

Karen's heart swelled as she looked about at the drab countryside. It was mixed up in her mind with something to come—something she longed for. She must be getting home to it. She had to hurry. Already it was getting dark. "Run with me, Jack," she said. For an instant he was going to, and she felt, with real excitement, that if he did so she would love him—she would have to love him. But he shrugged his shoulders. Embarrassed, uneasy. He could not understand her. He could not even see that there was nothing to understand. "Ah, Karen," he said, "that's for kids. You're not a kid any more."

"Please, Jack."

He saw that she was really excited. Her eyes were bright, blinking rapidly. Her expression was animated, pleased, an expression he did not think he had ever seen on her before. "Look at those birds!" Karen cried. They were dull, gray, shivering birds, fluttering out of the sky and to the stooped trees as though they were falling. "Someone's throwing them by hand!" Karen said. She hugged herself, smiling, looking around. "I want so much to love," she said, "I want to love— to love— I want to live— I want— I don't know—"

"You'll do those things, Karen," Jack said.

His voice for some reason depressed her. She looked back at him. "I suppose so," she said. They fell silent. "I hear a car coming somewhere."

The car's engine made a low, ominous sound. It seemed to have appeared from nowhere, already quite loud. "I ought to have driven myself," Jack said. "But I was afraid—I thought you wouldn't want to see me alone. After the trouble at Revere's—"

"Let's get a ride with this car," Karen said suddenly.

"Don't you want to walk? I think we have a lot of things to talk about."

Karen watched for the car. It was not yet in sight. "I've got to get home," she said mechanically. "My father— I have to do something with my father."

"What about me?" Jack said. "You make a gahdam fool out of me, don't you? Don't you? If I didn't know you better I'd think you did it on purpose and laughed about it later, or else did it to make me more interested. But it's not for either reason, is it? Is it?"

36

The car seemed almost upon them, yet it had not turned the bend. Karen waited patiently. She hoped it would be some-one they knew, perhaps one of the hired men. "Someday some-one's going to drag you off into the woods or into a barn," Jack said, lapsing back to the contemptuous, loose manner he had feigned in the tavern. "Then you'll wish it had been me. You'll wish you had somebody that loved you then. Even if it was just a bother to you. Gahdam son of a bitch of a—"

Karen stared at him. She could not tell if he was swearing at her or not. He stopped, licking his lips. They looked at each other. "When I used to kiss you," he said awkwardly, "you had it in your mind that it was somebody else, didn't you? Wasn't that why it turned out so strange? I mean . . . in your mind it was somebody else doing it. Who else was it?"

"I don't know," Karen said. She stared at the hard clay road, as if the answer were as important to herself as to Jack. "I don't know."

"Watch out for the car."

Karen looked up. The car was turning the bend, going fast. Very fast. It was a strange car—new, gleaming, flashing even in the waning light. "I'll make him stop," she said.

Jack pulled her arm. "Come on," he said. "It's nobody we know."

"I'll make him stop," she said. She raised her hand and waved in a deliberately childish way. Something told her the man was not going to stop, so she stepped out into the road. Jack lunged for her. "He'll stop, he'll *stop*," Karen said, strug-gling with Jack. "Leave me alone."

"Gahdam it, you want to get killed! I swear you want to get killed!" Jack cried.

The car rushed upon them. It looked absurdly large: a great silver front, headlights like eyes, broad curving windshield that distorted the figure of the man inside. Karen saw his shocked

37

white face in the instant before Jack yanked her to the side of the road. The car skidded in the frozen clay, turned slightly, screeched to a stop some distance away. "Hell to pay now," Jack said. "I sure do hope it wasn't anybody we know."

"He'll give us a ride now," Karen said. "Come on."

She ran to the car, leaving Jack to plod behind, muttering. "Mister," she cried, "mister, are you going— Are you going—"

She stopped. The man had gotten out. He stared at her with such undisguised hatred, such a malicious intent, that for an instant her voice failed her. "I ought to of kilt you, you little bitch," he said. "I ought to of ground you and that bastard both down. A son of a bitch of a country trick if I ever knew one."

He was breathing fast. A tall, pale man with black hair, straight black hair. His face looked as if it had been hacked out of stone with a blunt, murderous instrument. Before the purity of his anger Karen's whole manner, her persona, failed; she stood breathing shallowly, watching him, wondering if she would cry after all. When Jack came she turned and took his arm. "What the hell are you trying to do?" the man said. "Do you want to try it again? I'll be glad to try it again. This time I'll slam it into you, both of you. Goddam back-country idiots."

He turned to get into the car. "Just a minute," Jack said nervously. "You can't— She didn't—"

"We want a ride," Karen said.

"A ride," said the man. His face was amazingly blank.

"To the Herz farm. Do you know that? Are you from around here—or—"

The idea struck Karen about the same time that it struck the man himself. He was lighting a cigarette; suddenly he looked up at her. "So you're Herz, huh? Which one of you? *You?* Is the old man dead yet?"

"No," said Karen. She stared at the man. "I don't think so."

"I wisht to hell I never came back," the man said. Karen had expected a change in his manner, but there was none. Some of the savagery of his anger had faded, but his expression was as frozen, as malicious as before; he stared at her bluntly. He put her in mind of a hawk, one of the soiled, shabby birds of prey that circled the skies. "All right. Get in, then. I'll drive you home. Goddam back-country idiots," he muttered, too loudly for them not to hear.

3

After church on Sunday, with the voices of the choir haunting her and the vision of the priest holding aloft the sacrament burned into her mind, Karen would return to her room and go to her window and kneel. There she would close her eyes and clutch her hands before her. At these times her brain would be a chaos: buzzing with light, song, incantation, the picture of herself approaching the altar, kneeling to receive the sacrament. At her first communion she had nearly fainted when she returned with the other children to their pew. Her family had spoken of dizziness from hunger, of fear, but Karen remembered it to be happiness that had overwhelmed her. Her father had understood. He had said little but his eyes on her were fierce, bright, proud. When Celine had muttered something about showing off he had turned to her abruptly and ordered her to leave the room: how vividly Karen remembered that! But she had felt no triumph; she had felt only pity for Celine that this strange happiness, so new to Karen, was perhaps inaccessible to Celine.

Now as she kneeled she began to feel the warmth of her room. With her eyes still closed she tilted her head to let her hat fall to the floor—a round little hat made of mink, dark brown and soft. She unbuttoned her coat—black cashmere with a great puffy mink collar; she let it fall to the floor. Storming her mind were visions of the church, the smell of incense, the heraldic ring of the bells, the spontaneous joy of the congregation. Staring at the priest's back, at his gold and green vestments, Karen had felt the power of his words, his chant: he pulled them on, ahead, joined them into one when he turned and raised his hands to them. Powerless to resist, hearts swelling with the queer haunting song, the steady murmur of Latin, they had kneeled, closed their eyes, had felt themselves swept forward. . . . At the communion rail Karen knelt beside her father. She did not look up, but clasped her cold hands tightly. To her left the priest approached her. Her mouth was dry, her throat kept swallowing nervously, as if she had no control of it; all about her sound and smell and color threatened to distract her from her prayer. She forced everything away until she felt alone, small, an absurd figure braced against collapse by the strength of her prayer alone.

Release! Released, they turned away, heads bowed, fingers clasped. They followed the slow line back to their pew. Karen had felt dizzy with excitement; her throat stung her, tears threatened. Now in her room she pressed her forehead against the window and let herself breathe in short, shallow, soblike breaths. Prayers crowded her brain, demanded to be said. She remained kneeling for some time, her eyes shut tight, lips moving silently—the secret ecstasy of these prayers, their burning, breathless power, excited her so that only a shout from outside brought her to herself.

She looked up. Her eyes were wet, cheeks wet. She blinked against the sunlight. Down in the drive stood her father and someone—Karen squinted against the light—it was one of her brothers; they were talking about something. Karen's heart suddenly swelled with love for them and she got to her feet. She ran to her door. Descending the stairs, she caught sight of herself in a mirror: she looked pale, as if frightened. She opened the heavy door and ran down the steps, her shoes clicking on the cold stone.

Karen ran down to her father and brother. They turned to her. She laughed and took her father's hand. Her breath showed in a frenzied halo about her mouth. "I heard you all the way up in my room," she said.

"You look hot," her father said. "Are you coming down with a fever? And look at her, coming outside without a coat on! What did you do with your coat?"

"It's up in my room," Karen said. "How are you, Ed? We didn't see you at church."

"We went early," he said. Her oldest brother, a man of thirty-five with four children of his own, he had always seemed to Karen remote and uninteresting. But she felt this morning a strange compulsive interest in him. "The baby's got toothache," he said.

Karen's father put his arm around her shoulders. He was bulky in his storm coat: a giant of a man, some people thought, with a large, heavy head. Karen could see her father in Ed.

42

They had the same thick brows, though her father's now were iron-gray instead of black, the same gray eyes, the same hard-looking, prominent cheekbones. Karen with her light hair and pale, childish complexion, her gentle features, might have belonged to another species. But the difference between them did not discomfort her; it made her feel instead the force of attraction between opposites. "Had some trouble with my girl here a day or so ago," her father said. "It was like pulling teeth to get her to come with me to old Rule's. I told you he was sick, didn't I? My girl here didn't much want to go—got sulking on me. We brought him back some soup, though."

Ed nodded vaguely. "I heard he was sick. Who's taking care of him?"

"He won't have a doctor. Says he won't let one in. His son's back there now—Shar. You remember Shar?"

Ed shrugged his shoulders. "I don't know," he said. "Look, if you want me over this week you let me know. I'm glad to help. If I were you I—"

Karen laughed. "If you were him what? You wouldn't work so hard? Is that it?"

Ed looked embarrassed; their father laughed. Karen felt feverish. "But you don't work so hard now! And you're not him!" she said.

Her father appreciated that. Karen understood it in the way he laughed. "These women get out of hand," he said. "Look, Karen, I think you're getting a fever. I do for a fact. You'd better go back inside."

"All right," Karen said. "I hope the baby gets better, Ed. That's . . . Timmy, isn't it?"

"Billy Ray," Ed said. He looked more surprised than hurt that anyone should forget the baby's name. "Say, Karen, you been crying or something? You look a little funny."

"I'm all right," Karen said. She lowered her gaze as they

looked at her. Her brain was in a turmoil: she could not understand herself. She wanted to give herself up to crying, convulsively, yet at the same time she wanted to hug both her father and Ed—her father for his love, Ed for his slowness—and draw them to her.

"Jack's coming for dinner today," her father said, winking. "That's what's got into her."

"Oh. Jack?" Ed said. He nodded vaguely.

"It isn't Jack," Karen said. Her face went hot suddenly. "It isn't. It has nothing to do with him." For an instant her father's knowing expression annoyed her, angered her. Then she laughed at their grins. "You don't understand," she said. "It has nothing to do with him."

Hurrying breathless up the steps, Karen heard Ed's voice: "There's things to lift around, you let them men do it. That's why you hired them. Don't go messing with it yourself." Inside the house she leaned back against the door. In spite of her shivering she felt hot. "Damn him," she thought of Ed. "Damn him." Then she felt shame for it—for her sudden hatred of her brother. She could not understand herself.

Sunday morning was always different from the rest of the day, and from the rest of the week; and Karen felt its passing with regret. Since having quit school she had surrendered most of her life outside her home and she was jealous of the drain of energy the routines of life demanded—drawing out her father, for instance, into different roles, different masks, so that she could never hope to know him entirely; the morning at church pulled them back together, stabilized them, united them as it had in the dim past when the Herz pew had been filled with children. Once church was over its sanctity would not last long, not when there was so much to do: already people were drawn to other matters, other concerns.

44

And it seemed to Karen now, as it had in the past few days, that she could sense a peculiar rigidity, a tension, in her father that had not been there before. This tension she felt in herself, a secret inner waiting for release. She knew what it was, of course, and, standing at her window and staring at the featureless sky, she thought of the old man dying—it was his death they awaited. Its promise was with them everywhere. The timeless, ghostly sanctity of Sunday morning finished, now time took over again, and time had its peculiar eroding demands. Surely this was why her father looked as he did that day at dinner and seemed so distracted that his manner confused and worried Jack. Karen made herself talk lightly, she drew her father and Jack into conversation together, she turned to Celine often to exchange a feigned glance, to smile as if in the recognition that, being female, they had something in common. If Celine understood Karen's insincerity she did not let on. The meal did not last long, food lay uneaten on Karen's plate, cold and greasy; the men smoked; a clock ticked somewhere. So the meaningful part of Sunday came to an end.

Rule's son Shar had come to eat with them the day before. He had come in with Karen's father, silent, contemptuous, not even looking at Karen and Celine; he ignored everyone but Herz himself, and even to him he spoke with a brief shrugging manner that before long turned Herz cold. To his question about what Shar did, Shar had said simply, "I drive a car." The conversation had ended with that. At the end of the meal Shar had stood, refusing coffee, and to everyone's embarrassment insisting upon paying. . . . Karen had been unable to look at him. Since meeting him in the road that evening with Jack she had been unable to reconcile him with the memory of the thin, dirty boy who had lived back in the hermit's shack so long ago. He had fought in pear fights with Karen's brothers against impossible odds, he had stolen Herz's corn, tomatoes, strawberries. He had stolen pumpkins, only to throw them down on the rocky shore of the creek for everyone to see. Now friends with her brothers, now enemies, he had always been on the periphery of their lives—despised by their mothers, by the schoolteacher, alternately despised and admired by the children themselves.

Now, a man of thirty, Shar belonged to neither world—not the dim, safe past or the static present. What was he to them but a stranger from lower land, the region of paved roads and cities and, far away, the sea itself? Once so like her brothers, so joined with them in their harsh boyish insolence, he now revealed himself as a creature of another species, a stranger. Karen had felt, watching her father and Shar at supper that night, a sense of warning, of something unavoidable they must —together—defeat, and at the same time a sense of vague uncontrollable excitement, a desire for this violence to happen. "I drive a car," Shar had said—his face had been squinted against a haze of smoke. At that moment he looked to Karen sharply familiar. His face looked as if it had been finely drawn, line by inked line, features shaped out of his strong face by the delicate and painstaking strokes of a pen. No doubt he looked like his father at that age: straight black hair, dark eyes carefully lashed as if to emphasize his contemptuous secrecy. He had a simple, graceless manner, unlike Jack, and a series of repetitive gestures; he ate as if the food they gave him had no taste. After he had put some dollar bills on the table before Karen's angry father they had waited, silently, for him to leave. But as if he understood their anger and liked it, he hesitated; he said conversationally, "You people have a hell of a lot of dogs around here still. What do you do with them? Hunt?" Karen, watching Shar, did not see her father's gesture.

"I remember that black hound once, one of your boys' dogs," Shar said. "The kids were at school and I came around and that one—there—you," he said to Karen, as if he did not know her name, "—she was standing outside one of the barns and crying. I came over to see what it was and inside the black hound was rolling around, having puppies. You know how dogs are. And the little girl was about sick with watching it, and her face all wet and dirty, but she kept standing by the door; she stood there crying. I remember that." Karen looked at her father. "Did that ever happen?" she cried. "I remember it just as plain," Shar said. "It was me you told to make them puppies go away."

The memory of Shar's presence, the haunting fact of his father's impending death, possessed Karen as soon as the excitement of Sunday morning ebbed. The Sunday dinner had not been finished before she caught herself picturing Rule's cabin and the dirty bed in which the old man lay. How odd it was that she had forgotten him in church, that she had not prayed for him—as if his illness could not intrude upon the sanctity of the mass! Jack had had to repeat something to her before she understood—she was distracted, troubled, her strangeness annoyed her father; she was sorry. "Are you worried about something?" Jack asked. His collar looked tight and she wanted to reach out and touch his straining, nervous throat. "That old man is sick," Celine said softly. Karen was surprised at her sister's understanding. She looked over to her father and saw that he had not thought of that himself; his expression of annoyance softened. "Not much we can do about it," he said. He smoked his pipe with a complacent, comfortable sigh. "Girls her age worry about everything."

After dinner Karen and Jack went for a walk. They walked slowly across the grounds, not holding hands, not looking at each other. Before the impending seriousness of their conversation Karen could feel only dismay, boredom, impatience. When he suggested they stop, Karen insisted upon climbing the

47

hill to the Herz cemetery. "I used to go up there every day," Karen said, "for my mother. Now I forget about it or put it off." They climbed the hard frozen path. Karen could hear Jack's breath. At the top the Herz family was arranged in rows, some graves marked by intricate stones—one, Karen's grandmother's, had a child-sized angel. In summer the cemetery was kept well and had always attracted Karen; in winter old dead weeds, seemingly sprung out of nowhere, cluttered everything. Karen walked slowly along the path. "There. There are the babies," she said. For some reason children's graves were marked by tiny markers, some made only of wood. Two feet high and a foot across: they leaned a little forward, identically, as if they were trying to crawl down to the path. "Allan Henry Herz, 4 months 15 days, God's Will Be Done," Karen read. "That was one of my father's brothers. And here—'Ethan, 1 month 10 days'; no inscription for him. He was my father's brother too." Jack looked anxiously at Karen. But instead of being depressed by this she seemed, on the contrary, to be excited, almost feverish. She wore her blond hair straight to her shoulders, without any curl or wave, and now, when the cold breeze blew it against her face, she brushed strands away angrily. She seemed to have forgotten Jack. "But over here are ours," she said, crossing to a group of stones and markers beneath an oak tree. "See, 'Patricia Ann Herz, 3 years approximately. A Blessing to Her Mother and Father.' She was my sister—it could be me here. It could be me. And this one— 'Baby Herz, He Never Saw the Light of Day.' Never born. Never even born." Behind the markers an angel prayed with closed eyes and stiff uplifted hands. As a child Karen had squatted in the grass at the other end of the cemetery watching the angel, waiting for it to move; now she stared at it as if it had spoken to her. Jack nervously lit a cigarette.

"Here are two wives," Karen said. "His first one there. I

never knew her, of course. She was Ed's mother—Ed's and Cissy's. My mother's stone is better." They stopped before a fine stone, a hard, polished white, exactly like the sky. ELIZABETH ANN HERZ. Jack watched Karen as she stared at the stone. If he was afraid she might drop to her knees at any second he gave no indication, but smoked his cigarette in silence. "She was supposed to look like me," Karen said. Sometimes she had prayed, alone by herself here, but today it did not cross her mind. She was fascinated instead by the coldness of the day, the cold, hard stone with its chipped letters, the brittle weeds, the cemetery itself, as they compared to her own youth: what magnificent life she possessed, what health, what feeling! She turned to Jack in wonder and despair, and she could not help but think that in just such a way had her mother turned to Herz—turned to the big, smiling, strong man, the handsome man with the proud, selfish look. In just such a way had she given herself to him—

But Karen could not do it. The moment passed. She smiled in embarrassment at Jack's strange look and went on, looking back to the graves, "The other wives aren't here. Their people wanted them back. One of them has her own tomb, over in Tintern; we used to go visit it sometimes and take flowers. We haven't for a while, though. . . . I can't remember whose mother she is. Celine's, I guess." Jack followed along beside her. "That space is for him, for when he dies. He goes in the middle, under the oak. I used to lie down there, flat on my back; I don't know why. I used to cry about it. Then my grave will be—"

"What?" said Jack.

"My grave," said Karen. "It will be there—somewhere around there. I used to want an angel like my grandmother, but I don't any more. Birds go on them—you know—and the freeze shifts them around."

"Why do you think you'll be here?" Jack said. "What makes you think such things?"

"What makes me— What else am I to think?" Karen said. She turned to look at him. They faced each other, strangers, and their voices had turned a little sharp, perhaps from the cold air. "This is what I want."

"It's what you want?" said Jack. His eyes narrowed. "Staying here? Being buried up here? It's what you want?" She saw him swallow. "Not being buried with your husband? What about that?"

"Husband!" Karen whispered. "But I won't have one."

"What do you mean? Of course you'll have one."

"No. I won't."

"Of course you will," Jack said angrily. "What the hell is wrong with you? Of course you'll be married—all girls are— you're a beautiful girl, a—"

"I won't," Karen said. "I won't marry."

Jack stared at her. He finished his cigarette and let it fall to the ground.

Karen went ahead of him to descend the path. Below them coarse, thinning sheets of snow still lay on the ground. The brown weeds, like spikes, looked especially sharp against the snow. The farm buildings looked big and neat, and the house itself, on the highest hill, faced them with its high old-fashioned windows shot with reflected sunlight. A three-story house, made of stone: playing in the fields they had pretended it was their castle. Giant oak trees leaned over it, lightning rods protected it.

Far to the left there were cornstalks bunched together in a field in crooked rows behind the snow fence. Winding in and out of the cornstalks were strips of ice. Just beyond that was the thicket that grew by the creek, and in that was old Rule's shanty—hidden from sight. No smoke even eased up from it,

50

as smoke did from Herz's big chimney; and Karen was struck again by the queer thought that it would be pleasant to die there, lulled by the rushing of the creek, soothed by the chill sunlight. Then over here, here to the cemetery: Herz would put him along the side, probably, where some of the hired men were buried—homeless men, churchless men, men without faces. If only it were already done! Karen felt that then she might breathe again.

At the bottom of the hill Jack's unsteady voice showed that something had happened to upset him. He talked of going home now, of thanking her father for dinner, of . . . "You meant that, didn't you?" he said. Karen thought he was about to take hold of her. "About not wanting to marry. You meant it. You mean it. It's in your head that way—he's stuffed it in you!"

Karen stared. "What do you mean?"

"He's got you to promise something," Jack said softly, as if they were conspiring. "To take care of him in his old age—something like that. Sure. And you want to do it."

They looked at each other. They stood at the edge of the circling driveway, not far from Jack's car. "You don't want me to come back then," he said. His tongue flicked out to moisten his lips. "You want to forget about it. Do I understand you?"

"There's nothing to forget about," Karen said.

She spoke quietly, yet she was aware of the weight of her words and, though she did not watch Jack, she sensed the stabbing chillness that for a moment left him speechless and vulnerable; but there was nothing for her to do except wait.

When he did finally speak it was a disappointment—the same mock-robust, loose manner he had hid behind at the tavern. "Sure. All right. I'll see you then—you and your father. I'll see you around. Around the cattle judging."

"Good-by," said Karen.

She turned to climb the steps. Jack must have watched her

51

for a moment, then he said, in the same way, "I always knew you felt like that. Really. I always knew it. You never fooled me, or tried to—you told the truth. You always told the gah-dam truth, looking me in the middle of the forehead! Little girl! The old women in my family could tell it too and told me to forget about you. They said you were poison for me. Poison—you would ruin me—you would drive me crazy— And for what? For what? What are you but a child after all, a kid, a little kid! There's nothing to you! Some people even say you're queer in the head—and my brother doesn't even think you're pretty. He likes them fixed up and— He likes them *women*. What do you know about that? You don't know any-thing—anything—you're as cold as all your family up in the graveyard, might as well be dead! Might as well be dead right now!"

Karen ran the last few steps to the house. What emotion she felt was only relief, slight shame—shame for Jack himself, when he thought over his words. He had shown her now why he was not suited for her—why he did not deserve her; a few hours later, by himself, he would understand the nature of his confession.

But deep inside her brain, like a sliver of glass suddenly un-covered in the dark, secret earth, was the knowledge that much of what Jack had said was true.

That night Karen's father read to them from the Bible. He sat in his chair beside the fireplace. The old fireplace, begrimed by time, was consumed by a great fire: logs, kindling, embers, blasts of flame. The shifting fire put his face into an uneasy ar-rangement of shadow and glowing flesh as he read. He had read to his family every Sunday night from the Bible; Karen remembered when the room had been filled with children. Now only Karen and Celine remained, but he spoke as if to an entire room, his voice expansive and dramatic, poking into corners, forcing its way into shadowy cracks. He read to them from Genesis, the story of Abraham and Isaac:

" 'He said, "Take your son, your only son Isaac, whom you love, and go to the land of Moriah, and offer him there as a burnt offering upon one of the mountains of which I shall tell you." ' "

Karen listened intently, watching her father's face. Beside her Celine sat in a daze from the hot fire, dreaming, perhaps, or with her mind blank. Karen had heard this story many times before—her father's words put her in mind of other evenings, the big drafty room hushed with children, Karen's own mother over there in the chair in which she had sat to sew. But Karen resisted dreaming and listened to the words. They evoked in her mind visions of faceless people, humanity bound by stories, by parables. What strange dignity to fulfill one's destiny in that way—forever bound by the inhuman plot of a story, manipulated by God Himself! It was a queer thought and Karen did not really understand it, though she felt very clearly the power of its attraction. . . . Her father's voice was swelling with confidence as he neared the conclusion of the story; at the same words his tone always changed, as if there were a pencil mark in the text. " 'Abraham built an altar there, and laid the wood in order, and bound Isaac his son, and laid him upon the altar, upon the wood.' " This was pronounced evenly, steadily, as if Karen's father were reciting the ingredients in a recipe. " 'Then Abraham put forth his hand, and took the knife to slay his son . . .' "

Karen stared at her father's face. For the instant he was transformed by his reading, by the story of these ancient people. Karen read their anguish in her father's face, in his thoughtful eyes, the aging lines about his mouth; what did this transformation mean? Or did she imagine it? Had it carried her along with him, absolved of the trivial vulgarities of her life—of Jack's demanding love, of Rule's sickness, of Shar himself who somehow threatened them? The thought of an absolution of this life appealed to Karen strangely, eerily, so captivating her mind that she hardly heard the rest of the story. Really she did not hear it.

Her father closed the dirty Bible. Karen did not look up at him for fear of what she might see: an aging man, a man already old, forced to consider eternity by pains about his heart, forced to consider it alone; no one could help him. Karen herself could not help him. But the magic of the Biblical story haunted the chilly air about them, and the hot air about the fireplace, and suggested comfort—mysterious comfort.

Celine yawned and spoke of bed. And so that Sunday ended.

4

Afterward, when Karen tried to remember that night—her father's reading of the Bible, the fireplace alive with flame, Celine half dozing beside her—it was really so she might remember herself. Summoning those images back might give her the power to see herself as she had been: Karen at seventeen, sitting forward, staring at her father's face, her features belying her childlike fascination, her innocence.

The next morning dawned cold and gray, like all mornings in early spring. Wanting company as well as warmth, Karen went down into the kitchen where her father and the hired men sat at breakfast. The hired men were a good lot generally: most of them over forty, with vague, shifting pasts, strong arms, weathered faces, fatherly looks for her. It had come as a surprise to Karen when she had discovered years ago that other families did not have so many men around all the time; she had felt it somehow vulgar of them, and ignorant of their children to talk about it. Her father greeted her with surprise, since she rarely got up so early and rarely came into the kitchen when it was crowded. "She's got up to help us work, it looks like," he said. "Come here, Karen. Let's see if she's old enough to have coffee."

Karen laughed and waved him away. She did not drink coffee, she had never learned. No, she said, shaking her head, she had never learned. The kitchen was warm and pleasant and Karen did not think that the men had to change their conversation for her; they seemed glad to see her. She was about to sit where her father had dragged a chair for her when someone knocked at the back door.

They could see Shar's face at the pane. "Well, let him in," Karen's father said. One of the men put down the saucer of coffee he had been sipping at and, without standing, reached around and opened the door. "Come in, come in," Karen's father said. Karen's heart began to pound. She had not sat beside her father, but stood, staring at Shar; she felt now the mistake of her coming down here, the error she had made in forcing her company into the company of men. She belonged in her room, in her bed, safe in sleep or in the sluggish halo of sleep that came with dawn.

Shar brought cold air in with him. "Thought you'd want to know," he said, "he's back there dead."

"Dead?" said Karen's father. He put down his coffee cup. "Rule's dead?"

"Dead," said Shar. "What do you think? It must of happened sometime last night. I don't know. I never woke up till a few minutes ago."

Karen's father sighed and pushed back his chair. "All right. We'd better go back there."

Karen backed away as the men got up and put on their jackets. The sleepy vacuity of their faces, the complacence of her father, astonished her. A man dead so close to them—dead while they sat eating and joking! Her mind spun. She stood blinking at the scuffed floor while they mumbled and grumbled and put on their boots. Someone lit a cigarette.

Then the door opened again and they went out. Karen saw her father and Shar out on the porch talking and the other men waiting. She went to the door and put her arms out against it as if she were embracing something. Her father was telling Shar something, Shar shrugged his shoulders, looking around— he nearly saw her, his eyes flashed across the window and away. Then her father stepped down and Shar turned to stare at his back.

Karen turned. She thought of going to tell Celine; but Celine would only pretend to care. Celine would think it was queer of Karen to feel this way—and Karen did not know exactly how she felt. She picked up the thick white cup her father had left and turned it in her fingers; it was still warm. She set it down again. There was nothing for her to do. She tried to think of Rule but, inexplicably, only the old misshapen rock on which he had sat to fish came to mind—she wondered suddenly if Shar knew about it or remembered it, whether she ought to tell him in a few days. . . .

The door opened again and Shar appeared. He looked sullen. "I got to drive in to town to see the sheriff, your old man tells me. He says for you to come along."

"What?" said Karen.

"For you to come along," he said. He held the door open upon the glaring air. "To show me the way. I forgot the way to town."

"Do you have to go now?" Karen said. She stared at him in disbelief. "Now? When your father is—"

"I got to go now. The sheriff has to come out and look at him and I got to see about some other things too, your old man says. He says for you to come along."

Karen got her coat and joined him. The air was fresh, freshly assaulting. They went to the barn where Shar had parked his car. The automobile was a little dusty, but it was a kind Karen had never seen before: gaudy, magnificent, over-large, decorated with strips and twists of chrome that might have meant something in a secret symbolic language. The thought that Shar had money suddenly occurred to Karen, for all this vulgarity would not have come cheaply. She felt almost compelled by the size of the automobile to say something about it.

She got in by herself. Shar slid in beside her and slammed the door. They did not look at each other. Karen felt numb and cold and baffled, as if a fog had come between her and what she must see, so that she could not exactly understand what was happening. "I s'pose he was a little crazy," Shar said.

His voice was harsh. He backed the car out of the barn, jerked it to a halt, then rushed forward so that the tires dug into the loose cinders. She heard him take a big breath. She watched with a tightening sensation the way the trees along-side the drive careened toward them, tilting slightly from side to side as the car picked up speed. "Huh? Don't you think so?" Shar said.

"What?" said Karen in alarm.

"The old bastard was a little crazy."

58

The drive dropped to the clay road. Karen shut her eyes. She could feel the pressure of the door against her side, hard against her side, and could hear Shar's voice—as though from a distance. Suddenly she put her hands to her face. "I always thought so," Shar said in his harsh, morning-slurred voice. They turned out onto the road and approached the bridge. It was an old rusted bridge, built before Karen was born, spanning the creek with a rattle of boards and high intricate beams that looked like a parody of a real bridge. It had been struck by lightning many times and had been a favorite place for the boys to play—Karen remembered Shar jumping from the top beam —and though, when she was a child, she had screamed when they approached it, she had gradually come to accept and forget about it; her father had assured her, his hand on his heart and no fingers crossed, that it would never collapse while she was on it.

"One time I did something he didn't like," Shar said almost conversationally, "—chased the chickens around or something. And he made me go down to the crick with him and he got a big limb that was laying down there, half rotten. He said he would have to lick me. I took a look at that limb and told him he wasn't going to. I told him that. I was about twelve. So he stands there holding the big limb, with little black ants going crazy running around on it, and looks at it, and says he would have to lick me. But he never moved and just stood there talking to himself or maybe to me, I couldn't hear him. He was looking out at the crick too where there's the yellow birds flying around the stones—it was summer then, and the stones sticking up dry—and he stands there like he forgot me, so after a while I went away. He must of forgot about it. He never said anything. I s'pose the son of a bitch was crazy for years."

59

"He was your father," Karen said.

He drove faster. The hard clay road rushed by beneath them. "Was he my father?" Shar said.

Karen said nothing. They had passed over the creek and she had forgotten to look down it—to look for Rule's shanty, which was visible in wintertime from the road. "For all I know Herz could of been my father," Shar said flippantly. "Your old man got around a lot thirty years ago—did you know that?"

"What are you saying?" Karen whispered. "Are you—"

"Nothing," said Shar. "The old hermit bastard was my father all right. I got his goddam look. Just an accident, though, that he was my father. Or any of my kin—those bastards off somewheres, cousins, uncles—nothing to me. An accident I got born. You think my father and that slut he had were thinking of me when they—"

Karen stared at him. She could not believe her ears. Shar glanced at her and in the same voice said, "Which way do I turn now? To the left?" Without waiting for Karen's answer he swerved to the left. They were on a better road now. Now that they were driving, Shar seemed a different person. His sullenness had vanished; he apparently wanted to talk. Karen was confused by his manner. More than ever he seemed a stranger, not only to her but to the world to which she was accustomed. "Do you smoke?" said Shar. He had lit a cigarette. Karen shook her head. "What's your name? Karen? Karen, huh?"

"Yes."

"Well, you were the baby. Let's see. I remember you some. A passel of kids your father got over there. He wore out three women with it. Or was it four?"

Karen stared at the road. "Three or four, not counting some others," Shar said. "My mother too, so they say. She was a real country bitch— She went off somewhere and left me with Rule.

I guess I can't remember her, except the stories people told me." If he sensed Karen's disgust he gave no indication of it. He hardly glanced at her. The sun had appeared, glaring white. Its queer frozen light seemed to Karen somehow ominous. "Will you reach in the glove compartment for me?"

"Here?"

"Reach in there and get out my sunglasses, will you?" He waited for her to open it. "There they are." He took them from her and shook them open. "It keeps the sun off. I can't always see so—"

"Be careful," Karen said without thinking.

He glanced at her. She could see his teeth behind his slow curving lips. "I'm always careful," he said. He put on the sunglasses. "That's why I'm still here. . . . I'm not sure how you go about it," he said, "I mean the old man's death. I never had a dead person on my hands before. I s'pose they got laws for what to do and undertakers and a cemetery to buy into. Are all cemeteries with churches? I can't remember."

"You don't have to worry about it," Karen said.

"What?"

"My father will see to it," Karen said.

Shar stared at her. Karen met his gaze evenly. "He will? Where will he bury him?"

"In our cemetery."

"Why?"

"He said he would," Karen said.

"He ain't kin of yours, is he?"

"No," said Karen. "But he'll see to it."

In town Shar parked by the sheriff's office, though the place looked closed; it was too early. Karen sat by herself, shivering, and watched Shar go up to the building and rap mechanically

61

at the door. The air inside the car bothered her—smoke from Shar's cigarette—and she opened the window. The fresh air stung her eyes and awakened her to the knowledge that she should not be here. "This was a mistake," Karen whispered aloud, though she had no idea how she knew it was a mistake. She felt entrapped in a dream.

Shar came back. "I don't know where the hell they are," he said. He leaned in the window. "I got some other things to do. You want to come with me?"

"Where?"

"Out here. Get out. I'm going down there to buy something."

"No," said Karen. "I'll wait here."

He pulled his sunglasses down a little and looked at her. His eyes had little flecks of red in them, streaks of blood. She thought with surprise that he was a handsome man. "You want to sit here by yourself?" he said.

"I'll be all right."

"I'm going down the street. I might find the sheriff."

Karen sat without moving. "Well," Shar said, straightening, "do what you like. It wasn't *your* father, though."

He went away. About Karen the smooth gleaming inside of the car prodded at her vision: expanses of chrome, gaudy and useless, dials, gauges, handles, little knobs, buttons to press. Something about the clean hard shininess of the car made her start to cry. What had Jack said of her? People thought she was queer in the head. True. Perhaps true. It had been insane of her to come here; indeed, she could not think why she had come. In fifteen minutes she would be home, though. . . .

The walks in town were strewn with hay. The main street was all there was, really, to the town—it was made up of old high buildings of red brick and frame buildings with big glass fronts. Because it was so early few people were on the street. But some distance away, at the cross street where the high school was, someone was walking. Karen thought that perhaps she ought to go to Albert's apartment; he would help her. But she could not think why she needed help, or what she could say to him. Tears streamed over her cheeks; she tasted salt. She did not even know what she was crying about. She did not think it was for Rule.

When she looked around a few minutes later, she happened to see Shar standing on the sidewalk watching her. She only happened to see him; he had made no sound at all. She had the idea he had been there for a while.

He held a bulky paper bag in the crook of one arm and was eating a candy bar with a gaudy red wrapper. They looked at each other without expression. Finally Shar came around to the other side of the car and got in. He put the package in the back on the floor. He chewed the candy slowly and deliberately, as if he were not tasting it. "Do you like to cry?" he said. He started the car. He drove down the road, jolting at the potholes and bumps. Karen tensed herself against the ride, and against the chilly oppressive fear that had begun to take over: a nearly wild fear of not reaching home, a fear of reaching home and her father as if she had done something wrong. She wanted to ask Shar about the sheriff but could not. She leaned against the open window, crying, oddly ashamed; she did not know what was wrong. "Do you like to cry?" Shar said again. Karen did not look around. Her hair had begun to streak out in the cold wind. "I heard a song back there," Shar said, "the drug store where I got this." His spirits were buoyant; he seemed in a way pleased at her confusion. "The same tune over and over so it gets stuck in your head. Listen—" And she felt him touch her shoulder. He said softly in a pushing, tuneless voice:

"The more she looked, the more she mourned,
Till she fell to the ground a-crying.

63

> Saying take me up and carry me home
> For I am now . . .

"Like that. You know how that goes?" he said.

When Karen did not reply, he said nothing for a while. They were in the country now. Shar hummed to himself. He drove faster than before and seemed to know the way without asking her, without even hesitating. Karen was lulled by the rush of gray scenery, by the chill persistent wind against her face; she felt almost sleepy, as if sleep were something she could escape to. In a while she would achieve it: home again, home in her room, in her bed. They would not expect her to attend the funeral, if there was one, to see the old man's coffin lowered into the ground—they would understand. Her father would understand. He would understand too that the events of the last few days had frightened her, unsettled her, that she needed rest and sleep, protection from them.

Shar said suddenly, "Why don't you look at me?"

She felt his fingers against her shoulder, prodding at her. "Here," he said. "What the hell is it to you if somebody died? It's better off for him that he's dead, don't you know that?"

"Please," said Karen.

"Don't you know that?" He pulled her around so that she could look at him, but Karen stared sightlessly before her at the road. She felt sleepy and dazed by the morning and the speed at which they traveled, and by Shar's hand on her shoulder—still and heavy and warm. "You drive too fast," she murmured.

"Why do you cry?" Shar said. "Because of that old bastard?" He pushed at the accelerator, watching her; Karen felt the car pick up speed at once. "Are you afraid of me? What are you afraid of? Of death?" He steered with one hand and with the other held Karen's shoulder. There was something unreal

64

about the situation; Karen could not quite accept it. She stared at the hypnotic rushing of the clay road beneath them. "If I wanted to I could kill us both now," Shar said conversationally. "All I would need to do is swerve the car off the road—crash it into those trees—that would be the end. All there is to it. Didn't know you primped in mirrors and your mother suffered to have you so it could end like that—did you? Did you?"

He let up on the accelerator. Karen closed her sore eyes as if in prayer, but she did not pray; she did not think of it. "Why don't you look at me?" said Shar. "You haven't seen me for a long time and won't again. Don't you like me?"

He braked the car suddenly and turned off the road. Karen looked around in terror. They drove lurching along a lane—bare branches swept toward them, scraping viciously against the roof of the car. Shar stopped the car. Everything was silent. It had happened so quickly that Karen did not know what to say. Shar leaned back and looked at her. "Don't you like me?" he said.

"What are you doing?" Karen said faintly.

"Here," said Shar. He took her hand. Karen watched in fascination as he drew her hand to him and put it on his thigh. She could not understand what was happening. The sense of unreality pushed away fear, disgust, or anger—she only stared at him. "This is a good time for it," said Shar. "All right? I'll make it fast." But his hard, casual calmness was belied by a sudden shivering that crossed over him as he pressed Karen's hand against his body. "Oh, God," said Shar.

Karen pulled away from him. "What are you doing?" she said. Her voice was thin and childish. She felt that tears would help her, but she could not cry. "I don't want to be here," she said, "I don't want—"

"I seen you with that back-country bastard," Shar said. "Do you think he's better than I am?"

Karen shook her head uncomprehendingly. "I have to be home," she said. "I don't know what—what's happening—I—"

"I seen you with that bastard," Shar said tightly. "Who do you think you're fooling?"

Everything was still. Karen did not even think of trying to get out of the car. "Your father is dead," she whispered.

"Why did you come with me then?" said Shar.

"Come with you? You said—"

"What? What did I say?"

"My father told you I should. You said—"

"I said nothing. The hell with that."

"You told me so!" Karen whispered. For an instant she doubted everything; she must surely be going insane. "You told me my father wanted—"

"No," said Shar. "Your old man never said anything. He told me to call the sheriff. To call him from your telephone."

"No, no," said Karen, closing her eyes. "No."

"The hell with all that," said Shar. "We're here now. I'll be careful—I got something to use. Come on," he said. But he did not touch her. He waited. "I'll be good," he said, trying to keep down his anger, trying to speak evenly and hypnotically. "I'll open you up for that bastard. Come on. Come on."

Karen stared before her. They waited a while, as if their minds were blank. She could think of nothing.

After a few minutes Shar relaxed. "All right," he said. His voice was carefully empty. He started the car and backed it around to the road. Once on the road he drove fast again: sharp curves, dips, twists of the road, now a rock before them, now a great pothole. This time Karen almost liked the speed. Shar said nothing for a while but then, as if he could not help himself and did so reluctantly, he touched her shoulder again. She stared at him in terror. "I s'pose he never even did anything to

66

you," he said. Karen could not understand what he meant. "You're just a kid. You ought to of been my age when I was around here." He spoke softly, but there was a coarse, stern edge to his voice and the corners of his lips kept wanting to ease upward into a kind of grimace. Karen watched him. "It's a goddam shame I got to leave here today," he said, as if to himself.

She felt his fingers at the back of her neck: just punishment, he would strangle her, punishment for the wrong she had done. He tightened his grip and she felt herself being drawn back slowly. For the moment her shame and guilt might be transformed into pain, concentrated into physical pain; that way she could bear it. Yet in spite of herself she cried out. Her scream surprised and pleased Shar, who did not release her. "What's that?" he said. "Look around at me. Little girl. Baby of the family. Look at me instead of out there—you keep looking there, waiting for us to crash! Or are you looking for home? You'll be there in a minute. . . . What the hell do I care about you," he said angrily. He muttered to himself. But he did not release her. "A goddam little bitch like you, to get me going. Just a little bitch. The hell with it. I don't need you. I'm going back today; the hell with it. It's the same with all women. I don't—" Yet he did not let go of her. His fingers gripped her neck, played with it; she felt his nails digging into her skin.

Then Karen saw that they were heading up to the bridge. Almost home! Almost home! Hysteria seized her. She could see the house now, on the other side. Later she was unable to say what happened, but she remembered screaming: "You can't do this—not here—it's too close to— You can't— What have I done, what have I done—my fault—" They were up on the bridge now; the floor thumped beneath them vigorously. Karen felt Shar's arm slide about her shoulders and pull her against him, as if he could not help himself. She pushed against him, screaming. In her mind they were guilty, shameful; the ease of death about which Shar had spoken only a while ago seized her imagination, and she felt that both she and Shar must be punished. She pushed madly against him and took hold of the steering wheel. "Not here, not here," Shar said. Karen pulled at the wheel, leaning against Shar, her hair whipped into her eyes, and she felt the car rushing off the bridge and onto the road again, she felt Shar's fist strike her jaw and the clean swerve of the car beneath them, the tires screeching, shuddering, the road jerking off to their left—they were clear of the bridge now, she thought with savage regret—she felt the sudden terrific slamming of guard rails against the car and the groaning surrender of the car itself, spun helplessly off the road.

5

When Herz and one of his men made their way along the creek bank and emerged through a dense thicket, they saw Shar's automobile smashed through the guard posts and at rest, head first, down the fifteen-foot hill from the road. Herz cried out, but his words were lost in the roar of the creek. The hired man, a bald, slow-faced old man, listened gaping to Herz's snatched words. Both men ran stumbling forward. They had been in the hermit's shanty when the crash had occurred, and Herz could still hear the ominous sound of squealing brakes. When he saw Karen appear, miraculously, by the side of the car, he stopped dead in the brittle grass.

"Karen!" he said.

Shar came stumbling from around the back of the car, his hand to his face. "Look what she did!" he shouted. His face was white, bleeding beneath one of his eyes. The bright blue automobile, dented and misshapen and sprinkled with broken glass, gave off a sharp odor of gasoline. "Look at it!" Shar cried. Karen had taken a step forward to come to her father, but had hesitated; and now she cringed back from Shar, who approached her with his hands uplifted as if he meant to tear her apart.

Karen's father reached her first. He began shaking her. He said nothing: veins on his forehead were swollen, outraged. When Shar shouted something at him he turned and pushed Shar back, his hand opened upon Shar's chest. "You bastard!" Shar cried insanely. "What the hell are you doing?" His face was streaked with blood and Herz, distracted from his daughter to look at the man, felt in spite of his own anger that Shar might be dangerous—he might be a killer. "What is this?" Herz said. "What is Karen doing here?"

"I don't give a damn for it!" Shar cried, rushing at Herz. But he stopped before he met him and stood with his hands raised and clawlike, threshing the air. Behind Herz the hired man stood gaping in silence. "What? About her? Yes, she come along with me for a ride! The little bitch wanted to go for a ride! She was dying for it!"

Karen's father pulled her away from Shar. She stumbled with him down the hill, clinging to his arm; for an instant she even lay her head against his shoulder before he pushed her away. "You're not hurt," her father said. Karen could see the undisguised hatred in his face. "Get up to the house and stay there. I'll see about you later."

"I—" said Karen.

"Get up there. And you," he said to Shar, trying to speak calmly, "you can get off my land. I don't give a damn about you or your car or how you're hurt—go hitch a ride! Goddam you, get out of here!"

"Please," said Karen, "I—"

Shar ran to them and seized Herz's arm. "What the hell are you talking about, you miserable old bastard?" he cried. His eyes were bloody and wild. "I got to get out of here? What? Here—you goddam old—"

Karen tried to push between her father and Shar, but her father held her still. "I ain't leaving here until I get done," Shar said. He was wiping his face viciously with his hand. "She was dying to come out with me! Dying for it! I ain't leaving till I see to him back there— And my car, look what she did to it! And she never got hurt either, the little bitch! Little bitch! It's all downhill, how am I to get it up again—how am I to get out of this country without it?"

Before Shar's frenzy father and daughter stepped back. Karen could feel her father's trembling. She wanted to embrace him, protect him—against Shar's violence, against the shame of what she had done, if only in her father's imagination. "And I never asked her to come along," Shar said. "Damn her! All her fault for this! Her fault if I lay into you and kill you all! Look at my car, and me here by myself, and that son of a bitch back there laying dead— You ain't ordering me off of here. Herz, you try to tell me what to do, you try to tell me a thing, I swear I'll kill you! I'll wring your buzzardly neck till your eyes pop out!"

Specks of blood flew off Shar and onto Karen and her father. Shar continued shouting, and Karen felt her father's hesitation—she felt the rapport between them, still, in spite of what he thought had happened. She believed he was about to turn to

71

her, his eyes about to meet hers, accept hers, they would be unified against the insanity of this man's passion. . . . "You ask her! Ask her!" Shar cried.

When Karen's father did look at her it was not as she had hoped. He looked at her as if she were a stranger who had touched his arm in a crowd. "I'll have this out with you later," he said to her. She could see some of his gold fillings as he spoke, and his words so stunned her, so chilled her, that she felt once more a creature trapped within a dream, waiting for release. The unreal violence of the past few minutes rushed to a climax and exploded in her brain as she felt the impact of her father's disgust.

"No, please," she cried senselessly, "please, please. . . ."

As if infuriated by Karen's voice, Shar rushed upon her and grabbed her away from her father. He yanked her around, almost throwing her onto the ground. "Bitch! Bitch!" he yelled. Before Karen's father could do anything Shar had brought his bleeding hand down hard on Karen's head and face, and then he shoved her back to her father. "Don't you touch me," Shar said, pointing one finger at Herz. "I mean it. I'm going to take care of him before I leave; I ain't leaving now; I ain't leaving till I'm done. If you touch me I swear I'll kill you. I'll do it right here." He addressed the hired man, who stood with his feet apart and hands vaguely upraised. "I mean it," he said. "I don't care anything about killing all of you."

Karen's father said nothing. He pushed past Shar and started for the hill. The hired man awoke to movement and followed him: "You going back, Mr. Herz? What do you want me to do?"

Shar and Karen watched them leave, stumbling up the hill through the grass. The hired man scurried after Herz, craning his neck. At the top Herz turned briefly and said, "This is my personal business!"

Shar was sucking at his hand. He watched Herz and the man until they were out of sight, then he went over to the car and forced the door open. Karen stood, dazed, and watched him with a vacant stare. Her face was damp from the blood he had smeared on it. "Buzzardly old bastards!" Shar muttered. He straightened away from the car and tossed an empty paper bag over his shoulder. He was carrying a metal container and fumbling with its top, and he glanced at Karen, oddly enough, as if they were conspirators. "You better go up with them," he said.

He started back along the creek bank to Rule's shed. "What are you doing?" Karen said softly. If he heard her he gave no sign. She hesitated and then followed him. This was a path along which they had run as children: Karen and her brothers and sisters. Now it was grown over and sharp stinging branches fell against her, whipped back by Shar. "You get back with them," Shar said, looking around. "I told you to get back with them."

Karen ran after him. "He went to get his shotgun," she said. The rapids made a harsh, thunderous sound here, so loud it seemed to suck her words away. Shar, however, heard: he stopped as if petrified.

"His shotgun?" he said.

He picked Karen's hysterical fingers off his arm. She saw this with surprise; she had not known she was so close to him. "Don't let him kill you," she said. "Don't let him."

Shar hesitated. His expression was calm now, though blood from the scratches on his face gave him a bizarre, demented look, like a creature conceived in a nightmare. "The old bastard would do it too," he said. "He killed a nigger once like that. A nigger."

Karen could see the lightning rods glinting up at the big house. She waited for Shar to say something. But he said nothing—only waited another second—and turned back along the path to Rule's shed.

When Karen's father appeared at the end of the lane Shar had already set the cabin on fire. The mismatched boards and tar-paper roof, the junk cluttered so jealously around it, were dissolving into themselves and upward, belling out, expanding and shrinking, smoke black, clamorous, huge clouds of it drifting up through the trees to the pale sky. Beyond the swelling flames Herz appeared, seeming to materialize out of the fire itself. He carried the shotgun proudly before him.

Karen had meant to run to him, but something in his look stopped her. He was unfamiliar and savage—a giant of a man in oil-smeared boots and rancher's clothing, a stranger. As Shar moved out to meet him, his eyes took on a furious, stone-like rigidity. The kerosene-fed flames glowed warmly on his face and hair and on the stock of the shotgun. He did not look at the fire but inched toward Shar, his feet seeming to take hold in the ground, not gracefully, but firmly, firmly, feeling his way along while Shar waited. Karen wanted to cry out—she wanted their eyes to jerk to her, to leave each other, for she saw that they were killers; she could absorb their wrath, drown shuddering in their fury. She wanted her father to freeze suddenly, to think of something—anything— From where he stood now he could see much: the rushing creek and the plowed land on the other side, rich black land notched against the sky. But the men stared hungrily at each other.

They waited. Karen's father was nearly upon him. From so close the shotgun blast would tear Shar in two. With the barrel of the gun, now, Karen's father began to do an odd thing: he made a series of rapid, jerked motions toward the burning cabin, as if he wanted Shar to go into it. Shar stepped backward. He put his hand out slowly as if to ward off the shot. His face was blank and without passion, as if drained of life. He began shaking his head and saying something—it must have been "no."

He stopped and would go no farther. Herz motioned with the gun again, but Shar did not move. The wind blew flames lapping over the collapsed shanty. Karen whispered aloud, "Never the same again!" She clasped her hands as if in prayer as her father raised the gun to shoot.

Shar moved suddenly; the shot exploded, jarring Karen, and Shar had hold of the gun at the stock and was wrestling savagely with Herz. Had her father meant to miss? Karen could not tell. "Four more shots!" she cried to no one. "Four more! Four more!"

Shar seized the shotgun and swung it around, in almost the same movement. The gun blurred in an arc about his shoulders as he struck Karen's father with it, knocking him back and onto the ground. Karen began to scream. Shar turned and fired the shotgun into the cabin: the gun made a thunderous roar. Karen ran to her father as Shar turned and came at him. The old man was on his hands and knees, looking at Shar with a queer, surprised look, as if someone had played a joke on him. With a savage and impersonal energy Shar struck him again on the side of the head, and, crouching over him, he slashed at him again with the stock of the gun as if he were counting the blows. "No, no!" Karen screamed. Shar pushed her away and struck her father once more, his legs jerking with the effort. Then he turned and lifted the gun over his head and threw it into the fire.

He looked down at Karen's father and slowly drew his arm across his face. Without a glance at Karen he went by to the path and out of sight.

Karen knelt beside her father. He lay flat on his back, and in this position his chest looked queer and stuffed, as if only his breath had kept it strong. His face was bleeding and the blood was illuminated garishly by the firelight. Karen heard shouts somewhere: the hired men coming. They had heard the shots. She knelt and pressed her face against her father's. She could not cry. His breath rasped and bubbled in her ear. "Father," she said. "Father. . . ."

One of his heavy fists came up. She took hold of it and stared at him. His eyes looked bluish under the lids, half closed; then they opened, fixed themselves upon her. She saw the clarity of his recognition at once. "I'm all right," he said. His face was distorted suddenly by pain; it must have run through him like a current of electricity. "You—Karen—" he said, swallowing, "Karen—"

"I'll take care of you," she said. "I'm here with you. I have you."

"Karen— Get him." He closed his eyes and Karen leaned to him as if to follow him into unconsciousness. Behind them the men hurried, stomping through the grass. They cried: "Mr. Herz! Mr. Herz!" He opened his eyes and stared at her again; she leaned over him, waiting. "Don't come to me until you get him. Kill him. Kill him."

"Father—"

"Kill him," he said.

Then someone pulled her away, helped her up. Blinded by tears and terror, Karen could not see who. "Not me! Not me!" she cried. "Let me alone!" She pushed past the men. One of them stopped her, hesitating; then he let her go. She ran back along the path to the lane.

6

In spite of the chaos of the land about her and the surface buzz-ing of her mind, Karen felt that, deep inside, secretly inside her, she was able to think clearly and sanely. The fault did indeed lie in her, was of her doing: but it originated not in the deci-sion to go with Shar but in her deliberately resisting sleep that morning. That was so—she had pushed against sleep, pushing herself up out of it as though she were moving slowly up through water to the clean air above. She had wanted that clean, clear air; she had insisted upon it; she had wanted to breathe. Nothing else could explain her behavior. Now, as she ran feverishly across fields, sucking at air, her mind was able to function simply and damningly, as accurate as a clock ticking. Perhaps she had even understood the price of forcing herself up from sleep and, in going down to the men, the price of violating her role. Perhaps she had understood, without really being able to know, that the rejection of her child's bed would lead, after a series of insane, vivid scenes, to the picture of her father lying in the cold mud, bleeding, staring up at her—how right he was to judge her, to find her guilty! She understood his judgment and accepted it.

Though her thoughts arranged themselves in order and seemed to indicate that she was in control of herself, she ran through the fields like one possessed—her thoughts had nothing to do with her action, but ticked on mechanically. Once, hearing one of the men behind her—"Karen!" he had called, making her name forlorn and unfamiliar—she had ducked down into an irrigation ditch and lay flat against the cold ground. "Can't find me! I'll lie flat—flat—" she murmured, gloating; in the next instant she congratulated herself on her cunning. There was no sound. Her body was still and heavy, like a stranger's. She felt her heart beat, and pulses in her body, little throbbings in her fingertips.

"Karen!" the man cried, fainter now. "Ka-ren!" The word sounded ghostly.

She waited for a while. When she stood, all the blood seemed to rush out of her head, leaving her gasping and dizzy. She remembered then that she had been in an automobile accident, that she was probably hurt somewhere—somehow—she did not know. She examined the palms of her hands, as if that might mean something. They were dirty and smeared with dried blood. Staring at the blood, she thought again of her father's face.

Then she ran. Once she felt something cutting at her legs: looking down, pulling at her skirt, she saw a thin white streak that swelled gently with blood as she watched. She forgot about it in the next instant, for she had come now to the field where she believed Shar was. She did not exactly know how she knew this, but she felt no doubt. The field was unworked and choked with grass and bushes. The bushes were skeletal, edged with long thin expanses of dirty snow; everything was silent. Only Karen's breath disturbed the quiet, but she could not help it. She walked now, hugging herself against the cold, looking around and waiting to see Shar. She could not remember what he looked like. She walked stiffly and mechanically, her eyes fastened upon the colorless shapes and lines of winter, bush, grass, yearling tree, until they disappeared into a dark wood.

Out of the woods, or out of nowhere, Shar appeared and waited for her. "What do you want?" he cried at once. She saw him without surprise. "What do you want?" His face, smeared and crisscrossed with blood, looked as it had looked when he tried to wave the shotgun away: had she not suspected her reason, she might have believed she saw anguish there.

Karen came to him. He stared at her. It was with difficulty that she kept her eyes fastened on him—sometimes she stumbled and found herself looking at the dull sky or the horizon; she could not quite control herself. "What's wrong? What do you want?" Shar said. "Is he dead? Did I kill him?" He seemed to be breathing as loudly as she. "I seen you coming all the way," he said. Karen stopped before him and tried to focus her eyes upon him. "I watched you. What are you trying to do? What do you want? I told him to leave me alone," he said slowly, "I told him myself I would kill him. I did. He was trying for me. . . . Is he dead?" Karen, watching him, could

79

think of nothing to say. All her strength was consumed in fighting away unconsciousness, in forcing herself to stand. "What do you want with me?" Shar said slowly.

They stood quietly. Shar wiped his face. He was perspiring, though the air was still cold. He moved in a jerky, brutal way that seemed to her clumsily disturbing, and his voice, when it came, was disturbing too: "What do you want?" he said. Karen read the evidence of her own madness in this stranger's perplexed eyes. "You turn back," he said.

As if she felt she must do something, Karen lowered her gaze. Her hands, clasping each other fervently, were chalk white.

"Go back home," Shar said angrily.

There was a short silence. Then she could see Shar's teeth, before he spoke. "Go back home! Go take care of him! What the hell do you—" He bent suddenly and picked something up —an old rotted stick. He raised it. "Do you hear me? You go back home!" Incredibly—she had not planned to do it—Karen took a step forward. She saw Shar's fingers tighten about the stick and his elbow jerk inward, and something change about his face. She closed her eyes to wait for the blow. But nothing happened; she looked up to see him turn and toss the stick away. He walked quickly away and into the woods.

On the summit of the plain stretching off to their right, into which the woods slowly dissolved, fir trees stood in ranked clumps and stretches, their tops forming a saw-notched line brilliantly black against the sky. Karen, following Shar, could see birds among the branches—snatches of gray, fluttering wings—and for some reason her heart went out to these birds. They darted and sank in the cold air, their cries pierced the air, liquid and sharp and meaningless. She nodded as if in agreement with them.

Birds fluttered in the trees above her. Only when she caught sight of Shar again did she forget about them. She saw him just when he turned to glance back at her. His hair was black: blacker than the woods behind him. He was saying something to her. It occurred to Karen that if this was not a dream it was related closely to a dream—surely she had dreamed of a man in this wood, a man in any of the woods, awaiting her? He rushed toward her as if someone had given him a shove. "All right, you little bitch," he said, "do you know what I'm going to do to you? You know what I'm all ready for?"

His breath seemed to have control of him, to be shaking and jerking his chest. He rubbed his palms against each other, and against his thighs, as if they itched him. "Goddam little bitch," he said softly, "got me into this. You ought to pay for this somehow. Got your father chopped down too, didn't you!" he said with a grin. But the grin faded almost at once. He said, "What do you want?"

He spoke softly; before she even looked up at him Karen knew he was leaning a little forward, the way one speaks to a child. "What do you want?" he said.

Karen spoke clearly and with more strength than she thought she had. "I want you," she said.

Shar stared. He licked his lips, licking at the dried blood. For a moment his eyes blurred past her, and about her, and Karen waited, dizzy, within the abrupt shock of the man's gaze: it was as if she had said something so indecent Shar would not acknowledge having understood. Then he said, lapsing into his previous tone, "Go back home. I told you to go back home." His eyes avoided her face. Above them the somber winter birds cried out in brief, confused notes, as if they were lost. "Go back home. Go back home," Shar said, nearly whispering, and again he wiped his palms against his thighs. "Don't follow me."

He turned and left her. Karen began automatically to follow. For a while her eyes were fixed upon his back, then she lost sight of him. From time to time she stopped to steady herself and to listen to the silence about her. She half expected to hear someone crying, "Karen! Karen!" behind her; but there was nothing except the birds. In winter the wood was empty. She saw tracks of deer in the hardened mud, and other tracks —rabbits, probably—but none of the animals themselves. In spots the ground was covered with ice that glinted slowly, reflecting the white sky: the wood was so thin at this time of year that the heavy glare of the sky could not be kept out, as it would be in spring and summer.

Where the ground was soft it sucked at her feet. She watched them: muddy shoes, mud-scuffed legs, one foot came out and then the other, like the feet on a wooden doll. Karen began to experience a strange sensation then—that of being eased suddenly away from herself and able to watch from a distance her slow progress. A frail girl with blond hair blown ragged by the wind, and a blank, exhausted face, pale blue eyes that probably reflected madness. The day before she would have observed such a creature with pity, and now she was this creature —irreparably, completely; she could not go back. She clasped her hands before her and murmured, "Forgive me. Forgive me," to the dead wood and the birds and the remembered image of her father's face.

A memory of her late childhood came to her. It had been four or five years ago, an April like this though warmer and softer. The road to the country school had glistened with mud and water and the sky had been swollen with clouds. Fear came with the memory: fear of the school, of the children. Since she was the youngest child, Karen had no one to walk with; her brothers and sisters no longer went to this school. So she hurried along the edge of the road and pressed her school books against her chest and dared herself to cry. When tears threatened, she pinched her arm viciously. "Baby! Baby!" she whispered, the way her older sisters whispered to her when she cried. About her fields lifted away from the clay road, already plowed, and the earth looked dark and fertile in the early light. The sky was richly shaped, with great masses of cloud that looked boiled, so heavy were they with rain. Karen hurried.

The schoolhouse was in a muddy yard between two fields. It was a one-room building with a churchlike entryway, on one side of which coal for the stove was kept. A crumbling concrete walk led to the door. Karen walked up the walk. The school seemed unfamiliar without the other children running about and shouting before it.

Before entering the school Karen looked back to the road: no one was in sight. She hurried inside. The air of the school was chill and stale, and there was dust in the air—the schoolteacher had come early to sweep and light the stove, for he had been hired to do this work as well as teach. The man stood at the front of the room by the window and looked at her in surprise. Karen went to her desk and sat down. The teacher was a young man, but he did not act young, really: Karen thought of him as she thought of her father, a person beyond youth who had never had youth and had never desired it. He had a dark, thin, nervous face, glasses that made his eyes small, and teeth with slight cracks between them, as if they, too, were too small. Karen did not look at him, but put her lunch inside her desk and folded her arms on top of her books and stared at the blackboard at the front of the room. With the knowledge that she was safe her heart began to slow. She ran her eyes along the top of the blackboard, following the smartly gleaming placards of letters, A B C D, and on to the corner where the tarnished, spearlike top of the flag leaned, covered with dust. Above the letters were portraits of famous men, presidents, who stared

83

down at the children past streaked glass and always looked burdened by the heavy imitation-gold frames that contained them. One of the portraits, that of George Washington, had fluffy white clouds circling the man, as if he were peering down at them from heaven. The boys had said that he had been tarred and feathered and that was why he looked like that, but Karen preferred to think it was indeed heaven from which he looked.

The teacher walked slowly down the aisle on the other side of the room. She heard him clear his throat. "It looks like a storm today," he said. When Karen did not reply, he cleared his throat again and straightened out some books on one of the wall shelves. Karen sat with her knees up against the cold bottom of her desk. "Karen," the teacher said. She jerked as though he had touched her. "Why did you come so early?" He had moved behind her now, back by the old black stove. She heard him open the smoked door of the stove and prod around with the poker. "Is there some trouble I ought to be told about?"

"No," said Karen, but so faintly she had to repeat herself. "No." She remembered she had not taken off her coat, and got up to do so. The teacher, warming himself by the stove, watched her. His eyes were grave and colorless behind his glasses.

When the others began coming in Karen was looking through the book for her first lesson—an old arithmetic book of her brother's. All the answers were written in and other things as well—names and drawings. In uncertain inked letters on the first page was: JUDD HERZ GRADE 7. IF BY CHANCE THIS BOOK SHOULD ROAM BOX ITS EARS AND SEND IT HOME. Karen had written her own name above Judd's, also in ink. For some reason she felt pleased to see their names together—the "Herz" together—though Judd himself, one of the older boys, paid little attention to her.

Karen looked around to see the other children coming in. The smaller children were helped with their clothing by older brothers and sisters, who squatted to pull off boots with looks of hatred. Dirty mittens, tied together by long lenths of yarn, were pulled through sleeves and looped over hangers. At the last minute the older boys stomped in, important in their hunting boots and overalls. Their hands were big and moving, constantly moving. Karen looked around to her book, holding it tightly, and waited for school to begin.

The teacher self-consciously rang his hand bell and ignored the snickers of the big boys. When he went to the entryway (known to everyone as the "antry") to ring the bell again, the boy who sat behind Karen leaned forward and closed his fist in her hair. "You, there, Karen Herz!" he tittered. "Hey hey!" Karen tried not to cry out and waited for him to release her.

The first graders were taught first. They read aloud, first in a group (there were five of them), then singly. When the teacher's back was turned the boy behind Karen—he was a Revere, perhaps four years older than she and still in her grade—leaned to her and whispered, "You there, Karen. Karen Herz. Ain't you got pretty color hair now?" He poked at her shoulder. The other boys giggled. Karen tried to sit forward, staring down at the smudged pages of the book. Nothing happened for a while, then a piece of paper, folded in two, was tossed over her shoulder. Without thinking, she opened it. It was an obscene drawing with the label KAREN attached to part of it. The boys behind her giggled as Karen crumpled it up and brushed it off onto the floor. The Revere boy stooped and picked it up to save for later. "Hey, hey!" he murmured. After a while, when she did not respond, she felt their attention shift elsewhere.

Outside, one noon not long before, they had pulled Karen into a game the other boys were playing, running back and forth and around. It was "pom-pom-pull-away" and tags for "it" were allowed to be blows. Karen had tried to break away, and as she ran, the Revere boy had grabbed her by the collar and nearly ripped her dress off, yanking her violently around. She fell to the ground and cut her knee and the boys had run, laughing, around the schoolhouse. When the schoolteacher came out, hurrying clumsily, Karen had been sitting on the frozen ground and crying. The other girls inched away; they did not know her well, or like her; they shared their families' envy of the Herz clan.

Since then, at recess and at noon, she remained in her seat, reading a book. She would be conscious of the shuffling about her, children running down the aisles, footsteps slamming hollowly out in the entry. At noon that day, after she had finished her lunch, she sat with her head down on her hands, her cheek against the carved desk top; she pretended to sleep. The teacher moved about occasionally, crossing and uncrossing his legs. His desk was at the front of the room, by the first side window, in front of the old faded flag. He spent recesses and noon hour reading and coming out onto the concrete walk when summoned—he was the sole, if inadequate, protection for the younger children. Though he rarely spoke to the children, he now said to Karen: "Are you sure there isn't something I ought to be told about? Something you're afraid of?"

Karen looked up, blinking as if she had really been asleep, though she knew the teacher hadn't been fooled. "I guess not," she said. She shook her head slowly and thoughtfully. The teacher stared at her and pushed his glasses up further on his nose. "Why don't you go outside and play?" he said.

Karen shook her head again. "I don't know," she said.

After school she waited, putting her books into a pile on top of the desk and putting them back inside, back and forth, until the other children were gone. Then she stood and picked them up—she carried the same books, all she owned, back and forth to school every day. As she put on her coat the teacher approached her. His hands were stuffed awkwardly in the pockets of his corduroy jacket. "Karen," he said, "I think you and I should have a little talk. I think—" Karen went slowly to the entry and the teacher followed alongside her. Out in the entry they stopped. It was a narrow corridor with a coal bin to the left, quite dark. The boards of the bin were scarred with initials and drawings and words. "I think I know what you're afraid of," he said confidentially. Karen saw the Revere boy's name carved in the wood, clumsily and deeply, the dirty wood splintering outward around it. "The boys here, the big boys," he said. "That's the trouble, isn't it? You're afraid of them." Karen shook her head vaguely. She opened the door to the outside and looked out. The yard and the road were already empty.

"If that's the case I could do something about it," he said. "I could talk to their fathers. I would be glad to— It isn't because they don't like you," he said oddly. Karen glanced at him in surprise. "It's all right," she said. The teacher went on, "If I thought they were molesting you. . . . You might tell your father about it too."

"No," said Karen.

"Why not?"

"It's nasty," she said. She spoke so faintly he had to ask her to repeat it. "It's nasty," she said, "it isn't nice, it— They're nasty."

She stopped. "Nasty?" said the teacher. "How? How do they bother you?"

"I don't know."

"They make you afraid of them, don't they?"

Karen shook her head slowly.

"No? You're not afraid? Why do you stay inside, then?"

"I don't know."

"You don't know?" He tried to laugh a little. "You certainly are afraid," he said. "You're very afraid. What do they do to you?"

"I'm not afraid," Karen said.

"No?"

"I don't like him to touch me though."

"Him? Who's that, Revere?" he said. "The Revere boy?"

"Yes," said Karen. "But I'm not afraid of him. I just don't like him. I don't like him to touch me."

"Does he—where does he— What does he do to you?"

When Karen said nothing he went on, "It's a shame to have a boy that age still in school—he's so much older than you, and— Boys that age are—are getting to be—" His voice suddenly turned peculiar, a little hurried and guilty, slurred, so that Karen knew he was not looking at her but that his eyes were lowered. "He's so much bigger than you, he's— What does he do to you?"

Karen was leaning out of the doorway and looking down the road. She could see no one there. When she started to step down the teacher stopped her; he took hold of her arm. "Wait," he said. "Why don't you answer? Why are you like this? I only want to talk to you. Please don't be—don't be ashamed. I was watching you today. I felt sorry for you. I felt sorry for you."

"I have to go home," Karen said. She looked up at him. Surprisingly, his eyes behind the thick glasses were not like her father's or an older person's at all—they belonged to a boy. She stared at him as if seeing him for the first time.

"Won't you listen?" he said. "I only want to help you. I don't like to see you so afraid."

"I'm not afraid," said Karen.

He still held her arm. "Tell me—what does he do?" he said,

88

nearly in a whisper. There was something urgent about his voice that shocked Karen. "Don't be ashamed to tell me. Don't be ashamed."

"I'm not ashamed," Karen said. "I'm not afraid either." Her shock and discomfort were turning now to anger, though she could not have said why. She frowned out at the road.

"Tell me what he does," the teacher said.

"He does this!" said Karen impatiently. She pulled the skirt of her dress up and stared at the teacher's alarmed look. "I'm not ashamed of anything," she said, letting the skirt fall back. She thought, looking calmly at him, that she ought to say something more, but she could think of nothing—she felt only a sharp sensation of joy, of obstinate joy, in response to the alarm and shame she saw in his eyes. It was almost as if she had struck him: he stepped back, releasing her, his eyes at last rising to her face. "Now you leave me alone," Karen said. "You leave me alone too." In spite of her anger she knew that somehow she had done right, and that the teacher, shaken and ashamed, recognized it. Even in the face of the knowledge that she would be completely alone at the school after this, she could not help but feel a sense of bitter joy. "You leave me alone too!" she had cried, running out onto the walk.

Something moving drew her back to the present—to the woods: she thought she had seen something. She stood before a small gully, looking across to a pasture. Shapes defined themselves to her eye but she did not really see them; she waited only for movement. The gully was crusted with remnants of snow and rocks and looked as if it would be difficult to cross. She could not remember if she had played here as a child; probably she had not come so far from home. Some distance away there was a small grouping of buildings she thought she recognized.

After a while she began to descend the gully, steadying herself with her hands. Her mind went blank beneath a pushing, blood-pounding ache, and she lost her sense of time. She could not have said how long it was since she had left her home, and the fact of leaving—the pain of her father, the automobile accident before that—seemed unreal. Rocks gave way and she lost her footing. Her hands were scratched, one fingernail was torn back to show raw, pink, bleeding flesh that looked surprised at being uncovered. When she reached the top of the other side her head was pounding. She looked over to the buildings, which were in shadow: the sun was behind them. She stared at them, resting, and at the sun that must have fallen suddenly through the sky. Time had proceeded with gaps she did not try to understand.

As she crossed the field she heard something she had not noticed before: the beginning of the wind. It murmured sadly through the grass, a low, dwindling sound that never quite died. Birds back in the woods called out warnings to one another, as if they had just seen something that frightened them. As Karen approached the first of the old buildings—abandoned buildings of her father's—she saw, without any surprise, Shar appear around the corner. He seemed to be waiting for her. She did not hurry. She looked at him, neither with relief nor with concern, and from time to time her eyes slipped out of control and stared at the sky or the field or the barn again and Shar's figure before it.

She could already hear his voice. What was he saying? His words made no sense. Then she saw his expression suddenly leap to her, close, in focus, savagely clear. His words came like scraps of paper or leaves raised and slammed past by the wind. "Goddam it but I told you! I told you! I told you!" He ran to her. "I seen you all this time!" She thought he was about to take hold of her but he only went on, white-faced, trembling with anger: "Now you come all this way! For what? For what? Now what?" His face was still streaked with blood: Karen saw that. His hand was dirty, smeared, and he rubbed it restlessly against his thigh, his fingers outstretched as if in exquisite pain. He turned suddenly to look around. Something moved down on the road. He pulled Karen back behind the barn. She could still see, though, the wagon down there: a horse-drawn wagon, a small wagon with a man holding the slackened reins and turning on the seat to look at two persons behind him—two children, Karen saw, whose voices she could hear across the distance. She thought she knew who they were, neighbors of theirs. The voices of the children were thin and snatched and one of the children, a little girl, leaned over the side of the wagon with her hand outstretched to the moving ground. . . .

"All right," Shar said. They were standing before the entrance to the barn in what had once been worn, used ground; it was now crusted with grass. "Now you get what you wanted. Come here." His last words startled her. She looked up and then thought to cross the little space to him; this was what he meant. Shar's expression changed from its look of taunting hardness to one of slow, cold disgust, almost incredulous disgust, as if he could not quite believe what he saw. "My God," he said, staring, "how can you—" Then he quit. Overtaken by something else, he came to her, touched her shoulders, took hold of her. His touch seemed to awaken her: she felt the reality of the moment, the strength of the strange man who held her. She turned aside and put her hands to her face, shielding it, and looked back to the field and the empty road as if to frame their look.

When Shar opened the door of the barn and forced her inside, things ran away in the corners, fleeing the light. "Son of a bitchen rats!" Shar said in a vigorous, straining voice.

7

The store was in an old, barnlike building oddly close to the road, with an old-fashioned porch that ran its length and was cluttered at one end with discarded barrels and cartons. Inside, the air was cold and stale. Shar walked idly up to the front window once again, buttoning his shirt. His eyes were sore from the few hours' sleep he had had and he was trying to get rid of the taste in his mouth by smoking. At the window he rubbed the steamy dirt and looked out to the road; it was still empty. In the early morning cold the gingerbread posts of the porch were coated with a thin film of frost. Across the road a plowed field sloped up and ended in a chill white haze.

The owner of the store, a man Shar had thought at first to be old but now thought to be middle-aged, stood behind the counter, as if he were waiting to sell something to Shar. He watched Shar pace back and forth. He had spent the night sleeping out in this part of the store, in a roll of blankets on the floor, and these he had now piled on top of the counter. One looked like a horse blanket—it was olive-colored, filthy, and had buckles on it. Shar looked at the buckles with distaste. The man pulled his shoulders up with an effort and began to speak. "He'll be along any minute. Any minute now, don't you worry. I'm glad to do it. I don't owe Herz anything." When Shar did not answer, the man went on, peering up importantly at Shar, "It don't look so bad now you washed the blood off. Your face, I mean. Nobody could hardly tell there was anything wrong."

Shar leaned forward on the counter as if he were tired. He and the man looked at each other: the man's eyes were still and jellied behind his glasses. "I wish to hell he would get here," Shar said. "I'm sick of this place."

"Yes, yes, that's true," the man said vaguely. His hair was dark and thin and came down on his forehead in two flimsy strands. His chin was reflected on the dull scratched top of the glass counter. For some reason he seemed to like Shar; he nodded amiably at him. "But those state troopers won't be back any more. They know me; we used to give out gas here a while back, and they stopped in a lot. They knew my brother more but me too. . . . Did you like what I said to them?"

"Hell," said Shar.

As if this were an answer, the man went on chattily, "They must have patrolled the road last night, driving back and forth and stopping cars. Maybe they set up a roadblock for a while.

93

The kid will tell you if there's one now—it's all right. They wouldn't keep it up long. They'd figure you got out." Behind him shelves reached to the ceiling: boxes, canned goods, boots, grimy glassware, coils of rope. Shar let his eyes wander over the objects. "Your face does look a lot better now," the man said. He smiled seriously. "It was just the surprise of it, last night I mean, you coming in here like you did— My heart isn't so good and I—"

Shar looked at him. "What's wrong with your heart?"

"Why—why—I'm not sure—" the man stammered; he was obviously flattered. As if he did not want to ruin the moment by talking, he fell silent.

Shar lit another cigarette and strolled back to the window. There was nothing to see. "Those bastards will never find me," he said. Then he felt embarrassed for having spoken. Back at the counter, with his soft stomach expanded against the glass, the man would be nodding enthusiastically.

"Do you have—do you have insomnia?" the man said.

"What?"

"Insomnia—like me. That would help you." He stood in the same position, one fat hand on the pile of blankets. "I can't sleep much and when I do, I wake up before dawn. The birds do it—at dawn, I mean." Seeing Shar's look, he went on, "I mean, that would help you. If you have a long way to go and want to keep going straight through. Or anything you want to do and don't want to waste your life sleeping—insomnia would help. An ideal insomnia."

Shar turned back to the window. He hardly heard the man. "Think if you're fifty years old. That means you spent maybe eighteen years asleep. Did you ever think of that? All that time asleep, and lying flat on your back. . . . It makes me mad to think about it," he said. "I don't like to think about it."

The cold white glare began to hurt Shar's eyes so he came

back to the counter again. "Another thing," the man said, "a lot of things going on that you want to change—make better, I mean. Specially in a store like this where you're by yourself and people coming in and out all the time. Some ones of them only stop once, like you . . . like you're doing. Some things go on you'd like to change or give some help to. I mean, like this kid the other night. He was maybe thirteen or so, a runaway for sure, and freezing cold and hungry. Well, I happened to see him coming out there and couldn't think what to do—to let him in or not, to give him something or not. I couldn't think. I locked the door, though—without thinking—I got that done. He stood out there rattling around with it. I thought maybe I'd go up and unlock it but I never did. Because he was hungry, I knew he was *hungry,* so I was afraid of him. Then I thought he'd break in or throw a rock through the window, but he didn't. He was run away from something for sure—and had a face all gone thin like a hawk or an old man. They get like that."

Beneath the marred glass of the counter Shar saw opened cartons of cigarettes and candy bars and pieces of candy that lay out in the open, lengths of licorice and peppermint sticks. There was even a fly, dazed with the cold or just coming back to life, that crawled over one of the peppermint sticks.

"I ought to have tossed him out a candy bar!" the man said suddenly. He gave a shrill, brief giggle that stopped when Shar stared up at him. "Well," he said, resuming his nod, "you don't need to worry. Not a bit. I'll do just what you say."

"What about the boy?"

"No, he won't say anything. I'll see to it."

Shar watched the fly. Its wings beat slowly, tiny pulsations. It crawled with intricate steps over the candy. "All right," said Shar. "It better be that way. Once I get out of here I don't want to come back, or send anybody back for you."

95

"Of course. No—no. That's right."

"If I was here," Shar said, "I wouldn't stand for it but would get the hell out of here. Like I did when I was a kid. Give it all up and leave—burn it all up and leave."

"Would you?" said the man with great interest.

Shar shrugged his shoulders, sorry he had said anything. He tapped on the counter. Beneath the glass the fly remained still, as though paralyzed by the sound or the vibrations. "The hell with it," he said. "Nothing would hold me anywhere. I wouldn't give it up to no one or anything to hold me. Without being free—" He paused and looked away. The man waited. When Shar went on it was about something else, and he could feel the man's queer disappointment. "It better be a good car," he said. "I don't care what it looks like but it better be good underneath."

"I don't know much about cars."

"Well, I do. It better be good for what I'm giving you."

"There's some risk involved for me—"

"Risk!" said Shar. For the first time that morning he felt angry. The sensation pleased him. "Mention that to me again and I'll stuff those goddam peppermint sticks down your throat— You'll wish to hell you'd given them to the kid then."

"The kid?"

"The one outside—the one wanting to get in," Shar said. He stared at the man in distaste. "You're a bastard not to give him anything."

"But he—he might have— When people are hungry they're not the same," the man said, pretending to be flustered but obviously pleased by both Shar's attention and his contempt. "They do things—they might do things to you. A person can't take a chance."

Shar yawned and looked around. The other wall of the store was also filled with shelves and merchandise, and before it there was another counter, stacked with half-opened boxes. A pile of shirts like the one Shar had just put on—heavy woolen shirts with leather buttons—had been tossed down, and there were work shirts of denim, and overalls, and shotgun shells, and leather gloves. "I got a lot of things stored up here," the man said. "Some of them been here a long time—when my father had the place, even. They don't move fast. Like that shirt I gave you and them gloves—they got fur on the inside. We had some ladies' stuff but it never sold so we got rid of it. They'd rather go in to town for that—rather get the same stuff there. I never could figure out why."

"How long is he going to take?" Shar said impatiently.

"It won't be long now."

"I wish to hell he'd hurry up. It's been light now for a couple of hours."

As if summoned, the man came around the counter. He was nearly a head shorter than Shar and fairly heavy, with thick neck and shoulders. "He had to wake them up down there," he said. "They aren't used to people coming around so early. But it oughtn't to be long now. I don't know what's keeping him."

Shar looked at his watch. It was cracked but ticked faintly. "It's been about an hour."

They waited, side by side. Shar stared mechanically at the window. Outside, the morning did not seem to get lighter but stayed the same—it had a dull, heavy look, as if a fog were pressed up hard against the building. Shar thought he would be glad to leave this country again, but he thought too that he would probably remember it in spite of himself: cold air, hard earth, mountains at the horizon, his father's shanty, an abandoned barn with rats scuttling around for an hour or so. And, last night, a back door opening fearfully and this man staring out at him with a look of such terror that Shar thought for an instant the automobile accident must have disfigured him. . . .

"There's something coming, there it is," the man said. He sounded a little disappointed. He went up to the door and opened it. "Yes. It's him."

When the kid drove up Shar stood back from the window. The car was black, an old model, mud-crusted, with one door wired shut. "All right," Shar said. "I'll go out and— No, wait." He drew back. "You go out and get rid of him."

Shar watched the man and the kid talking. When the kid glanced toward the window Shar turned aside. After a while the man came back in, carrying a bundle of clothing. "Could he get hold of everything?" Shar said. He took the clothes from the man; they were not folded but were wrinkled and damp. "How's the car?"

"Good, good," the man said, rubbing his hands. "You want to check it? But it's good—I know it. They got a good bargain, they wouldn't try to cheat you. I mean, to cheat me—it's all right. Don't worry. . . . Those things are from the guy's wife, that has the car lot. He said she put some good things in."

"All right," said Shar. "I'll look at the car in a minute. Get rid of the kid."

"He's gone."

The man followed Shar to the back of the store. "He's my brother's kid, works for Harry down there—Harry's got the car lot. He's smart and knows what's what; he won't talk. I told him."

Shar pushed a door open with his foot and went through, stooping, with the man clumsily behind him. "You ought to have got that blood off her hair," the man said. "I could do it myself now if you want."

"What?" said Shar.

"That blood on her hair—"

The room looked as if it had been a storeroom before being

converted into a bedroom: there was light only from a small high window that had neither a curtain nor a shade. Shar went to the bed where Karen was lying beneath a pile of dirty quilts. Her eyes were open slightly, so Shar had to stoop to see if she was really asleep. There was no pillow and her head seemed flung back at a painful angle. Her hair was matted and dirty and lay about her head in pale strands, spread out as if expressing surprise. Shar shook her. "I could get a washcloth," the man said.

"You stay where you are," said Shar. He let the bundle of clothes fall and shook Karen; he pulled the quilts off her. The man, watching, stepped closer. Shar saw him in the corner of his eye. The man's white pudgy hands were lifted as if he wanted to help.

"Like I—like I said before," the man began, moving a little closer to Shar, "there's things happening here you'd want to change, or to help the people— Some things . . . that you could do some good to." He stood watching Shar. "When they're young people, especially then. But I—I—"

Shar pushed him back. The man gasped in alarm, clutching his chest. "But I can't! I can't!" he said. "I can't do it!"

"What the hell are you talking about?"

"Why, you can see them starting, and how they'll go! You can see them like a map with red pencil on it—things to end with clothes all soiled, in a gas station somewhere, or a public rest room, or the back of a store with candy up front—those old pieces of candy there, stale and hard as rocks, stuck in that counter for so long—"

Shar had jerked Karen to her feet and she now leaned against him, her hair fallen softly forward. Without glancing at the man Shar said, "What the hell are you talking about?" He was trying to get Karen to stand by herself. Something about her dazed eyes, her pale, transparent-looking skin, transfixed him; he saw that her lips were moving as if she were whispering to him, to lure him closer. "Damn you," Shar said, "stand up. Stand up. How much time do you think I have?"

He was picking at the buttons at the neck of her dress, then he gave up and took hold of the dress by the collar and ripped it open. She lifted her arms against him slowly, but he pushed them down. "Hand me that thing there," Shar said to the man. The man awoke to action, already nodding, and gave Shar a dress of dark, cheap cotton, smelling of dampness. Shar tossed it beside him on the bed and turned back to Karen, tearing at the rest of her dress. He could see the man leaning to him and could almost feel the pressure of his body against him, and the weight of his look behind the glasses. "I don't know what it is to you," Shar said, "but it isn't the end of anything. It isn't any end. It's only now begun."

SUMMER

8

Strolling along the main street of Synderdale one day in mid-summer were two young men, one a Negro employed by a racing company and the other an ex-college student, a big, pudgy, pleasant-faced young man who had quit school to experience life and who had managed to become employed by the same company that owned, or hired, the Negro. The Negro, Mitchie, was neat and cleanly handsome, and carried himself with pride: he was being groomed for racing. The other man, Ponzi, who had anxiously applied for a mechanic's job and whose ignorance had not yet been discovered, carried himself with pride also—but it was a perverse, insolent, grinning pride, as if he were pleased with his slouching posture and damp clothes and the sweat that seemed to seep out of his skin, as well as the more obscure fact of his accompanying a Negro obviously his superior, obviously more attractive to any women they might encounter.

It was the morning of the Synderdale picnic and race. The two were not really connected: the picnic was sponsored by volunteer firemen in the county to make money and the race was controlled by people outside Synderdale who rented the old fair grounds for the day. As Mitchie and Ponzi walked through town they enjoyed the sensation of being strangers and of being looked upon as superior. Groups of teen-age boys crowded along the street and looked at them, wondering if they were drivers in the race or owners; no one dared ask them. "A hell of a hot day for a race," Ponzi said, wiping his face. "He'll lose ten pounds on that track."

"I heard he lost eight or so one day," Mitchie said. "That was before I was with them."

Traffic moved slowly through town. There were groups of people in uniform: they wore satin and gold braid and carried musical instruments that gleamed importantly in the sunlight. Drum majorettes, some of them not more than children, ran giggling along the sidewalks in short shiny skirts. Tassels on their white boots jiggled in their excitement. Catching sight of Mitchie and Ponzi, the girls whispered together and peeped at them slyly and surrendered to gales of laughter. "These country girls," Ponzi said, grinning.

A fat man in the street, dressed like an army officer of high rank except for the splendid scarlet of his uniform, blew experimentally on a tuba. Perspiring men carried flags of various colors and dragged drums across the street. One of the drums,

Ponzi saw, said MARCHEN COUNTY CORPS. Still in the back of a pick-up truck was another drum, a newer and larger one, that said MEDINA FIREMEN. Little boys pounded on the drum with their fists and, just before Mitchie and Ponzi passed by, began to kick it angrily. People shouted. Someone had arranged for music to be broadcast throughout the town by means of a loud-speaker system, and the music got suddenly louder: it was a popular song, twangy and persistent, a woman's voice straining against a background of frenzied guitars and electronic instruments. She sang:

"The way love is it treats you wrong,
It don't care for hearts that break.
Take your burdens to the Lord. . . ."

Teen-age boys in roaring jalopies drove up and down the main street, waving and shouting. Someone on the sidewalk picked up a big stone and threw it after them, but it bounced harmlessly across the street; one of the uniformed firemen, tacking up a poster, looked angrily around to see who had thrown it. Before a drug store a sound truck had been parked, decorated with red crepe paper. A man dressed in a suit and tie stood on a platform with a microphone in his hand, interviewing a young girl and grinning and trying to draw into the conversation the group of people who stood silently watching. As Mitchie and Ponzi passed by he said, "Now folks, folks, this is a busy day in Synderdale; a busy morning in Synderdale; there's folks all up and down the street, and out in the park the firemen and their wives are getting tents set up, and games set up, and the big chowder kettles are filled with— chowder—and everything is getting ready for the parade! The parade is at one o'clock! The parade will be led off by the Synderdale Consolidated High School, and I have the young lady here who is president—what?—vice-president of the baton twirlers. A young lady who—" The girl wore white with gold braid. She giggled behind her hand. A woman in the crowd, probably her mother, nodded anxiously as if she were trying to tell the girl something.

Young girls strolled along the sidewalk, four and five abreast, with linked arms. Some of them wore shorts and were barefoot, others were dressed as if it were Sunday, in high heels, and others wore the gleaming short skirts of the baton twirlers: approaching Mitchie and Ponzi, they pretended to look away and to talk breathlessly among themselves, but at the last moment they would turn on the men their neat, hard, sharply sweet looks and release each other so the men could pass by. Ponzi smelled their harsh perfume. He heard them giggle something about "that nigger." Again he felt a thrill of insolent pride, and glanced at Mitchie to see if he had heard.

Mitchie wore sky blue and white: he looked careful, even cautious, about his dress. A solemn necktie of gray gave him the look of a professional man. His hair was cut short, hardly more than a dark film on his head; his face was clean, a little shiny from perspiration, and his eyes and teeth, astonishingly white, seemed to hide themselves: he had the look of being on view and yet not self-conscious, as if he had been prepared by someone other than himself. Ponzi, walking proudly beside him with his chest out, wore a stained shirt of yellow, open at the neck, and khaki pants that were too big for him at the seat and knees and were stained with grease. His arms swung militantly back and forth as he walked, and his hands, clammy white beneath the grease stains, sometimes caught each other in mid-swing and for an instant clasped together, caressingly or nervously. "When did you say they're coming? Why aren't they here?" he said. "Shar's been here for a day. What is he like—Max—will he notice me? What is he like?"

Mitchie did not look at him. He seemed to feel embarrassment for Ponzi's anxiety. He said softly, "Don't you worry any about him. It's most likely he won't even notice you."

But this was not what Ponzi wanted to hear. "What's he like?" he said, leaning to Mitchie. "Is he— How old is he? What does he look like?"

Mitchie shrugged his shoulders. "I don't know him too well. I don't do no business with him anyway."

"But what is he like? Doesn't he ever talk to you?"

"He does sometimes," Mitchie said. "He told me he'd heard some good things about me, about my driving. He said Shar was the one told him that." Mitchie could not help glancing at Ponzi as he said that. "Shar himself told it. Shar clocked me going around—"

"But Max, I mean Max," Ponzi said. "What does he look like?"

"He's a big man," Mitchie said slowly.

A horde of boys stood about the sidewalk, smoking. They watched Mitchie and Ponzi silently. Behind them, as if protected by them, was a poster advertising the race: the garish picture of a racing car and a helmeted man who seemed to be lunging out of a halo of flame. The man's eyes were hidden by his goggles, but his mouth—open, grinning, twisted—shouted of terror. The poster had not even been defaced.

For some reason a truck came down the street with banners draped about it—bright colors, red and blue—and boys of about ten years sat with legs dangling in the back, waving condescendingly at people on the street. Stones were thrown at them; some bounced up against the cab of the truck. One of the boys, who had been shouting and waving white fists, was struck in the face and scrambled up and started to cry. The truck passed out of sight. Horns blew, cars drove grandly down the middle of the street. They were filled with passengers and sagged gently.

Activity increased. As if spurred on by the frenzy of the music, new groups appeared around corners, drove down the street. A bus stopped to unload teen-agers, some of whom carried lunch bags. One of the baton twirlers stopped to ask Mitchie for a light for her cigarette. She was perhaps fourteen, but big for her age: her white satin outfit strained to contain her. She had red-blond hair and eyes outlined in black. As she inhaled the smoke she bent her head forward, making her white throat arch. "I never seen you here before," she said. "You two in for the races, ain't you? You got something to do with it?"

"Mitchie might be a driver," Ponzi said at once. He grinned, sweating. He put one arm around Mitchie's shoulders. "How do you like that? He might get to drive."

The girl stared in awe. "No kidding?" she said.

"Me, I crawl in the grease. That's what I do. I roll around in the grease." Ponzi laughed extravagantly, as if he had said something funny. Mitchie pulled away so that Ponzi's arm hugged the air. "It's goddam safer there," Ponzi said.

"No kidding you might race?" the girl said to Mitchie. "Is that no kidding?"

"I'm not the driver," Mitchie said. He did not look at the girl.

"You're not? Who is it then? Is it somebody around here?"

"The driver's here. He's here. Do you want to meet him?" Ponzi said. "Do you want me to take you to meet him?"

"Jesus Christ," said Mitchie. He stared out at the street.

"No kidding you could?" said the girl. "He ain't married, is he? Where is he?"

Seeing Mitchie's look, Ponzi suddenly calmed. He said sadly, "I guess I can't just yet. Maybe later."

"Later when?" said the girl. She followed them along for a

108

while. "Listen, mister, I never met a driver before. That's the truth. I never yet met one. I—"

"Later on," Ponzi said. "You come by later on."

The girl called after them for a while, but was lost in the crowd. More people appeared, many of them in uniform. Some men blew noisemakers. The golden gleam of braid and buttons and musical instruments filled the air. Before a hardware store a girl who looked hardly more than sixteen stood on top of a chair, holding her baby up to look around: the baby, eyes closed and face as blank as if it had been erased, moved its lips helplessly. There was a smell of hot dogs in the air.

Mitchie walked in the street to get away from the crowd. Ponzi, hurrying with him, walked in the gutter. Mitchie began to talk suddenly, though his face showed no sign of expression: "Shar says it's only fire that worries him. I thought about that too. If it could be a crash and everything over at once, all the bones broke you're going to have, over at once—that wouldn't be too bad. But the fire comes right away and keeps on. That's bad."

Ponzi had begun to pant. "Fire?" he said. "What about it?"

"I don't like it none myself. Dream of it sometimes."

"A big strong nigger like you?" Ponzi said. "Hell, don't let it worry you. I wouldn't let it worry you."

"I ast Shar if he dreamt of it too and he said he did a few times, when he first started. But then he said too after you die worms and things eat you; if you was burnt away they couldn't get at you. You got to think of that."

"Shar said that?"

"Shar got it all thought out."

"He doesn't like me much," Ponzi said, grinning.

"Telling that girl I was the driver, like you did, it got me to think for a minute I *was* it. Scairt me some."

109

"Hell—"

"Sure it did. That's how it is," Mitchie said. They stopped in the street and Mitchie lit a cigarette. Ponzi saw some people watching Mitchie: he was a tall, handsome Negro, and people could not decide whether he knew it or not. "Now," he said, tossing away the match, "Shar told me one time we were drinking together something he thought out. He said, 'Why should anything be safe?' I wondered that too; why should it? Who says so? A man fell in love with a car, like some of us, he don't owe it to himself for things to be safe. They ain't worth it to be safe. I understand that."

"You're a hell of a lot smarter than me if you do," Ponzi said.

His irony was lost on Mitchie. He did not even think Mitchie heard him. "Now, even a piddling race like this one today, even with no special guy to beat, Shar takes it the same as any other. 'Course Max and them want him to practice up for the Fourth of July race; but Shar don't think of that. He just thinks of the car. You ever seen a driver around a car so much? He come in early with it himself and balanced the wheels himself. He won't let anybody else at it, he checks over the parts himself. He does it every time. How many guys, got up to be drivers, would bother with that? They'd s'pose it was below them. He told me how a man has got to love his car or else he won't win."

"Love his car!" Ponzi laughed. He looked around as if for an audience. "I heard different about your driver!"

"This first race we had he mostly burnt his foot off, taking the car around that goddam gravel track at Jasper. But he kept on going till he won."

"A hell of a stupid thing to do," Ponzi grinned.

"His foot was about cooked from all that heat, but he said it was just numb. He said he never felt it so long as he kept on going, but Max got mad as hell, told him he ought to take care of himself more; 'cause Max loves him," he said oddly. "I seen that. He takes it hard, any trouble of Shar's. But you got to love the car! I know that for a fact. Look at them all, Shar and the other drivers—their hands all blisters and eyes burnt, cars about ready to explode or fall apart—wheels, axles, anything— but they love it all the way! A man puts in years out on the track—in ten minutes he gets that much living out of it. And you see how Shar takes a race. All quiet, like he was under a shot."

"Nerve but no nerves," Ponzi announced, as if he had just thought of the phrase.

They found Shar and another driver standing on the pavement outside one of the bars. Ponzi squinted at Shar while at the same time trying not to be seen, because something about the man worried him. It might have been his closeness to mutilation and death. Shar and Mitchie nodded solemnly to each other; Ponzi, behind Mitchie, nodded too. "Weather ain't getting any cooler," Mitchie said. Ponzi had been surprised at the amount of attention given to the weather by racing people, but he was grateful for it too, since it was something he could understand. Shar, wearing sunglasses, stared coldly at him as if he could read Ponzi's mind. "You," he said to Ponzi, "what the hell time is it?" He held out his arm and they compared watches. "They're late. They're an hour late," he said to himself. Ponzi wondered if he wanted anything more from him. In Shar's presence Ponzi's self-mocking slovenliness ebbed; he no longer thought himself funny, or thought anything very funny. "Who's late?" he said.

But that was a mistake. Shar turned away as if he did not

like the smell of Ponzi, and did not even answer. Mitchie made a face at him. "Goddam big mouth," he said. "Why do you pretend things all the time?"

"Did he mean Max?"

The other driver was about Shar's age, but already balding. He looked nervous. Shar stood staring out at the street and the man talked behind his back, loud enough for Shar to hear if he wanted. "We were hoping for a little rain this morning, to keep the dust down. Hell, they might not even have sprinklers here —this is a two-bit track. My first time here too. I'd like to be in the Cherry River race—that's Fourth of July—but my manager had some trouble getting us in; I might get in, though."

"That's a good track," Mitchie said cautiously.

"Cherry River, yeah. That's good. The money's good too," the man said, winking. "But the competition's bad!" He laughed, glancing around at Shar's back. Shar did not turn around. "I was telling your boy here what some local bastard is doing. Did you hear about it? The seats in the stands go for a dollar or more, and they let kids and people sit around on the grass by the track for half a buck. But this bastard—runs a shoe store in town—got up the idea to rent some space there, and paid five bucks for it, nobody any wiser. So what does he do but put up some kind of goddam stand himself! Made out of pipes and things, like in a kid's playground where the kids climb around on them, going up in the air, so he figures to put thirty people on it, not counting little kids, and the ones right on top can see as well as anybody in the stands. A hell of a wise bastard—somebody ought to teach **him** a lesson. And he figures to make a lot by it—him and some friends are in the bar there laughing about it, and how they put one over on the racing people. My manager will be mad as hell when he hears of it."

Shar turned. He had lit a cigarette. Ponzi thought idly that he did not look so calm—his face looked strained, pale, his lips turned up in a tight, mocking grimace. Whether he was angry at the other driver or at something else was not clear. "Jesus Christ," he said.

"Yeah, it's a goddam thing," the man said, as if Shar had agreed with him. "Nobody knew what he was up to."

"You talk too goddam much," Shar said.

The driver blinked at him. He laughed nervously. Shar said to Mitchie, "If you see them tell them I'm at the hotel. I had enough of this waiting."

"I'll sure do that," Mitchie said. When speaking to Shar he looked down at the man's feet, as if he thought looking at Shar's face would annoy him.

"Good luck this afternoon," the other driver said as Shar left. He shrugged his shoulders and moved closer to Mitchie and Ponzi. "He's really a son of a bitch, isn't he?" he said cautiously. "I mean, gets mad pretty fast. He told somebody's manager inside there he'd send his boy spinning off the track today, dump him right in the guy's lap. Nobody knew how to take it—serious or not. Shar wasn't smiling much when he said it."

Mitchie frowned and licked his lips and looked away. Ponzi pretended to be angry at what the man had said about Shar and glared at him. "He doesn't joke much," he said importantly.

The man ambled back into the bar, wiping his balding head. Outside the bar the sidewalk was crowded—there were firemen perspiring in their gaudy uniforms, and boys in tight, surging hordes, and small children, barefoot, and the girls who would march in the parade: proud and slyly shy they were, sipping soft drinks from perspiring bottles, looking at the men, ignoring the boys, now and then lifting arms to caress their hair and to show the little half moons of perspiration under

113

their arms. Ponzi was drenched with sweat; he seemed to glow in it and in the crowd's excitement. He liked being jostled, especially when one of the girls pushed against him, and he even liked the incredible wailing from the loud-speaker, a voice that could have been either male or female, screaming about love:

"Searching, searching,
I spent my whole-life-through
Searching, searching for someone
Just like you!"

Ponzi saw the automobile at about the same time Mitchie did. It had been edging in and out of traffic down the street, traveling fast, and approached them with its horn blaring impatiently. Four or five old women scurried to safety on the sidewalk, gasping for breath; in his haste to get away a boy on a bicycle fell over, hard, right on his side. Uniformed men in a great friendly crowd pointed at the boy and roared with laughter. The boy, his face almost swollen with blood, ashamed, trying not to cry, dragged himself painfully over to the gutter.

The car was black—a black convertible. People pushed out to look at it. It was piled in back with boxes and suitcases and a man sat on top of the pile on the left, smoking, looking at the people who stared back at him. In the front seat sat a neat-looking man with black hair, driving, honking his horn without any show of impatience, judging from his face; next to him sat a big man with a pale, dough-colored face, looking at the town as if he were delighted with it. Beside him, pushed against the door, was a girl with blond hair who sat with one arm outstretched, fingers idly spread to catch the warm wind. All wore sunglasses, even the man in the back, who nodded mysteriously at people on the sidewalk.

Up the street someone stepped off the sidewalk: it was Shar.

114

He waved to them. The car screeched to a stop, dust rising immediately around it. The man in the back seat stood and began yelling something but no one paid any attention. Shar opened the door and pulled the girl out, leaned across to talk to the heavy man with the big, pale face for a minute. The car started and stopped again, rocking. The man in the back seat picked up some suitcases and handed them to Shar, but Shar refused to take them; they were put back in the car. The little man in the driver's seat, dispassionate and hardly glancing around, now started the car again and drove away.

Shar and the girl crossed the street. On the sidewalk Shar embraced the girl. She allowed him to hold her: Ponzi stared at them through the thin, hot, dusty air. His eyes were stinging a little. He stared at them, though Mitchie wanted to go—they stood on the sidewalk with people passing and looking too, Shar holding the girl anxiously and the girl in white high-heeled shoes, with bare white legs, straining upward, leaning forward against Shar's chest and straining up to him, her black skirt showing the backs of her knees, her blouse pulled out and up in back by Shar's embrace so that Ponzi could see, below the wrinkled blouse and the wrinkled cotton of Shar's sleeve, the girl's bare skin.

"He'll be all right now," Mitchie said. "He'll be better now." He even smiled at Ponzi, he was so pleased, so relieved. But Ponzi, struck by something—it might have been the girl's youth—felt strangely depressed. He pulled his collar away from his throat. The excitement of the crowd, titillated by Shar and the girl and the magnificence of that automobile, no longer interested him. For a moment he felt afraid, though he did not know why.

9

Rich orange sunlight glowed against the drawn shade of the room in which Shar lay with Karen. Down on the street there were shouts and murmurs and a sound like firecrackers being set off, but in the room it was quiet, still, even a little restrained. Shar lay beside Karen and looked at her: her hair was outspread on the pillow, as it always was, sleek and fine, her eyes matched his in their seriousness, her lips were a little open as they were when she slept. Their reunion had been violent— Shar felt he was hurting her—and the knowledge that she felt little, that she did not really share in the sensation that overwhelmed him, had made his brutality more unchecked. Now, watching her closely, as if he did not see she was aware of him, Shar thought of the few times he had been able to draw her along with him: the memory shot through him, a pang of excitement. "Are you happy?" Shar said. Karen smiled gently. "Will you watch me out there today? Will you?"

"Yes," said Karen.

"How was your drive down here? Jerry drives all right, doesn't he?"

"It was a good drive," Karen said. "I wanted to come with you, though. You shouldn't have made me stay behind."

"No, I had to do it," Shar said seriously, "I had to work that car out by myself. I don't put enough time in it. I got to know it before I can drive it."

"I wanted to come with you," Karen said.

Shar hardly heard her. The smell of her hair and of her body enchanted him. He touched her face; she held his hand gently. In his violence, when desire was so strong it made him anxious, almost desperate, Karen's gentleness did not soothe him but goaded him—as if deliberately; he felt himself entrapped, falling, incomplete until he gave himself to her. At night he would wake from dreams of Karen so vivid he could smell the rich perspiring warmth of her body and remember her expression: frank, innocent, brutal in its simplicity. It was only in his imagination that she lured him to her; Karen herself did nothing, or seemed to do nothing. He thought that at times he could touch the queer love she had for him, but they had never talked about it. Only in the last two months, when Shar had begun racing for the summer, had they begun to speak much to each other. Their conversations seemed incomplete, as if they could not really understand each other's language. Much of what Karen said Shar understood to be paraphrases of things he had

117

said, or anticipations of things he would say. When she spoke he would listen to the self-assured sweetness of her voice and watch her face, allowing himself to be enchanted. Now she spoke about something: it did not matter what she said, what mattered was the manner in which she said it, luring and captivating him, and at times Shar believed she understood this as well as he.

"Do you love me?" Karen said.

Shar sat up and lit a cigarette. The smoke would clear his head; he had to think. Immediately his mind filled with the race, the grandstands full of people, the relentless dirt track. He felt something—a queer little force—drawing at him, luring him into the center, to death, but he did not understand what it was. Death for auto racers came not through surrender to the center, but through surrender to the outside—to centrifugal force, a sudden careening off the track. Green infield, dotted grandstand, blue sky: these would reel before him, narrowing to the white retaining wall and then to the flash of impact. Shar had awakened out of various nightmares upon the moment of impact, drenched with sweat, his fists clenched on an invisible wheel, his legs and feet straining to keep him in, keep him in. . . .

He turned to Karen as if he had not heard her. She looked serene, complete; she gazed at him with satisfaction. Little he said or left unsaid seemed to have any effect on her. "You scare me sometimes," Shar had said once nervously; he felt Karen oddly like himself, for she reflected his surface calm with her entire being, while Shar's mask did little more than mock his feelings. It was as if she had designed herself so: a woman imagining what would attract him, entrap him, and creating herself in that image, hair and eyes and mouth and body, and the hints of a soul that Karen revealed.

Shar remembered that she had not always been like this.

118

She had emerged out of a week of pain and hysteria, attended by Max's doctor, to claim him. When Max had demanded what Shar wanted to do with the girl, what point there had been in abducting her, ruining her health, almost ruining her sanity, Shar had really been unable to reply; he did not know. He had not thought about it. At the back of his mind he felt that she had wanted it, but his common sense rejected that and his expectation of Max's outrage silenced it. Shar had not had time to think about it, and now the familiar image of Karen's presence obscured all thought. At times he could not remember ever having been without her.

As if she understood his thought, she moved to take him into her arms. "Come here," Karen said. Shar let the cigarette fall on the floor with the dirty clothes and empty whisky bottles and came to Karen. He embraced her with his body. Anguish overtook him that he would not be able to make her feel as he did, then frustration, then the beginning of his mute, angry violence: she resisted him at the same time she gave herself to him, he thought; she did not love him, she mocked him, she used his infatuation to degrade him. In the face of such mockery Karen's gentleness, her silence even to his deliberate coarseness, irritated him until he felt like striking her, forcing her to cry out—as she sometimes did—in sharp, surprised pain. But her body had adapted itself to him now, he could hurt her only from time to time, and as he did it he was tortured by the fact that he wanted to do it; he could not understand. Anger at himself expressed itself in anger at Karen, who accepted it as she accepted everything—not bravely but only silently, innocently, as if everything he did were normal, as if these were the rituals that passed between a man and a woman in love! It was indecent—dirty—Shar thought, his outrage rising, it was dirty, dirty, he had made himself dirty in doing it, yet he enjoyed it, he loved it, he was obsessed by it! Karen, stained by his exertions, exhausted by his energy, was really untouched by him: he could not reach her. In desperation he gave himself up to the hot sucking softness of her body. He could stand it no longer; he cried out, he sobbed helplessly against her tensed face, he felt her small limbs brace him as if to prevent his doing violence against himself.

Some time later when Shar awoke he found that Karen had pulled the sheet over them and held him in her arms. His face had been against her shoulder; her skin was wet with his saliva. Shar drew away. "Christ, it's hot," he said. He felt strangely irritated. "What time is it?"

Karen reached for the watch on the night table. "It's five after twelve," she said.

He sat up and reached for his cigarettes. He did not look at Karen. "What the hell is that noise down there? It sounds like firecrackers." A slow uproar was sustained down on the street, punctuated by explosions and horns. Someone on the sidewalk three stories below was laughing hysterically. Listening to the laughter, Shar glanced at Karen: she was watching him steadily. Her face was damp with perspiration, her hair a little darker with it around her forehead. For a moment he sat with a lighted match in his hand, looking at her. He wanted to appeal to her, cringe before her, bury his face in her stomach, hide his eyes. He did not know why. He wanted to beg something of her, but he did not know what it would be— she was little to him, after all, new to his life and temporary to it; he had had other women longer than this. Before her pleased silent gaze he felt helpless. Even his strength was help-less. It occurred to him that if he wanted to be free of her he would have to kill her.

This thought bothered him. "Hell," he said aloud, lighting his cigarette. He tossed the burned match onto the floor with the rest of the refuse he had accumulated—crumpled candy bar wrappers, soiled underclothes, bottles, opened newspapers. His shoes, white with dust, lay against the baseboard of the wall as if they had been thrown there.

"I'm going out to the track," Shar said. "I'll see you after the race."

When he looked around he saw Karen trying to hide a small yawn. The movement of her arm, the sleepy luxury of her expression, touched him; he smiled at her. But his smile stopped when he felt with alarm his body preparing itself for her. He looked away. He got up. What did he want to beg of her? It might have been freedom—freedom to rid himself of her, clean himself of his intoxication for her, so that he could approach her as a man. Never had he made any choice about her: she had happened to him as accidents happened to him, immediate and complete. He had talked to Max about it. In the past Max had helped him with everything. Max listened to him, asked him questions, shared in his life; sometimes Shar felt that Max wanted too much, crowded Shar a little, but Shar had grown almost as dependent upon Max as Max was on him. He did not understand the relationship, he was not interested in understanding it. Shar's experience in racing, his experience with violence, with women, certain events in his past—these Max had shared, had drawn out of Shar so they really did not belong to Shar any more. But of Karen Shar had been able to tell Max little. He could not talk about her with anyone. She belonged to him, she seemed to have no life except with him. The thought of this maddened him, made his brain buzz and flinch—he had tried to explain it to Max but had grown so angry that he had been incoherent. And sick with desire for her. He could not escape her. He felt that she was nothing apart from him, she had nothing of herself but what she gave him, she was nothing in herself but what he touched —unlike the other women whom he could not even remember

121

now—she did not turn away in secret, she did not avert her eyes, did not think of other men when she was with him. She gave herself to him at once, and constantly; even the expression of pleasure she revealed from time to time was no more than a part of Shar, of what he created in her.

Shar chewed on a piece of chocolate candy left on the bureau and went into the bathroom, leaving Karen to herself. He was angry with her and he knew she understood, though neither of them could have explained. Under the shower he thought of sweat running off his body, dirt licked free, the intense heat of the bedroom exorcized by the water. He would be free of that; he would be ready for the race. Systematically he began emptying his mind of all things irrelevant to the race. First there was Karen: there was always Karen. On the verge of sleep at night he confused her in his mind with other women, with all women up to the first girl he had had, years ago; she blended with them, distorted their faces to hers, usurped their roles. A baby of three running fatly in her polka-dot clothes, blond curls, plump soft legs, busy fists! That had been Karen too. Remembering her thus strained Shar's sanity; he could not believe she was the same person. He had tried to explain it to Max: "I picked her up and handed her to her father that day. I was about sixteen—I don't know. She was two or three. She couldn't talk sense yet. Can you believe it's the same person?" Max thought it delightful; he had wanted to hear more. For the first time Shar resisted his questioning. Gladly, zestfully, had he reviewed his experiences with other women—Max had listened impassively—but something dulled his energy when he started to betray Karen. Max had asked his usual question: "Did you make her happy?" Instead of saying, as he usually did, "You're goddammed right I did," he had fallen silent; he did not know what to say. "Not like with the others," he had told Max finally. At the start he had been able to say, when Max asked him how it was with Karen, that it was wonderful, beautiful, that he "couldn't last five minutes with her"—Shar's tribute to a beautiful woman—but after a while he had shrugged his shoulders, he had not wanted to answer. For the first time he felt that Max wanted to know too much. "The fat old son of a bitch!" Shar growled into the shower—inexplicably, for he really liked Max.

There were other things he must cleanse himself of: his hatred for the people who crowded the street and who would be watching him this afternoon. A grandstand filled with hungry faces, murmuring lips. What delicious pleasure it would give them to watch him die! He knew them; he understood them. But he must not think of them, for anything beyond the pure experience of the speed alone was degrading. It was a private ritual—Shar shared it with no one, with none of the other drivers, certainly with no one in the crowd; he shared it, perhaps, with Max, but only partially. Max, who sat propped up with pillows in a chair, fingering pages in his innumerable books, fearful of his heart, of heat stroke, of cancer, of anything—Max could feel the beauty of Shar's experience only in his imagination, while Shar felt it in his very body. At a certain point the speed became his body: he was one with it. Those who sat sweating and chewing popcorn and drinking beer in the stadium watched the drivers tear around the track, but what they saw had little relationship to what really happened —to the private experiences of the drivers, who moved in a world apart. "Safe from those goddam bastards!" Shar said with immense satisfaction. And on the track he would be safe from entanglements with anyone—with himself, even, his usual self, the mortality in him that linked him to other men. He would be safe from time, lifted above time, he would be free of human bondage, of hatred, of jealousy, of anger, of lust, most of all, of love!—free of love! For him there would be dust

123

and the smell of oil and the terrific reality of that dirt track and the speed at which he moved above it. When the race was over, when he came back, he would feel cleansed, exorcized of fragments in him that were not really himself, that cluttered and obscured his vision. It was good to work up the speed, good to give it up, to return to the normal world of time: it was good to see the sun perfectly still in the sky.

If he could return from a race and meet Karen for the first time, then it would be possible for him to love her; he felt that strongly, angrily. If he could approach her without lust, without fear, he could love her. He did not know if he wanted to love her, if he was strong enough for it. He realized now that he had never loved anyone before. But he did know that his bondage to her was driving him insane, splitting him from what had always been essential in his life—a simplicity of vision, and simplicity of emotion—and that he had to free himself from it. Again the thought came to him that his freedom would be the same as Karen's death. But he shook his head in disgust; he did not believe it, he did not want to hear about it.

Emptied of the past, he prepared himself carefully for the future.

10

At one time the several acres of land north of Synderdale that were set aside for county use had been the site of the annual county fair, but now everything but the racing track and its stadium was abandoned. The track had originally been used for horse racing—farmers and their sons had showed off their horses with great pride; but for the last several years the track had been used for auto racing and, more often, for stock car racing—spectacles that attracted great crowds even on the hottest summer days.

On this day the dirt parking lot was filling up early with cars and pick-up trucks. Children rode bicycles and parked them in the grass. Old buses, of the sort usually seen transporting migrant farm workers from place to place, showed up filled with strangers from cities to the north. Hot-dog stands were crowded, cotton candy was sold, beer, soft drinks, souvenir flags and whistles, racing caps and goggles for children, straw hats, noisemakers—all were for sale. It was impossible not to feel the intense excitement in the air.

The impending communion in such a spectacle, well worshiped by most of the people, gave them a sense of brotherhood. Gangs of boys sought each other out, young girls drifted about in slow loose clusters, smiling at everyone. Many of the older people, still dressed in their fine uniforms and flushed by the joy and success of the firemen's parade, argued and shouted and slapped one another on the back with great gusto. They eyed with suspicion and admiration the big, well-dressed, rich-looking man who walked in conversation with the beautiful young girl—no doubt his daughter. These two were strolling slowly through the old fair grounds, waiting for the beginning of the race to near. The man kept looking at his watch. He wore a very light gray suit of a rich material, unfortunately a little too tight for his big, almost fat body; his shirt was cream colored and his necktie a modest blue. For all his bulk he walked delicately, as if he were not used to it or as if he feared it might somehow injure him. From a distance his face looked merely blank, and of a bloodless, stony color; at closer range his face was heavy and burdened with many tiny lines about his eyes and cheeks. Wrinkles of delight and of anger had imprinted themselves into him, running from his massive jaw and mouth up to his nose, out from his eyes in a fan-shaped spread, and across his forehead in irregular precision.

126

One of his pockets was stretched almost to bursting by a small blue book that he had stuffed into it.

The girl wore blue linen, a dress that did not belong exactly to summer or to the race track, and about her neck a necklace of silver hung catching the sunlight. Her pale hair hung straight to her shoulders. Her face was small, childlike, yet at the same time elegant—so people thought who stared at her. Sunglasses hid her eyes, and the careful vacuity of her expression, the deliberate set of her reddened lips, hid any feeling she might have had.

Automobiles were beginning to fill up the lot in which they strolled, so they turned away. Flies and mosquitoes buzzed in the air. They passed old buildings: the biggest, with most of its grimy windows broken, declared itself in a long weather-stained sign before its entrance: DAIRY CENTER. Now the doors were open and led into nothing but sunlight and buzzing flies. The man, who fondly called himself Max, spoke confidentially to Karen with a forefinger raised, as if he were delivering a lecture.

"You are thinking you have fooled me!" he said merrily. "You think to yourself—a fat man on a hot day, what a fool he turns out to be! Sweats himself away in little dribbles. Ah, that's true," he said, wiping his forehead, taking off his sunglasses either to wipe his eyes or to peer at Karen. "Heat, this heat disintegrates me—given a high temperature, a man caught in it —what happens to God at such times? So far away— Impossible— Just like no man with a toothache can be a believer."

Karen smiled to show she appreciated his humor but did not believe in it. Max's eyes, intent upon her, were startlingly small, small within the harsh pasty expanse of his face, and like the eyes of an animal, without much thought or perception: a deceit Karen knew he did not contrive. "But you are fooling me!" he cried, taking her arm. They passed through parked cars now, heading back to the stadium. "Who was it that took care of you in your hysteria? Was it Shar? Shar was drunk! It was I, and I understood you then, and I thought—a clever girl, a very intelligent girl, he is drunk and sick to death because he doesn't know what to do with her! I thought—she is a strange girl, but she will come around to me, she will see I am her friend; she will see that we are kin. Our minds are kin. I am positive of that."

Small boys ran shouting about them, intent on a game. Max stared at them for an instant in terror; but they did not notice and ran away behind the cars. Karen noticed his fear with a slight impulse of pity, but she said nothing. She had been trying not to surrender to pity for herself and, more immediately, to block Max's subtle probing into her mind, his groping for her secret. The effort to resist him had weakened her. "But when I say you are fooling me it is not just about this—you realize. No, it is about yourself—your very being. Your very being is a puzzle to me, a most delightful puzzle!" And he smiled to show he found her delightful. "You are the second to come down out of those mountains and to me—the first was Shar, a very young man then, no more than a boy. And you— You are a delight to me, you have made us very happy."

They passed by an old statue, overturned in the grass at the end of the makeshift parking lot, which was little more than a field. "Look here," Max said. He put his big hands on his thighs and grunted with the effort to bend and read the inscription on the statue. It was of a bearded man perched on a crumbling stone platform, with eyes of hard stone, rigid and consciously blind, who held in his lap sheaths of wheat. A collie dog with tongue breathlessly exposed sat leaning against his legs. The entire statue was discolored, crumpling, and children had defaced it with chalk. " 'Out of our land' it says there;

128

very nice." Max straightened with a luxurious sigh. "Very nice
—it reminds me of a graveyard piece; his eyes are angels' eyes."
Karen stared up at Max. She had had the same thought. "Now,
my dear Karen," the man said, smiling, "if you say that you do
not want my man to examine you—and he is a fine doctor, a
very learned man, you must not think that his giving himself
up to me—to my atrocious health—means he is inferior—nothing could be more misleading— If you do not want him to examine you I can only conclude that you are indeed pregnant
and that you will have to tell Shar about it, or I will have to
tell him, one or the other; maybe both. Both of us at once.
That would be nice, wouldn't it? It would make it less difficult for you. I know you are—you are worried about— Shar is
sometimes— But still you must do something about it. You
agree with me?"

"I have nothing to say," Karen said.

"But you fool me so! Not a one of them fools me like you
do," Max said, touching her chin. He held her face for a moment. "A very beautiful girl, it's no wonder you are as you
are! I suspect you have been pampered all your life and I agree
with that—that is absolutely correct—you are made to be pampered and that is why we pamper you like we do— That is why
I enjoy your persona, your little mask! Very discreet and
learned. You think, I will make them think how stupid I am,
how little I know! But you do not know how other women
are—how . . . completely, happily stupid they are, how the
wind whistles through their minds! Maybe Shar does not
know, or Jerry or my doctor, but I know; I know. I know
everything."

Where the stadium ended and there were no refreshment
stands or parked automobiles people were sitting peacefully in
the grass. Many of them had picnic lunches and were drinking
beer. A strange device had been set up: a stand made of pipes

on which people were sitting, crowded happily, waving to people on the ground. There were perhaps fifteen people, including small children and even babies, on each of the five levels. Those on top had field glasses and straw hats to shade their eyes from the sun, and looked about proudly. Some of the men grinned down at Karen as she passed. They waved beer bottles.

"Do you see those lightning rods?" Max said. He pointed to the rods gleaming frantically on the old section of the stadium. "They are supposed to have been hit by lightning many times. Something to see, wouldn't it? Have you ever seen lightning strike?"

"Yes," said Karen. "It just goes into the ground."

If Max was disappointed by this, he gave no sign. He seemed to take on the excitement of the crowd, and his walk became more spritely, almost youthful, as they approached the gate. "This will be a fine race, fine practice for Shar," he said. "A good day for him. He's beautiful to watch, isn't he? I am the only owner who follows his men around, the only one who loves to watch them! I suppose they say I am queer—touched in the head."

Karen smiled grimly. Max's reputation, among his own men and among people who knew him, was not tempered by whimsy. His origin unknown, his motives inscrutable, he had worked his way into auto racing by force alone. Karen had not asked about him, but she had heard vague remarks: he was supposed to make his fortune in gambling. Wherever he traveled he was accompanied by two men: one of them Jerry, who drove, and the other Max's own doctor, a blank-faced, silent, morose man of about forty who looked after Max's imaginary illnesses. Max's love was for Shar, however, and since Karen meant so much to Shar she deserved his love too; he had explained this to her carefully. "You will open my heart," Max had said once. "You must not be afraid of me. I am prepared to

130

love you—I want to love you. But you must not keep yourself from me."

Their seats were near the wall, in the shade. Jerry and the doctor awaited them. Max complained merrily of the heat to the doctor, Jerry asked if there was anything he wanted done, any messages run down to the garage; they arranged themselves in a row. "My grandmother's silver necklace," Max said, pointing to Karen. "Never did it look so good on anyone before! She is a beautiful girl." The doctor, sitting on the other side of Max, leaned over to stare without interest at Karen. He had thinning hair, a bald spot at the crown of his head. His eyes were sunken, flesh hung in loose folds on his face. On his lap, nearly embraced by his long arms, was the black bag in which he kept medical oddities for Max and liquor for himself. He said nothing. On Karen's right Jerry sat, his legs crossed, his smartly polished shoes gleaming. He nodded sagely at Max's remark and looked sideways at Karen. Karen did not meet his gaze. "Maybe she will grow more beautiful still," Karen heard Max say to the doctor. "She has nothing to tell me. We will have to wait and see. She keeps secrets, she keeps to herself."

Jerry lit a cigarette and said to Max, "It's Shar you ought to of talked to. It's his goddam fault. The way he acts you'd think a baby come out of a haystack one morning; he never did have any sense."

"He isn't very discreet," Max said sadly.

"He'll catch something one of these days," Jerry said. "You can have the doctor shoot him full of something—good for all ailments."

Behind them the stadium reared up gigantically, swarming with people. The frank, excited murmur of the crowd put Karen in mind, as it always did, of the danger that was impending; the delight of the crowd depressed her, oppressed her, she felt the bitter certainty that this would be Shar's last race. She had seen many races, and each had promised to be the last.

She tried to put the noise out of her mind and sat gazing at the slow melting of the sky above the curve of the stadium. Sunlight slanted down across the weathered roof of the stadium, sheering off the lightning rods and the dull rotting shingles onto the track and the dry green infield. There were billboards and posters on the stadium walls, shredded by wind and rain. The wall to Jerry's right was covered with scrawls and obscene drawings, some of them in lipstick. Karen stared at them guiltily, as if they were something she had done. She closed her eyes. She was exhausted: Max's presence exhausted her, threatened her, the impending trial of speed exhausted her —paralyzed her mind. She felt the brutality of the contest.

Down at the garage Shar would be in the car, and one of the men, perhaps, leaning in the doorway of the garage enclosure; the barbed-wire door, eight feet high, would be ajar. Someone's cotton gloves, smeared with oil, would be stuck through the fence. Oil would lie on the ground in shallow pools. Shar's face, partially concealed by the helmet and the green glasses, would have taken on the aspect of a mask, and except for his repeated grimaces, his lips grinning and relaxing, he would seem no more alive than the slender car. One of the men would be patting the hood of the car, showing his devotion. The gleam of the hood would look cold in the hot sun. The other men, the mechanics, would watch Shar curiously, though not with concern, since they could not believe he was like them; they could not sympathize with the man who stared out at them through the green glasses. Perhaps they believed, as Karen did, that Shar had yet to learn fear, that he required someone to teach him. A gust of wind would pick up dust and blow it hotly against the faces of the men—they would blink against the pain, a tribute to their mortality.

A voice over the loud-speaker announced the race with great pleasure and zest. Karen opened her eyes reluctantly. "Let's feel your hand," Jerry said. He took hold of her and said, grinning, to Max, "She's afraid of this one." Jerry was a short, slim, neat man of about thirty-eight, though he looked younger. "Her hand is like ice."

"Let go of her," Max said without looking around.

The sound of the crowd, its delighted roar, brought Karen back to reality. She forced herself to stare down at the track. She awaited the familiar roaring. The voice over the loud-speaker identified the drivers and their cars lovingly. "Here it goes," Jerry said, craning his neck.

For a moment the roar of the autos filled the air; then it seemed to be yanked away. The car designed by Max's company was silver, and gleamed in the sunlight with a fine, sleek cleanliness. It sped above the dark earth with such precision and power that Karen felt, as always, the suggestion of something unnatural—almost mystical—in what she saw. "Beautiful, beautiful," Max murmured, clasping his big hands together. "A fine start."

The crowd cheered. Shar drove in a whirl of dust, through the dust, around now to the turn, and the dust wove through and behind him, for a moment obscuring the soiled white of the outer retaining wall, as though the wall itself had turned to swirling dust. Because of his record Shar was placed last at the start, and ahead of him the uneven string of cars seemed to jerk and glint in the light, veering from left to right. Seeing Shar approach them, the crowd yelled its encouragement, as if they supposed Shar was behind because of his clumsiness and was now making a move to catch up.

The lead cars were so far away that Karen could not see their numbers. She heard Max and Jerry exchanging information that meant nothing to her; Shar had an enemy some-

133

where, one of the drivers. One of the men. Now Shar's approach steadied and it looked as if the distance between him and the lead cars was static. All the cars looked as if they were set motionless on a great revolving disc. "He's waiting for something," Jerry said. Races made him excited, like a child; he began them coolly, ended them in a passion. "There. He's starting in to move."

Karen felt the excitement of the crowd begin to pulsate within her. The cars were at the far turn and reeled now back toward the stadium. Sunlight flashed off the hoods, then was obscured by a thin floating cloud of dust. "There, there," Jerry said, reaching across to grip Max. "What did I tell you?" They clasped hands in their excitement. Shar was still behind the other autos, but he had begun to swerve his car out carefully toward the retaining wall so that he could inch up on the others. For all his speed, he moved slowly and painstakingly, as if he were able to draw himself forward only by a dizzying rapport between himself and the next car.

"Look at that," Jerry said. "Beautiful driving! Did you see that?" Karen did not understand. Out on the track Shar began to overtake the others more deliberately. He moved above the dirt in the little car as though he were willing the movement—Shar with his look of neat, useless, splendid artifice, his shielded eyes, gloved hands, the stiff appearance of his fireproof clothing. The crowd pushed him ahead with their encouragement. Their strained voices were tense with anticipated pleasure.

The silver car moved up alongside the others, passing them with effort. Fragmented clouds of dust blew against it. Karen's throat was dry. The voice out of the loud-speaker suddenly announced something: there was an accident out in one of the fields, there were spectators involved. He asked for calmness, for people to keep their seats. Everyone, even Karen, wanted to brush aside his words, as if they hovered like insects about them, distracting them from the race. "Accident!" Max said. "A terrible word! The man should be punished, to use such a word at this time!" They heard the wail of an ambulance; one of the ambulances down by the track turned and moved out of sight. Again the voice asked for calm, and then it too returned to the race.

Jerry gripped Karen with his lean, strong fingers. "Son of a bitch!" he said happily. Shar was overtaking the others. Karen stared: she thought at any second she would see him swerve out of the groove and into the pile of tire dust at the turns, and then swerve and spin helplessly to the outer wall, his figure within the careening car a blur—the crowd would scream in delight, Jerry would stand—suddenly—swearing— But nothing happened. He passed three cars; another; he was moving up skillfully on the outside. It was queer to think that Shar performed this game as if he were nothing to her, as if none of them even knew him. He might have been a stranger, reeling around through the blinding dust and the hot smell of oil; and for an instant she felt the fear of losing him, greater than the fear that he might die. What could draw that man to her, what could strengthen the rapport between them, jerk it taut like a length of wire? "Shar, Shar," Karen murmured aloud, her heart pumping as the stadium shivered with excitement. She felt the people behind her, hot and damp, crying out to the drivers. She felt herself ease in among them, her own body wet like theirs with perspiration. The muscles about her mouth were taut as she tried not to cry out.

The silver car moved up into third place, on the outside. A long trail of dust lifted behind it. Four cars swerved around the turn at once. "There," Jerry said in alarm, "look at those sons of bitches. What did I tell you? That's him—that's the one." The two lead cars raced side by side; Karen gathered from what was being said that they were from the same company. She could not understand most of what was going on and took no interest in it except at this time. "What did I tell you?" cried Jerry to no one.

Racing down the stretch toward them now, the cars were still together; they sped in a tight, shivering clump, slowly drawing closer to one another. Now Shar, on the outside, raised a hand to signal for something. He wanted the car before him to move over. They sped past, swerving around the curve. The other car—it was bright red—slid out a little, but before Shar had time to ease into the space the other car came back. Beside Karen Jerry sat striking his palm with his fist. "The sons of bitches," he said. "Small-time hicks with two drivers." Shar had drawn up close behind the outside car and now he eased his car forward so that it touched the other, gently; everyone saw the man's helmeted head jerk around as if he were terrified. "My good God," Max said. In astonishment his hand crept to his chest, as if to soothe his pounding heart. The man in the red car made a motion for Shar to get back. Shar prodded the car again.

Now some of the people in the stands got to their feet. "Get him! Get him!" they shouted; Karen did not know what they meant. The smell of food and perspiration seemed to be pushed forward by their noise. "Look at those sons of bitches," Jerry said, "think they got it all planned! Aren't they asking for it? Why won't that guy let him through? Don't they know who he is?"

Jerry was grinding his hands together, flesh against flesh. In reality he hated Shar, but at races he adored him; like most of the men, Shar included, he seemed to come alive only at this spectacle of danger. "There! There!" Jerry cried with pleasure. "Now he's coming." Everyone stood. Max helped Karen up, taking time to smile down at her. A murmur rose to a swell and broke as Shar prodded the red car again—this time the car gave way, easing out to give Shar room. The driver turned and motioned for Shar to pass. The people cheered. They felt the silver car had made its way forward against all obstacles, that it deserved to win. "Good, there he goes," Jerry said. Shar had begun inching up into the space. The lead car whirled around the turn as if trying desperately to get away from him. Shar was a few yards behind it, and the red car, on the outside, was a few yards behind Shar; the fourth car had dropped behind. They made the turn and raced now down the stretch. Karen could see, shielding her eyes, that Shar and the driver in the red car were making signs to each other. "What are they doing?" she said aloud. No one heard her. The red car began to drop back deliberately. It gave way to Shar and the crowd took this with disappointment; someone cried, "A coward! A coward!" The car dropped back again and Karen saw—at first without comprehension—that Shar too had dropped back, as if to tease him; they raced now side by side. At this maneuver a group of men in smart gold and maroon uniforms knowingly broke into applause; they grinned and nodded at one another. This was something to see! This was how it was done!

Max reached across Karen and touched Jerry. "Get down there," he said. "Have them tell him to stop. This is enough." Jerry leaned across Karen and said with a pained look, "What the hell? Do you think I can tell him anything?" "Have them down at the garage write 'don't' on the blackboard—go on. Do it," Max said, showing his teeth.

Jerry got up and went somewhere. Down on the track Shar was bumping the red car. The red car tried to speed ahead to escape, then tried to fall back to escape; Shar kept even with it. The lead car strained to get away from this trouble, and behind the two struggling cars the others rushed in a flurry of mute order, stung with dust.

Max and Karen looked up to see Jerry return. "I can't get down there," he shouted across to Max. "I saw the pit, though. Mitch is out there holding up a sign." Behind them the crowd roared continuously. Max strained to hear Jerry. "He's got something written on it for Shar—I can't do no more." "Can't you even get down there?" Max said. "The exit's blocked with kids," Jerry said. "Besides, I can't do no more. Let him have his fun." Max stared. Veins in his forehead had swollen. Karen, looking at his big face so close to hers, felt sudden revulsion for him. "You could tell him a tire's going. You could tell him to come in," Max said. He spoke calmly. "I can't," Jerry said, "Goddam it, I told you the exit's blocked."

Max sat back. Shar and the driver in the red car were approaching the turn before the other wing of the stadium. Shar eased out to give the car another prod, then he pulled past; he straightened out and began to move away. The crowd showed its disappointment. "Ought to show the bastard! The coward!" a very drunken man behind Karen screamed. Though the spectators seemed to think the fun was past, Jerry said into Karen's ear, "Watch this. Watch your boy." Karen stared as if there were something down on the track she ought to be seeing. "Here comes an accident if I ever saw one," Jerry murmured. "That son of a bitch!" And then it happened, as neatly and as surprisingly as if it were truly an accident—no one could blame Shar for this: at the turn, the silver car, going a little too fast, swerved out and sideswiped the red car, not very seriously. The silver car, shaking for a moment, regained control of itself. The red car seemed all right—everyone screamed, but for what, for whose sake, Karen could not tell—and, as if in answer to the crowd's secret desire, the car spun suddenly out of control. Out of the invisible ring of pressure it flew, and as Shar and the lead car sped away, the red car traded ends, dust exploded up like a bomb, the volume of the crowd's delight swelled to burst-

138

ing. All eyes followed the stricken car as it headed for the retaining wall. For an instant it looked isolated: it seemed to hang against the dirty wall, a little off the ground. Then it jerked back into motion and, bursting into flames, scraped along the wall like a discarded toy, farther and farther along the wall, perhaps for a hundred feet, skidding, with its yellow flames almost obscuring it. What was left of it slammed finally against a concrete jutting and stopped.

Karen sobbed aloud. A siren began to wail and people shouted, individually now—behind her, beside her. At the wreck masses of flame licked up against the glowing concrete. Across the track fuel ran to the infield grass, already burning; clouds of dark smoke had begun to rise. Max had hold of Karen's arm. "An accident, an accident," he murmured. "An unfortunate happening."

Unless wreckage interfered with the race the other cars would not be flagged down; so far as they were concerned nothing had happened. Karen had witnessed this before but still could not understand it. She watched the untouched cars reel in their frantic order, glad to be alive. Shar was in the lead now, and dust roared up behind him grandly. The cars rushed, one by one, through the screen of black smoke and fire. "Look at that," Jerry said, laughing. "Going right through. Like driving through the poor bastard's blood." Karen put her hands to her face. They were cold, shocking. "My God, my God, Shar," she whispered, "don't let it be yet . . . not yet. . . ."

The line of cars passed through the boiling smoke unharmed. Sunlight touched them, illuminating their colors in spite of the dust that had covered them. At the wreck men moved about slowly; the ambulance had been backed up to the wall. The fire burned with gusto. It looked as if the car had stopped tilted on end, its top in the air. Men battled the flames energetically, with the air of people who are being watched.

Yet the horror of what had happened did not really dawn on Karen until she heard, a moment later, Max's murmuring voice. His forefinger was upraised. "What keeps them on it?" he said philosophically. "By common sense you would expect them all to fly off like that—drawn off—so!" He made a deadly flicking motion with his wrist and looked at Karen. She stared at him. Her eyes burned in her head. "It's the law of the circle, the one pressure on the outside and the other on the inside, they push together—the little car, it is caught in the middle. The two pressures keep him there. And the speed he makes, the little engine, and the pressure up in front of it, weight he has to push into—" He looked down at Karen, his mouth about to expand into a smile. "Amazing thing! Amazing, the two pressures, one pushing in, the other pushing out. That is how our lives are!" He stood, his face twitching with the discovery and the delight his words were leading him into. "Yes—see—the pressures are opposed, they fight each other. The law of the circle, that keeps the planets, you know, on the circumference, the other wants to draw them out and off somewhere—off somewhere, lost— Two forces, one to live and one to die— An amazing thing! A most wonderful thing! You see today how it works, like lines drawn to show you— Our Shar is full of life, he cannot be killed. He is filled with life."

The cars were finishing now. Shar won by a considerable distance. The crowd applauded dutifully; some of their attention was drawn to the burning car, some of it to Shar and his triumph—for, though death fascinated them, victory was an admirable thing and they wanted to share in it. Karen said clearly, "Shar is a killer."

Max turned to her. They were still standing, like everyone else. He put his hand to his wet chest; he pretended he had not heard her. Karen knew that he, too, was a killer, and that his past consisted of brutalities he never had to watch or to account for. "And you disgust me," she said, staring at his little astonished eyes.

"Why, Karen— I can't hear you—what did you say?"

"I said you disgust me," Karen whispered.

Max's face was wet with perspiration. It had gathered like dew on his forehead and hung in little salty drips on his broad nose. Behind his expensive sunglasses his eyes protruded a little, blinking against the unbelievable crudity of Karen's words; as if for her sake, for her own good, he seemed reluctant to have heard her. "You disgust me!" Karen cried, so loudly that people around them turned to stare in amusement. "All of you! Disgusting—dirty—you don't even clap to see men die, or pant for it—like the others—you're beyond that— It's a theory to you, it's nothing to you— Shar kills a man and it's nothing to you! Shar is filled with life!—Shar is filled with death! Shar is filled with death!"

Max took her arm. "My dear child, my child," he said. "This was an accident."

Karen snatched her arm away from him. "Not all things are accidents," she said coldly, staring at Max's bewildered face. She understood, beyond his polite bewilderment, her own fate —she saw him dismissing her with a flick of his wrist, then turning fatly to open a book, sitting propped up with pillows in the sunlight; but she did not care. Even the child growing within her—a speck of life, a ghostly image, a mockery of life —would not escape his wrath; but she did not care.

11

That night Max sat with his back to the wall so that he could see everything that went on in the crowded place. He ate melons luxuriously: pale green melons, smooth as skin, that the waiter—a boy of about seventeen—kept bringing him. Seeds had spilled out onto the table and on the front of his shirt, though he did not seem to notice. He waved the big glistening knife at them as he spoke. "This child was frightened by the race—her hands were cold, ice cold." He made a move to embrace Karen, a symbolic gesture. "She cannot get used to it.

Every race is new to her. She cannot believe you will survive the race!"

Shar was leaning back in his chair. He had been drinking for some time and, as usual, the liquor worked to quiet him in preparation for later outbursts of rage. He smiled tautly. "A woman's love is a beautiful thing to see," Max went on, licking at a sudden rivulet of juice that ran down his chin. "She is transformed by it, absolutely transformed. That has never been part of my experience—I know you will survive the race, I have no doubt in you. My mentality is masculine and objective, but hers—hers is possessive. She fears she will lose you."

Max's bright, merry words evoked a painful smile on Karen's face. She avoided Shar's eyes. With a flourish Max finished this melon and took a deep breath and called for the waiter. "Another one of these," he said, sighing helplessly. The table was wet with juice and scattered seeds that the boy—a rushed, alarmed-looking country boy with long hair—did not offer to wipe up. "You must tell me how the race was for you," Max said, laying a damp hand on Shar's arm.

The place was already crowded, yet more people came in continuously. At the bar a child had been lifted up so he could look around, squinting through the drifting clouds of smoke. His mother, whispering something to him, evidently meant him to see Shar. Along the bar and at the other tables, and milling about at the door, eyes would be directed toward Shar with great wonder and pride, as if he were somehow a credit to them. From time to time men ambled over to congratulate him and, for some reason, to congratulate Karen too. She would stare at them with cold astonishment.

Music from the jukebox exploded into the room. Mosquitoes and flies scattered to the ceiling. The sense of well-being that pervaded the place showed itself most explicitly on Max's face as he bent forward to listen to Shar's words. Shar talked of the

143

race in his low, hypnotic voice. These recitals had always alarmed Karen, for she felt there was something unhealthy about them; excluded from them, her isolation pointed out as if Shar and Max were staring hard at her, Karen sat in a flurry of smoke and music and insects, pretending to be interested in something across the floor.

At the bar Jerry stood talking with some women. He had a neat, smooth head, smooth skin that looked ageless; his eyes were small and bright, like buttons. Whatever he said made the women laugh—they turned to each other helplessly, sighing in their laughter. From time to time Jerry glanced over at Karen and, as if stimulated by her blank, weary expression, was inspired to charm the women even more. One was fairly old—perhaps forty, with fantastic red-blond hair that lifted away from her head as if electricity were coursing through it. The other, quieter, her expression sly and pleased, had long black hair curled at its tips. Her face was large and amiable, teased into prettiness by minute plucking of her eyebrows and intricate work about her eyes, and a violent, exotic outlining of her lips. Whenever anyone fended his way over to see Shar, to attempt to shake hands with him, Jerry would straighten quickly, ignore the women, and watch to see if he was needed: this would be indicated by a flapping of Max's big hand. So far there had been no trouble. The men connected with the garage whose car had crashed were not around—they were believed to have left right after the race. When Jerry saw that everything was all right he would relax and his grin would come back, bright and mischievous. One of the women leaned to him and asked him to light her cigarette.

In one corner a few couples tried to dance. They seemed to gallop together, violently; feet kicked the floor, kicked the air, tangled together and left the dancers hugging each other and gasping in ecstasy. The jukebox glowed grimy colors: red, yellow, green. Karen, who had been forcing herself to drink, felt the hot pulsations of the music lull and soothe her, easing her gently away from herself. Max and Shar talked together, heads conspiring. Shar had a hard, handsome face. His eyes were dark, shadowed by the strange light, and his lips, twitching up into a grin from time to time, looked hard, as if chiseled out of stone. He blew smoke luxuriously about him. "Did you hear the people much?" Karen heard Max ask. "Did you hear them applaud you? They were mad for you—they were in ecstasy for you!"

The boy returned with another melon. He carried it balanced up beside his head in one hand, without ceremony, as if it were a rock. Karen saw Max's tongue skim his lips as the melon was presented to him.

Max picked up the wet knife, brandishing it aloft for a moment as if he were pleased by its look of competence. With a sigh that reached every part of his vast body he bent to the melon and sliced it carefully; juice ran out onto the table as if shocked. Max cut a slice out of the melon and offered it to Shar, who shook his head; then he offered it to Karen, who did not understand for a moment. Then she too shook her head. Her fingers tightened around her glass. Max lifted the slice to his mouth and bit into it: for a moment his expression hesitated, judging, tasting; then it was found to be good. A good melon. His eyes swam with the pleasure of its taste and with the delight of such company—such beautiful young people. "What he tells me is fascinating—it is as if I had been there myself," he assured Karen. "He makes me relive it. Perhaps at night I will dream about it—who knows? I will be stuffed in the little car, my stomach pushed up into my face!—driving and winning a race to make people cheer!" He laughed at his humor, Shar grinned mockingly. Karen waited until their dialogue began again and looked away.

Sitting alone at the table next to them was Max's doctor. His black bag beside him, ready for use, he sat gazing vaguely toward Max; he drank with perfunctory regularity, as if he were taking medicine. Something had happened to make his frizzy hair stand up, for it framed his bald spot like a tiny halo, glistening with perspiration. His face was slack; he was silent. In the months Karen had been associated with him, in company with him, she had never heard him speak to anyone but Max, and then only when he was addressed. He seemed to live in a trance: even tonight, when women or even the girls still dressed in their satin outfits approached him, merry and teasing, he stared at them with silent fury until their smiles faded and they backed awkwardly away. Never did he act outside of his role except to follow Max around with his black bag and to pour out liquor for himself, which he did fondly yet without emotion. Once, in his role as a doctor, he had examined Karen herself; he had seemed a different person then. But it was long ago, before she knew who he was, and at a time when she had almost lost her capacity for memory. . . .

A fat man in a maroon uniform, unbuttoned on his chest, pushed his way through the crowd to get to Shar. His face was red and shiny, as if polished. "Did they glue it on? Eh? Did they glue it back on?" he cried, winking at Shar. "Glue what?" said Shar. "That guy's head! I heard the top of his head was sheared off!" the man exclaimed. "Oh, but he ast for it! He ast for it! Listen, mister—" Shar stared up at him. "Listen, I think you done right—in a race like that was—I—" "What the hell are you talking about?" Shar said. "I know what I know," the man said. He winked at them all again but his enthusiasm had begun to ebb; he turned to go. " 'Course couldn't nobody be sure of it—that's smart that way," he said. "I'll come to see you any time you're here."

He disappeared. Shar shrugged his shoulders. "There is something about you that appeals to them," Max said. "I'm not sure what it is—perhaps they sense you are like them, I mean originally—from the country, like them. They distrust people from our civilization!"

"Nobody could judge if that was on purpose or not," Shar said thoughtfully. "Nobody could tell, least of all me. They think they would have done it out there, if it had been them; but they can't speak for me."

"Did you hear that?" Max said to Karen. He was impressed by Shar's words, which were indeed thoughtful for Shar; the liquor had taken hold of him. "Very well put! I thought that myself."

"Nobody in the world could do that on purpose," Shar said. "Not going around a turn like that. The car acted by itself—by itself. I might have been thinking of it, just *thinking*—and then it acted by itself!"

Karen looked at him in disgust. He met her gaze with a mocking grin. "I had power out there," he said, leaning forward, "I felt that car moving with me, me moving with it, all the same thing! The same soul! A good way to die, that would be—to turn the car toward the stand, slam it into all those fat faces, shovel it into them! Not a driver but that he thinks of that—wants that. A good way to die when it comes time."

"You are no one to speak of dying," Max said, eating his melon. "You have a long life before you—many lives before you. You will live many times."

Shar looked at Karen. His face was hard and empty. "But what good is that," he broke out, "if all of them are different—all those lives—if you can't put them together! One good car after another, one car better than another, and every time I take them out I'm better than before— But a race is no sooner started than it's over, another one over. There isn't enough time for it all!"

147

Max wondered at him. "There is time for everything," he said sententiously.

Shar finished his drink. "I never had any trouble finding the right car," he said to Max. They looked at each other seriously. "Some guys spend their lives looking for that—I found it right off. I found it with you. I took it to the limit, the first one—until the rear hub wanted to come off, goddam threads cut the wrong way! I wasn't seventeen when I begun it and I'm still alive now—still alive now, and how many of them are dead! Poor goddam bastards! I force them—force them— Cars or people or myself, all the way out, to the limit, as far as it can go without killing me. I force it! What the hell is it any other way? Are you alive any other way? I know how much the car can take, but not what I can take. I never yet found my limit!" he cried.

This was taken up by Max with great admiration. He turned, nodding, to Karen. In a voice meant to be confidential he murmured, "You hear him? He is a fine man, he is filled with life. You must not try to pull him off—you know—I spoke of that before to you— You must cherish him."

"I cherish him," Karen said.

"She sucks me to death!" Shar said. He got up and went to the bar. Max and Karen watched him; Karen had begun to tremble.

"He is angry with you, he doesn't know why," Max said, licking his lips, pretending to be sorry. "You must tell him soon about the child—if there is a child—I'll help you with it, I'm good with him, he will listen to me. He won't be angry if I tell him. I'll tell him—it would be like a grandchild to me, a child related by blood to me! Related by the soul! He is filled with life and will understand what it is like to spread life—to give birth, to reproduce himself—"

"You're insane," Karen said.

148

Max wiped seeds off his chin. "You are hard on me," he complained. "Do you think I'm insane? What is insane about me? I am given to reading too much; I sit too much in one place; I eat too much—a shameful glutton, a vice inherited from my great-grandmother, who weighed three hundred pounds! Will you blame me for her? Did she know you, would she be judged by you? A fine, respectable woman with her own bed built especially for her! —You are my delight, Karen, my puzzle, my mystery, I could dream of you at night! We must know each other better; you must tell me of yourself. You must tell me what you dream—like Shar does; some of the most fascinating hours of my life have been spent listening to that man talk, allowing him to lead me through his mind, reveal himself to me! You look away—you seem ashamed— what are you ashamed of? That Shar reveals himself to me? That we are close, that two human beings are close? That we love each other? Do you think all Shar's passion is for you? He tells me of you—he describes his feelings with you, his—"

Shar was coming back, so Max fell silent. Karen stared at his averted eyes and at the hungry gleam of his big teeth. What he had said alarmed her. She was struck by a sense of terror greater than any disgust. "Tells you of me!" she wanted to cry. She wanted to seize him, shake him, shout into his face. "What does he tell you of me? What does he say?"

As if Shar knew what was going on, he faced them with a mock grin. He sat down heavily and poured a drink out of the new bottle he had bought. "Karen?" he said. She said "no" and turned aside.

As the hours passed, the tavern became more crowded and noisy. It was a small, shanty-like building out in the country, not far from a swamp, which Max had noticed on the way into Synderdale and had admired for its authenticity. His own money made by investments in gambling spots and taverns of

149

a more sophisticated nature, Max showed unashamed senti-mentality about country taverns. He liked, he had explained, the kind of people one met there; he liked the muddy floors, the jukeboxes, the country girls with their big smiles and strong arms. He liked the old neon signs and the old-fashioned bars and rickety tables and the proud photographs, yellowed by time, that showed local hunters with moose and deer and bears subdued by their guile and skill. "I love their lives," he cried, waving at the boisterous crowd. "I love to see them so—they're happy, they enjoy themselves! They don't think about it —they drink, they dance, the floor shakes with their joy!"

It shook now, not only with the feverish dancing at the far end of the place, but with scufflings and aborted fist fights. Karen watched them cautiously. She had seen men eying her, at the same time, and in almost the same way that they eyed Shar: it was an envy not far from open spite. At the bar Jerry sat drinking, perched up on a stool with the black-haired woman leaning seriously toward him. The doctor had been forced to move and now sat behind Max, though not at the table with him and Shar and Karen. Groups of men circu-lated, laughing importantly, calling out friendly insults. Mos-quitoes buzzed about the lights as if driven insane by the noise. Karen tried to close her eyes against the whirling faces and eyes and smells, but she was jerked awake by the slow, fond conversation between Shar and Max that was drifting toward her. Max was saying, "I have talked with her and I believe we are getting to know each other better. We are beginning to communicate. She has opened my heart wider, I will see you more clearly, more completely, through her—"

Two men appeared at the table to interrupt this. One was a young Negro, absurdly dressed; he looked like something pro-fessional—doctor, minister, schoolteacher. The other was a

150

slovenly young man with wild hair and a slack, pouting face and clothes stained with grease. From the conversation, Karen gathered that these men were employed by Max. One of them, the Negro, seemed favored; Shar invited him to sit down. The other pulled up a chair as well. Both were fairly drunk.

Max was eating oysters now. He offered them some: the Negro declined graciously, the other scooped out an oyster and stuffed it into his mouth. Watching him, Karen felt a swirling of nausea. She saw that as he ate his eyes wandered over to her and—incredibly—seemed to hint at recognition, comradeship. She looked away. The talk now centered about the race: moments were relived, details repeated. Snatches of conversations with other people were told. The plump young man—his name was Ponzi—talked with skill, evoking imagery and impressions that showed his imagination. Max and Shar listened to him in silence. The Negro put a hand on his shoulder, looking a little embarrassed, but Ponzi ignored him. "Found me sitting in his room! I was sitting in there when he came in—him and a woman! Such a woman, such big blond hair!" Ponzi said. "He got mad and asked me what I wanted and damned if I could think of it—couldn't think of it." He hiccuped sadly. "Found me sitting in the dark. I used to sit in the dark, by myself, in one of the upstairs closets—had to get away from them."

Jerry came over to the table, followed by the women. They touched their hair, looking at Shar. One of them, the sly-faced one with black hair, crowded in next to Karen. Ponzi, instead of giving way to these people, instead of taking the hint his Negro friend gave him—that he was annoying Shar and Max—began to talk louder, not even giving himself time to eat any oysters. Jerry reached over Shar's shoulder and took an oyster, dipped it in the sauce, and ate it with obvious satisfaction. The

151

women, offered some, demurred sweetly; they made tiny gestures with their long painted nails. Clouds of smells—perfume and beer—made Karen feel faint.

Ponzi was still talking. "The goddamnedest thing! Mitchie here told me not to tell it—says he ain't got the stomach or the ears to hear it— Those people on the grass. I went out back just in time to see it—wasn't trying—hell, I didn't know it would happen. How would I know that? Did I come on purpose to see that, or the accident either? Mitchie says he took care of two cousins of his that lived with them, that had—that were—" He tapped his forehead decisively. "Says he got along with them good and played with them—so he can take care of me; thinks I'm a little loony! He does!" He gave the Negro a playful punch. A girl dressed as a baton twirler appeared behind the Negro, gripping his shoulders; when he looked around she bent and smiled into his face as if they were well acquainted. With the approach of this girl the two women tensed. They had hardly noticed Karen. "Well, these people piled up like sardines in that what-do-you-call-it—a homemade grandstand some bastard built out of pipes or whatever it was," Ponzi went on, louder. "On the top they had bottles and were dumping them out on the ones beneath, to make them yell. And they had bags full of lunch, too—eating like pigs. Mostly men on top, a couple of kids. There were five levels. A lot of kids, they jiggled it—probably caused the trouble. A whole lot of people. The cars were going around the farthest turn and somebody probably leaned over to look, or maybe some of the kids scuffling around—and the goddam thing begins to tilt! Starts tilting! Everybody screams. Did you hear that? Or maybe you couldn't—too much noise already. The people sitting down in the grass around it point and gape like mad and watch it come down—slow as anything—there was enough time for a couple of men to scramble off and jump off the back—they

152

got away. It fell over and crushed them all together! Poor bastards!" Ponzi cried. Karen saw that there was something peculiar about his face—it was mocking and anguished at once. The young girl—she was about Karen's age—put her arms around the Negro's neck and leaned against him, peeping over his shoulder at the rest of the people. She had big arms, a little flabby at the tops, but was pretty in a broad, blunt, happy way; her lips glistened. Karen saw Shar watching her. "They screamed and screamed—two or three of them were dead right away, broken necks, and some others had backs broken—or cracked—whatever happens to a back," Ponzi giggled shrilly. "I don't know. And wriggling around! Wriggling with arms and legs sticking out of the pipes, wrapped around the pipes, some of them crawling out—blood in their hair— I got over there—some people came to help—I helped them—I—" As if this were saying too much, he returned to his earlier tone. He said with mocking relish, "All around them people sat on blankets, drinking beer and eating chicken—cold chicken! You could smell it! Some of them gave us their blankets, some came over to help—the ambulance got there then— Most of them kept right on watching the race and eating. They wouldn't be bothered. I got a blanket away from one of them—dirty bastard!—I put it over a girl to hide her, her face was—it was— She didn't die, I don't think she died," Ponzi said, "but she was— She couldn't scream, even, it was so—"

Jerry, catching a glance from Max, went to the young man and poked him in the back with a finger. "Outside," he said. "You can puke it up outside. We had enough of it."

"But I was just telling you!" Ponzi said, blinking as if sweat had run stinging into his eyes. "Thought you'd want to know! Didn't you want to know?" He leaned around clumsily and looked at Karen, who had drawn back from the table; she

153

stared at him as if he were a creature in a nightmare. The women looked at Karen as if she had just appeared beside them. Shar stared at her—furiously. Karen murmured, without thinking, "You've suffered."

Ponzi was herded outside. He seemed to go without any protest. Mitchie followed him—he explained to them he had promised to keep Ponzi out of trouble. He wished that crazy white man had let him alone—all white men told him their troubles, that was because he was Negro so it didn't count. They could tell him anything they wanted, no matter how bad it made them look. Later on, if they decided to hate him, that was all right too—they would feel good about it. It joined them to the brotherhood of white men! Mitchie got his laugh and turned to leave; he was liked by them, Shar and Max approved of him, though as soon as he left he was forgotten. The girl in the satin outfit sat down plumply in his seat, smiling in a veritable sweat of anticipation.

"A loud-mouthed bastard," Jerry said, reaching for another oyster. "I'll drown him in a pan full of grease tomorrow."

Shar had not spoken for some time. During most of Ponzi's monologue he had been drinking steadily and staring at Karen. When he put down his glass she saw that his hand was trembling. He pointed across the table at her. "What did you say to him! You said something to that fat son of a bitch! I heard you!"

The women shivered deliciously; the girl, her mouth opening wetly, looked around at Karen. She blinked to see Karen there—she had not noticed her before. "She was sorry for him —nothing more— As we all were," Max said, putting a hand out on Shar's arm. To his chagrin, Shar jerked away.

"A bitch! A cheap bitch!" Shar said. Karen saw how he hated her. "Come crawling to me for it! Left the old man bleeding like a pig—flat on his back in the mud! She did that

154

—she did that! She sucks me," he said, "sucks me— She kills me—"

Max looked alarmed, but Jerry, standing back, just watched in amusement. The doctor's eyes wandered briefly to Shar's face and then drifted away. Karen sat, feeling everyone's eyes on her, in a trance of fear—yet, beyond the fear, her mind worked clearly, without confusion; she knew who she was. "Sucks me dry! Sucks me dry!" Shar shouted, showing his teeth. "She wants to kill me!"

Max stood, jarring the table. It was his intention to get Karen out of the tavern, but Shar, yelling across the cluttered, seed-strewn table, kept on, his voice climbing to hysteria: "Sucks me! Sucks me! The old man flat on his back—mud— the other one shriveling up to a bunch of ashes! She comes to me! She comes to me!"

Max and Jerry got Karen out. They fended their way through the fascinated crowd, Karen closing her eyes against the looks, against the hungry faces of the men around her. At the door Max cried out: some kids were playing with a long, limp snake. "Get it away! Get it away!" Max screamed. When Jerry had taken care of it they went outside to the car. They only had to wait a minute for the doctor, who ran up, panting, and climbed in the back seat. Driving away, they heard a happy roar of music and voices.

It was fortunate the doctor had come, for Max soon had need of him. To quiet his nerves, to ward off an attack of some sort, he accepted pills that the doctor gave him—his big fingers, still sticky, trembled as he raised them to his mouth. His breath was labored and frightened and he seemed to have forgotten Karen. Jerry, on Karen's other side, drove fast; he was sullen and angry. "What the hell is he going to do with three of them!" he muttered to himself.

12

She could not believe that in the morning her life would not continue as usual. Back in the hotel room she had stood for a while at the window, looking down at the crowded street with the curtains held aside as if she were expecting someone down there to glance up at her suddenly. Her isolation made her feel viciously powerful, yet she was conscious always of the gentle, sickening loss of her power, a failure she could not admit, as she had never been able to admit when she was a child that after some trivial argument her father had really forgotten about her and was not going to seek her out to ask for-giveness. Behind her the room was cluttered, the bed rumpled and dirty. In the sullen light nothing looked familiar, though it was the same room—it was always the same room—she had lived in for months.

It was not the thought that something was going to happen that paralyzed her with anger, but rather the knowledge that she could not control it. She took a shower, wasting time, standing with her head bowed and her eyes closed. She played back to herself things that had happened that day, thinking of Shar and of Max. Their faces appeared in her mind's eye like faces in comic strips or cartoons, creatures bereft of life and soul, therefore invulnerable. And had she come so far, she thought angrily, to discover that he was not vulnerable? In the bathroom mirror she watched herself without interest, dry-ing her hair, combing it out. The ceiling light cast shadows down upon her. Little lines appeared about her mouth and un-der her eyes. She looked older than her sister, her face like a mask as indifferent to itself as to anyone else. Staring at that face, she understood that Shar would not be with her tonight; and she did not wonder at him. He was with another woman. And yet, she thought, her face twisting, becoming so ugly she had to look aside, he would not forget her that easily. He would think of her, just as she thought of him. The fact that she thought of him would force him to think of her; he would not be free. In the other woman's face he would see her face and when the woman touched him he would feel Karen touching him. . . .

She walked slowly about the room, pleased at her own calm-ness. Now and then she stumbled into something and drew back dreamily, setting it straight, picking it up and staring at it, letting it fall again to the floor. She had not just recently learned the value of forced, feigned calm; it had been with her for

157

years. Her father had taught her that. Had she not witnessed the perfect control with which he had faced death?—her own mother's death, when Karen was still a child, and she and the others had been forbidden to enter that queer-smelling room for so long. Men spoke of his steadiness at hunting; there was some story, some vague story of a wounded bear, she remembered, a dog torn in half, and her father . . . her father doing something, something unexpected and brave. She and her brothers had tried to envision that scene from the fragments they had been given; it had inspired them to ecstasies. Her childish nightmares pitted bear against father, a match of insane brutality that she could not stop, could not look away from, as if the blood had fascinated her. From these dreams she had awakened sobbing with terror, the bedclothes twisted around her like arms or legs, struggling to hold her down.

The bed was still a little damp. Karen pulled the sheet up and lay on top of it. With the overhead light on—a grimy, fly-filled globe—she lay in a stupor approaching sleep. She knew she should turn out the light but she did not want to get up. At the point at which sleep began her mind warned her against it and jerked her awake. It was as if she were being drawn toward a great dark hole, a kind of mouth. Dreams and fragments of dreams crowded her mind. Shar in the silver auto —Shar with his helmet, his green goggles, walking somewhere as precisely as any machine—yet when she approached him he turned and was someone else. He snatched off the goggles and stared at her in dismay, as if he too were sorry they did not know each other. Karen was seized by a sensation of hatred, and she thought for the first time in her life that hatred charged her, nourished her, prodded her along. She hated all strangers. She hated the vast, strange world that she could not control, that her family could not control, that her father did not even know about. In this town her father might wander down on the street, alone, unrecognized. . . . "I hate all strangers," Karen said.

This woke her. She sat up suddenly as if she supposed herself in danger. Her arms and legs were stiff and her throat dry. When she went to the window and looked out she sensed that it was hours later, perhaps almost dawn. The street was deserted and the hotel was quiet. Her hands clasped before her, she looked around as if she expected to see Shar. In the light the room was yellowed and tattered, the wallpaper stained at the ceiling with brown watermarks. One of them was in the shape of a gigantic cockroach; this caught her eye. She wondered what she would say to Shar in the morning. For the first time silence might fail her. It might not be strong enough. She had always felt her silent, limp passivity to be powerful, a bloodless power she knew was not admirable but could not be matched by real passion. Shar's violence would burn itself out, but Karen's silence was static and could not be wearied. When, after a one-sided argument, Shar would seize her and press his face against her and tell her he was sorry, he was sorry, she felt how precarious was his strength and how tormented he was by her quiet assurances that he had not hurt her, she was all right. She would pretend not to understand his anguish. Yet if he came to her in silence and did not hide his face, if he simply looked at her in this ugly light, judging and assessing her, she did not believe herself strong enough to face him. Her fingers twitched. They might have been yearning for something—the scissors in the kitchen drawer at home, the fishing knife one of her brothers had found.

But at the back of her mind, dreamily, was the stubborn conviction that nothing had changed. He could not have gone to another woman, she did not believe it. She could not imagine it. Had he really so much freedom apart from her that he could do things she could not even imagine? She did not believe it. It

159

was impossible that she could be unfaithful to him—she was disgusted by the thought—and so it was impossible that he could be unfaithful to her. Before this knowledge her superficial worries ebbed dizzily. Such things did not happen. Yet, at the window, she closed her fist in the curtain. If it were true, somehow, it would still mean nothing. At the instant of his passion he could think only of her—in his imagination it would be Karen who held him. He would never be free of her.

She opened the closet door. Idly she looked through her clothes, as if they might tell her something. The blue dress she had worn to the race: once she and Shar had been walking somewhere and she had had that dress on and she had noticed him glancing at her—how fiercely proud she had been, how she had wanted to take his arm and feel his hard muscle under her fingers! And the white dress, now a little soiled. Karen had bought it one afternoon by herself, wasting time again until Shar was finished at the track. In the store mirror her smug little reflection had stared back at her coldly, contrived by her art to look ageless. She had been isolated, complete; a stranger. The other women in the store were commonplace, they bustled about and touched things, asked prices, chatted with saleswomen; not Karen. She had felt feverishly isolated. What pride, what ferocious satisfaction! The ordinary lives of those ordinary women trailed in and out of the store and were not capable, even, of assessing Karen; she had felt that. Watching herself in the mirror, her shoulders taut, her eyes deliberating, avoiding the pleased face of the saleswoman at her shoulder, she had held her jaw so rigid that her teeth had begun to ache. And now she remembered what she had thought then, what had come to her suddenly without preparation: she had thought, I am losing my mind. She had wanted to lean forward and touch the mirror, perhaps embrace her image in it, but of course she had done nothing. She had stood with her arms stiff at her sides and her jaws paralyzed until the moment passed. Her terror had been such that she might have been staring out into some future room, that reflection staring past her and into the future and yet seeing nothing. So that was her mirrored self—a face unrelated to her, to her soul, a mockery of what she knew she was (for she knew who she was, always; inside her, somewhere in her heart, or in her brain, somewhere, was her true self), a distraction. Only to herself was her soul revealed. It was defined only in terms of what it had surrendered itself to: to claims of blood and duty, to love, to religious ecstasy. In itself it had no existence. It was like, she thought wildly, the things that lay about this dirty room— clothes, shoes, suitcases—things that had no existence without her to see them. "We are kin," Max had said to her once, seated fatly in some other hotel room just like this one, when Shar was away. And that was true, Karen thought. For just as Karen realized she had no existence without the greater presence of someone to acknowledge her (her father; God), so did Max realize that his existence depended upon the life of others. If some men supposed themselves free it was only because they did not understand that they were imprisoned—bars could be made of any shadowy substance, any dreamy loss of light.

Karen turned off the light and lay down again. There were footsteps out in the hall but they went nowhere. She listened to them, her heart pounding in excitement; but nothing happened. The sky outside the window had not lightened. On the bureau there were pills, sleeping pills Max's doctor had given her. But she would not take them. She despised pills. She wanted no help. If there was pain, she would feel it. If the pain belonged to her, she would feel it; it was hers. Then, abruptly, she was dreaming. A child had died. It had been growing inside a closet, on the dusty floor, a clothes closet with bright summer dresses in it: tubes ran in and out of the child's body, plastic veins, queer bright colors of red and blue and yellow, a transparent chest so that one could see the damp red heart. A plastic heart. But she would not cry for that, she thought angrily, it was a trick to make her pity herself, or pity someone, when pity was disgusting! Pity withered one's heart, bore into one's stomach. Pity ruined love. "God!" she said, grinding her teeth. Her heart was hardened: she could feel it turn to stone. She would pity no one. Certainly she would not pity herself. She thought of the fragmentary stories of men and women in the Bible, people who must have been in another world and yet who seemed to her, had always seemed to her, bizarre, wild-eyed contemporaries of her own. No pity. No mercy. Nothing. Had she been born for this, come into the world for this, that she should pity herself? On the contrary, someone was telling her, it was herself she must forget. Did she not know that the universe had contrived her life, her father had planned her birth, so that she might be here tonight in this dirty hotel room, alone, waiting? Of course the mind jerked away from such thoughts, but that was only because such thoughts terrified. Better to look into an empty drawer, stare into an empty hole, than to discover oneself looking into a darkness filled with shape! She began to twist her body as if someone were struggling with her. How much easier to look into a darkness that meant nothing than into a darkness that was really an open, straining mouth, a vast waiting hole that claimed her! It was as if God were struggling to appear to her, not in sunlight but in darkness. If she had ever expected to see God (and she had expected to see Him, as a child) she would have supposed Him to come in light, in fire. Not in darkness. But now she ground her teeth together savagely, twisting on the damp bed, and just at the moment when it seemed to her she would suffocate, her dream snapped clear and it was Shar who struggled with her. He lay above her, hard arms and legs, his hard wet body so familiar that she did not at first recognize him as someone apart from herself.

She forced herself awake. She was frightened, damp with perspiration. Someone was crying out, somewhere—far away. She listened; nothing. An automobile's brakes screeching. Now her heart began to pound with fear, for it was true that Shar was with another woman. He lay somewhere now, drunk, asleep, peaceful, safe from her. The realization that he had truly betrayed her seemed to clear her mind. She would be all right. She could deal calmly with the truth. And, as if her failure with him endeared him to her, made him seem much more a man, she lay back again and thought of how they had first met: of Shar's strangeness, his look of having come from another country. Then her father, and that trip to town—yes. Yes, she thought, how well it had all worked; she might have planned it herself. Shar jerking and straining to escape, but Shar trapped by her all the same! The fields, the barn, the back room of that country store, and after that, as if by magic, another room in the city—and Max's ritualistic behavior, his grave gentlemanly concern for her that she had distrusted for so long until she realized he was somehow seeing Shar in her, and that she was valuable to him because of this. She had been in bed then, attended by Max's doctor. Perhaps they had expected her to die and were waiting calmly. Perhaps everything had been arranged: a coffin, a grave. But she had not died. She had waited as they had waited, day after day, more patient than they. Max had brought her newspapers and magazines and a radio, then some books. Karen had turned the pages of the books idly, too weak to read. When she saw that the books had been charged out of a library in the city she was struck by a sense of disorder, of wonder, as if it were somehow absurd to have to see her bed and this anonymous room in relationship to a larger city, a coherent world of governmental design that in turn related itself to the world of her family. Max would talk to Shar about Karen, fondly, in her presence; he admitted himself quite fascinated with her. "She suffers without knowing it," he said often. "A strange thing. That endears the sufferer to us, but also makes us fearful of him—sometimes contemptuous!" And he had winked at her, as if they shared a joke Shar would never understand.

Shar watched her but seldom spoke to her. If he spoke, it was usually to Max, with Karen as a third party who might or might not be listening. Now and then he would glance at her as if he expected her, in those moments, not to notice him. He said things like, "It's warmer out today." "It's raining out this morning." "I had some stuff to do downtown." Always his words were accompanied by queer silent pleas, questions. He would stare at Karen secretly, indulge himself in long heavy-lidded examinations masked by clouds of smoke about his face. His legs, seemingly so idle, were really tensed to keep him on guard, protect him, get him out of the room if necessary, if the preposterous situation in which he discovered himself were suddenly too painful, too dangerous. Karen, dizzy with her own pain and with a despair so overwhelming she knew it must approach sin, absorbed his senseless, unanswered remarks and his looks as if she were older than he, stronger and wiser.

They had surveyed each other carefully at this time. Shar's first impact upon her had been physical: he had appeared as a body, a presence. Smears of color—lines of movement, a peculiar awkward grace—certain gestures with his fingers, which had struck her as nervous, nervously appealing. Beneath his contemptuous control there had always been distrust—he had learned that distrust as a child. Now, sitting with her in Max's presence, forced to sit still, to meditate, to stare in disbelief—and, in spite of her condition, with lust—he emerged in a sense from his body and created for her an image of himself that she

164

had learned to cherish as time passed, since it was only at such times, in perfect stillness or in sleep, that he appeared to her so. It was strange that even then, even when she could not have known clearly what he was going to do with her (whether she would be sent back home on a bus or abandoned somewhere in the city or passed around to the innumerable men who, it seemed, stomped about on the periphery of Shar's life), she thought of the various shades and complexities of his person as possessions of hers. It was almost as if he were offering himself to her, shielded as he was behind nervous clouds of smoke and by the rigidity of his being. "Remember, I am a stranger," he seemed to say. But he was already familiar: she might have known him for years, watched him secretly for years. The man who had, in a final vicious exasperation, made love to her that morning was not lost and did not belong to a painful nightmare, but sat with her often, gazed upon her with bewilderment and calculation, and identified himself always as the same man. He sometimes seemed to sweat with inertia; he could not move. The fat man who pampered them both seemed to sustain, witnessing Shar, a mild and delighted astonishment, as if he too were recognizing something: but what was happening? When Shar was gone Karen had the idea other people were watching her, spying on her drugged composure. Time passed. Reality slipped from her, she could not even soothe herself with tears for the life she had given up—she knew in her heart that she had not given it up—but the center of this new world, the force that controlled it, Shar, sat firmly and familiarly at her bedside, offered himself in mute impatience to her examination.

He was to her lean and hard: his physical presence blocked the light from the window, scattered and diffused its rays, so that his body, even in relaxation, had a precarious and threatening solidity that did not belong to other objects—the chipped

165

bed railing or the shade at the window. On Shar clothes lost all identity, became at once colorless and nondescript. Karen could never, in her imagination, see clearly what Shar wore— he wore wrinkled clothes, soiled clothes, perhaps; what was important was that she could not recognize any detail about him that was not inescapably himself. His leanness was expressed especially in movement, and in the taut look that suggested hunger and dissatisfaction, the uneasiness of the predatory beast that suspects he can never achieve satiation. His hardness came from other sources—from within, behind his eyes. He was to her a strangely beautiful machine, a creation shaped by hand, perhaps carved out of stone: the hardness had been set in him too, placed deep in his brain like a tiny pebble or seed. It inspired all his movements, all his words. Whatever he might say to her—and everything he said to her was abrupt and self-conscious—resulted from the angry agitation of this secret hardness, its friction against other oiled and clicking parts of his being, the parts that had run him for years, had initiated him to a pattern of reacting and understanding that was now being violated. She had not been too delirious to sense the irony here: upon whom had that violation been performed? It was true that her body was changed, but this change was not really within her experience—it was abstract and theoretical, like tiny points in a catechism lesson (to daydream during so many minutes of Mass was a venial sin, so many more minutes a mortal sin); certainly it was to this bitter forlorn man that the violation was real, and all his minutes with her in that gloomy room must have grated upon his brain and body, mocking his strength, establishing for him that personal dislike for her beyond his impersonal infatuation that he still showed now, months later. He had spoken as if always astonished by the fact that he was speaking at all, that he was recognizing her as a reality in his life, and as if astonished by the stupidity of whatever he said. "They got some stuff on the road, some junk, black tar that gets all over everything," he had said once. It was an effort for him to speak to her. He had the air of a man apprehensive of being fooled. "I went out to the garage to look at the car," he would say, his words getting harder and tighter instead of relaxing, "and had a talk with this friend of Max's, the one in the downtown precinct, and he says nothing—no news, nothing. Like nothing ever happened." He might have wanted to add, "Why aren't they looking for you?" but he did not. At such moments he would stare at her and their eyes would meet helplessly. Karen thought they might have been two people condemned to an eternity in each other's presence, lovers or criminals who had sinned together on earth but who could not understand precisely what they had done, or why, or in what way it was a sin demanding damnation. "But what are you doing here? What do you want with me?" Shar asked with his silent, baffled, murderous eyes, and his fingers would pick nervously at one another as the hard, diamond-sharp little pebble in his brain pressed and maddened him. It was not that Karen obscured the rest of the world from him that alarmed him, but rather that—she could only guess at this—he had come to feel that in some way she exemplified the rest of the world, or somehow invalidated it, so that it became irrelevant. Karen took his hatred for her as a token of their growing familiarity, something he revealed to her constantly while she revealed nothing to him. She would smile faintly and murmur, "Yes . . . yes . . . I think so . . . That man told me . . ." and allow her words to disintegrate, pushing at him the burden of carrying on this performance. She took courage from the simple knowledge that she had not abandoned anything of herself and so was in a way protected; she understood too that the looks they exchanged, the brief meaningless words they exchanged, were blind moves in a game of some sort, like the elaborate and cunning games of chess her father and brothers sometimes played at holiday reunions—and that Shar did not know the rules of the game.

It was Karen's icy reserve that controlled the game, precisely the secret in her that commanded her degradation and did not even require hysteria to narcoticize it—her knowing that if some morning Shar or the strange fat man were to see her crying, pleading for help, pleading not to be abandoned, not to be returned to a world that would never forgive her shame, pleading, above all, for Shar himself—then the game would be finished, the pieces swept off onto the floor with a slash of Shar's victorious hand. But they never found her this way. Even alone, awake for hours, she never gave in. Despair tempted her but it was a dry, hollow despair, the anguish that must lure people on the brink of death when tears and frenzy would change nothing, the despair one might experience upon seeing his heart snatched from him, slit and opened and turned neatly inside out, empty as an old soiled change purse. But Shar never detected that despair in her. If he hid a sharp, glinting knife in his insides, waiting to be turned upon her, she hid her knife also and did not even grimace—as he often did—when its brilliant edges cut her. The question in everyone's mind (so clamorous as to be almost vocal) was what Shar would do with her, and if Karen herself posed this question she did not offer it to him but thrust it upon him—not as a question but as a taunt, since she knew that nothing less than this could touch him. He was a man of violence, a stranger to her life, a man who could not even sit comfortably but must always be dreaming of air and space and speed—yet she was so arrogant as to suppose herself a match for him. She was so shameless as to show him that she knew his feeling for her, exactly what he wanted from her. There was nothing secret about this; it showed in the sweat on Shar's forehead, in the hot icy

168

gleam of his eyes that held her rigid while his voice went on to speak of other things—"No news today either. Max has five papers down there and reads them through." He would sometimes squirm in his chair, and if Max was in the room he would look around at him with a gesture that made Karen understand that his eyes showed anguish as soon as they were turned from her. The game continued for days, weeks. She did not know how long she was drugged; she took as a familiarity the equally drugged look of Shar's contemptuous, disbelieving face, turned upon her with a strange baffled urgency, as if they were conspirators and had no one but each other. One day Shar abandoned the game. Karen was not quite sure of how she knew this, but it was true. He abandoned it and admitted defeat, as if with a sudden uplifting of his hands toward heaven. Karen, by then accustomed to a life that began nowhere and headed nowhere, geographically or morally, understood that she must not abandon the game herself but must continue to play it in secret, plotting and calculating her moves until victory was hers.

When Karen felt well she and Shar went out for long, aimless, yawning walks. It was an effort for Shar to walk slowly enough for her; he was always straining ahead, peering enviously down alleys, up at the tops of buildings. They did not touch, and to a passer-by it might have seemed that the two of them—a man of about thirty with tiny perpetual lines of disapproval on his forehead and a girl of uncertain age, under twenty, who blinked at the sunlight as if unaccustomed to it— were not really aware of each other but simply happened to be going in the same direction at the same time. Shar expressed in his gestures and in his walk the brittle, impatient nervousness of the man who is frightened at his loss of self-control and cannot understand it. He was happy only when in control of some sort: driving his machines, drinking himself into a stupor, see-

169

ing the tabulation of his threatened violence on another's face. He never touched her, as if her skin might be poison to him, but she understood his slanted looks and felt victory approaching—he would not be able to resist for much longer the generous acquiescence she promised, could not help but promise, and the rich anarchy of the control he would then achieve over her. If he did finally surrender to her it was no more than himself he was surrendering to—already he must have thought of her as an appendage of his, an extension of his own body that he craved if he was to exist for other things. So in her presence he was alone; he contemplated her as they walked, puzzling and accusing the image of her that he carried with him, glancing over now and then in surprise at the actual young woman beside him. Karen caught these moments of surprise. "How do you feel?" Shar would say. His fingers would rub at his cheek, at his nose. "Are you tired yet?" Hopelessly they fell into silence. Shar would buy newspapers and sit in cheap diners reading them, frowning seriously, while Karen sat with a cup of coffee untouched and cooling before her. Shar leafed through the newspapers impatiently, reading only headlines and looking at pictures. When he was finished he threw the papers down and sat, smoking, looking out the grease-specked windows to the street. It did not occur to him to offer the papers to Karen; he might not have known she could read. In her role she could not ask him. She had no idea what was happening in the world, if anything was happening. She had withdrawn from history and had no interest in it, just as Shar, though he glanced at photographs of diplomats and African leaders and automobile accidents, had no interest in it, having created his own pastoral history out of the strength of his own body. What he looked for were items concerning Karen—GIRL REPORTED MISSING, GIRL SUSPECTED KIDNAPED—that he never found, and all other events baffled and angered him, as if their

170

space in the paper had usurped the place of the other ghostly story.

They walked through the slummy downtown of the city, and idly over toward the great cinder-strewn parking lots of factories, and across railroad tracks, and past fences topped with barbed wire, and through soot-darkened residential neighborhoods, and past schools with windows decorated with flowers, rabbits, and trees. Just as all external details disappeared in Shar's presence, so did Karen's vision of what they saw disappear. Shar walked impatiently through a vacuum composed of store-window reflections of himself and the silent girl beside him, and when there were no store windows to give him these reflections he must have contrived them himself. He smoked constantly, waited perfunctorily at deserted street corners before crossing, glanced with a dull, angry gaze to notice little corner stores that sold pretzel sticks and candy and popsicles of various flavors—orange, raspberry, root beer, cherry. If it was warm, they would stand on the steps of these stores while Shar, frowning in thought, sucked at a dripping popsicle and children straddling bicycles a few yards away ate the same thing. Karen never asked herself the question, "What is he? What kind of life does he lead?" Of course he had no life, he had nothing, he was simply himself. Other men hurried out of factories in the late afternoon, or were to be seen on errands, going somewhere, having come from somewhere, but Shar came from nowhere and went nowhere. He seemed also to notice nothing. Beside his muscular propriety the ordinary world paled and fell away. He was a sojourner here, and never confused the intricacies of this surface world with the reality of his own world, which consisted of himself. His simplicity, Karen thought, made him dangerous, for to him the world of man was not valued for its uniqueness, nor was human experience judged to be good or evil, nor was sin possible: there was

171

only Shar's will, the deadly whimsical range of his desire. He was as perplexed as she by his strange refusal to dismiss her. He wanted her gone yet he did not want her gone, not so simply. Once he had turned to her—they were near a mud-splattered excavation site—and said, as if he were only now thinking of this, "When are you going home?" Karen stared at their feet and pretended to be thinking. Shar had hard, big feet, dirty shoes with frayed shoelaces. After a while he said, "Max can fix it up for you. Buy the tickets or drive you right up there himself." Karen's silence forced upon them both the realization that there was for them in these roles no common language. Daily he was being drawn to her, his initial failure to escape her had decided everything; it was only Shar's simplicity that blinded him. "I can't leave you," Karen said, still staring at their feet.

His affinity was with machines, though none they saw were so finely geared and meshed as he. He loved to watch excavating machines and great straining trailer trucks maneuvered with astonishing skill; he even watched men repairing streets, enjoying the vibrations and the roar of the air drill. In the smelly bars they wandered in and out of he played machines—gaudily-colored pinball machines that seemed to Shar to be challenging him personally. When he was not with her, over at the garage, Karen believed he was trying to blot out his confusion over her with the blunt, exhilarating performance of machines. But he reappeared to her always, and something in the repetition of their days—they began to eat together, they had periods of real silence that were more intimate than anything Karen had ever experienced—seemed to satisfy him. One morning they went out walking, again in silence, but Shar was humming to himself and Karen had the numb feeling that something had been decided. They walked in a park bordering a cemetery. The air was fresh with spring, the grass vividly green. Karen touched her hair, her cool face, feeling herself unrevived by spring, pale and lifeless, unattractive, while the man at her side had to hold back his energy and could not stop his eyes from staring at the tops of trees and beyond them into the blue sky. Something had been decided, Karen thought. She had won. They wandered through to the cemetery, where the spongy ground and the cheap gravestones looked oddly healthy. Karen felt in the warming air that she had no right to be here, that she had really died; she had escaped illness and insanity, perhaps, but she had really died somewhere in the past. She could not help but stare at Shar's back with a kind of fond contempt—clumsy, ignorant man, to suppose he could understand her! She saw him looking about with a precision not ordinarily his. He said nothing, there was nothing hurried about him, and though later she would be able to sense, by the sudden rigidity of his jaw, exactly when the bitter pressure of his obsession overtook him, she did not understand until he finally touched her what his intention was—it must have been, up until that moment, ceremonial and plotted, an act his mind and not his body had prescribed for him. "I'm not well," Karen said. "I'm not— I might bleed—" She had begun to tremble convulsively. Shar urged her down and knelt beside her. He gripped her shoulders as if listening to her heartbeat. "It won't hurt," he said. But he waited. Karen felt her eyes harden; she looked behind him at the bare tree limbs stretched out so absurdly against the sky. As her strength ebbed out of her, the trembling lessened; she might have been fleeing her body, plotting to leave it behind with Shar in order to please him and cheat him at the same time. Shar touched her hands, her arms, her shoulders; very gently and seriously he stroked her body as if trying to bring her to life, while Karen closed her eyes and felt her soul contract itself into a tiny pebble-like thing safe in her brain. Her hand reached out and groped against his chest. She slid

173

her fingers inside his shirt and touched his skin, and in that instant she felt her trembling pass over into him. Still he crouched over her and stroked her limbs and her body, so gently and lovingly that, so long as her eyes were closed, she felt no shame. It might have been night, she might have been asleep, and this lover come to her made innocent by his being only a dream, something over which she need have no control. Suddenly he was like Jack and the other young men she had known who had tried to make her love them, tried to make her feel something for them—though they had never dared to do what Shar did to her. She wanted to take hold of his wrist, but she knew she did not have the right. She pitied him for trying to evoke in her a feeling she would never give him, just as she had pitied Jack and the others, though contemptuously, and with her eyes still closed she reached up to touch the nape of his neck. Then she heard something overhead—an airplane—and opened her eyes suddenly. She squinted and stared up at nothing. Then she looked at Shar's face and what she saw there made her lips jerk up in an angry, disgusted grin. Shar stared at her. He was breathing through his mouth and she could see his teeth. Then he straightened and brought his hand around and slapped her face. "Look at me like that, you little bitch!" he said. His face was white. Karen was frightened, but she could not change her expression. Her lips seemed frozen in their grimace. Shar slapped her again. She shut her eyes, her face turned away, while he raged above her. This was something real, something she could understand, the selfish little pebble in her brain rejoiced in it because it could make her hate this man so much more clearly. The memory of his patience was dissipated now by the violence of the pain she felt. They grunted together, Karen squirming backward in the damp earth, Shar grinding himself against her. Karen felt her hair tangle in the wet grass. "You little bitch! Little bitch!" Shar sobbed. Karen

174

heard cloth being ripped. She pushed against him, her forearm against his face, but he ducked under it and brought his face down hard against hers, blindly, his teeth wet, the hard deadly pressure of his skull holding her still. "I'd like to set you on fire like I did to *him*," he said, "take a match and set you on fire—burn everything—your clothes catching on and burning —you screaming for help, you little bitch! And all burning up, hair and insides, so you could see inside and see the things burning there, melting away, burning—" He was enlivened with rage as with charges of electricity, grinding and lunging against her, as if his murderous spite were trying to bore its way out of him and into her.

Karen woke to hear someone knocking at the door. She could not think for a moment where she was. She was alone, and she could not remember being alone. The knocking was soft and discreet. "Yes," she said vaguely. She did not move. Sunlight streamed in the grimy windows. After a moment the knocking began again. Karen pulled the sheets up to her chin and said nothing. Her heart had begun to thud. Then she heard the sound of a key in the lock. Knowing it was not Shar made her feel reckless; she did not even look around.

"My dear Karen!" Max closed the door behind him. He was fat and apologetic. "I was waiting for you downstairs—I thought you might come downstairs."

Karen said nothing.

"But my dear child," Max said, shifting his weight from one foot to the other, "you must look at me. Here. Yes, like that. How pretty you are, even after last night! I'm sorry to tell you this—it's hard for me, very hard for me, a strain on my heart— Are you listening? Shar is gone—I'm sorry to be the one to tell you, terribly sorry— He's gone, he said for me to tell you. He—"

"He isn't gone!" said Karen.

"It's difficult enough for me to tell you this," Max said, though his pert, benevolent expression seemed to suggest he was enjoying himself, "I could hardly eat breakfast, thinking of it; my appetite is gone. I thought of you up here, my poor forlorn Karen, and it made me think of the other women, the young women that Shar— It made me think of you all together, and made me think of how old I am— I told him he should be the one to tell you himself, but—"

"He isn't gone," Karen said. She stared angrily at Max. "I don't believe you. He can't be gone."

"But he is gone," Max said, lifting his palms in a gesture of defeat, gently, smiling gently, "he is gone—and you will never see him again. For your own good and his. Do you understand that?"

13

Max had been sitting in the sunny corner of the hotel lobby for about half an hour, awaiting Karen. He had arranged himself in the creaking chair with much effort and tenderness, hesitating many seconds before he let his legs slide out from under him. He wore a suit of light, faint blue, buttoned across his chest and stomach. His face was newly shaven and looked a little raw, as if he were being seen in too exposing a light. He crossed his short, thick legs with an effort, sighed unhappily, and opened a book. In a minute his reading so engrossed him that he chuckled out loud and took a pencil out of his pocket to mark something in the text.

A few people walked past but he did not look up. Jerry came downstairs and sat heavily in a cracked leather chair not far from Max, but said nothing. Max did not look up. The sunlight brightened, pouring warmly on his head. His fair, thinning hair had been dampened, and now the sunlight played minutely about it. Jerry, gazing blankly at his employer's head, put his arms behind his own head and yawned. Outside, automobile horns blared angrily.

As soon as the sound of sharp clicking heels came to Max's ears, he looked up. Karen passed by, heading for the street. He called to her; she turned quickly, showing her desperation. But in the next instant Max felt he had misunderstood her—she stood staring coldly at him, her lips firm, her neck very tense. She wore white: a hard, dazzling white. As if to mock him, the silver necklace he had given her gleamed proudly back at him!

"You must understand that he is gone—he is gone," Max said. She stood before him now, looking past his head. He was tempted to turn around and see what she was looking at. Jerry, slouched in his chair, watched her with the sort of helpless look Max had noticed in him when Karen was in their company. "You must learn to forgive him," Max went on, inspired by the pathos of the scene. He had felt it a delicious, dramatic moment—yet Karen, after the first instant of her surprise, showed no emotion, as if she had thrust upon Max the burden of making this difficult. "It has been difficult for him—I saw this coming in him, before he realized it himself. That was one of the reasons I talked to you yesterday—"

Karen's young, clever face showed nothing. Max was amazed as always by the clarity of her eyes—faint blue, modest blue, refusing to shift away under the impact of fear or shame.

Perhaps he had always misjudged her, and what he thought to be shrewdness in her was simply ignorance—profound ignorance? She did not even relish what suffering came to her; she did not seem to always know it was supposed to be suffering. Max was not sure if this was admirable in her or if it was an indication of her vulgarity.

"You will allow me to help you," Max said, getting to his feet. "I will be very happy to help you—to see that you return home safely. And to see that your health is good. Of course it is no business of mine, but—" He saw, to his alarm, that she was about to turn away. "Where are you going? At least let us talk together. Let me help you with your grief."

Karen did not appear grieved, but in a daze—a hard, tearless daze. She looked at Max as if she had never seen him before. "Perhaps I can tempt you into coming to breakfast with me," he said. His appetite now had returned most powerfully. "We can talk there. You surely can't be in a hurry to go anywhere —why, where would you go?"

In the murky coffee shop of the hotel they sat in a booth by one of the high, grimy windows. Max's doctor was already in there, sitting languidly at the counter; he turned and nodded to Max when they entered. He stirred his coffee endlessly. "This looks fine, by the window," Max had said. He sat across from Karen and Jerry, smiling hospitably at them. "Such brilliant sunlight! It woke me early this morning. I had difficulty with sleep—some trouble with my nerves, trouble as always with something! I'm afraid my health is disintegrating," he said.

Karen wanted nothing; Jerry ordered coffee. Max read off an order for breakfast from a fly-specked menu he had been given, then leaned forward, pressing his stomach against the table, to look seriously at Karen. "First of all, my dear," he said kindly, "you must not think of desperate measures—of violence against

179

yourself. You must accept what has happened. It is for the best —certainly—ultimately for the best; all things are. If you were to have a baby, if you had been pregnant—" He spoke now as if this were a possibility that no longer existed. "If you had been pregnant, Shar's reaction might have been—violent, or— He is governed by his passion, his emotion; he doesn't think. Exactly like a child. I have always considered him a child—the young man from the provinces, seeking his fortune. What sense is there in him of his condition? The whole world is shrunk down to fit him—he carries it around in his head! Exactly like a child! He is the child who does nothing, to whom all things are done. Whatever happens to him he hasn't deserved or earned—good or bad—whatever—these things simply happen, accidents. And that is true for you as well!"

Max smiled as if he had made a brilliant point. "We others— we who are more worldly, who aren't, properly speaking, from the 'provinces'—we realize that life is something else, that we are always responsible for what we do. But you children—you do not!—and that is what I love in you and respect very sincerely; I assure you I do. It is innocence. It is lost to all but children."

Jerry, who did not seem to be listening, took out a pack of cigarettes and selected one carefully. He lit the cigarette with a heavy silver lighter that was designed with small intricate hearts. His expression, professional and deaf, would have been the same had he been sitting alone.

"That is something you cannot understand," Max said softly. "A lost innocence—you cannot understand it. Those who are protected by innocence are not even aware of it; they know nothing. They *know* nothing. Yet you are innocent, my dear Karen, in spite of your knowing quite a bit—and you know these things, incredibly, without understanding them, without having been transformed yourself by the knowledge of them!"

180

He wiped his forehead. "That is what is incredible. . . . Nothing either you or Shar will ever do will have anything to do with you; all things are accidents to you. You heard Shar talk of the accident yesterday. Precisely! No one could say what had happened—Shar least of all. He would be the last to understand — He operates from his stomach."

"And I do too?" Karen said.

It was impossible to tell how she meant this. Max believed she was serious. "Perhaps not your stomach," he said, making a kind of gracious bow with his head, "that sounds . . . indelicate . . . for such a pretty girl. Your heart, perhaps— You operate from your heart."

"That is true," Karen said queerly.

The waitress brought their orders. Jerry accepted his coffee without looking up, Max the first part of his breakfast—a grapefruit, cut neatly in half and seeded—with a fond, condescending smile for the waitress. He ate with relish. The grapefruit was sour, even after he had put several spoonfuls of sugar on it; but still it was fresh and good. He understood that fruit was good for a man in his condition. He talked for a while of the grapefruit and of fruit in general, then reverted to his subject. "I sometimes think," he said philosophically, waving the dripping spoon at Karen, "that children like you understand the world best. You are perhaps most sophisticated, after all. To take life as an accident, and everything in it as an accident—what sophistication! Why should there be any logical pattern of events, any distinction between an earthly order and an . . . oh . . . eternal order? Why, indeed? We religious people—" He noted how Karen's eyes narrowed as he said this. "We religious people search for meaning, and we are humbled. What brilliance there is in a child, who takes the world as chaos and never thinks about it! *There* is innocence—it is impossible in anyone else, in anyone who believes."

181

Jerry sipped his coffee and blew on it when he found it too hot. From time to time he glanced up at Karen, but his face was expressionless. He never looked at Max or seemed to hear him, though Max's words gained momentum with his excitement. He finished his grapefruit in a burst of enthusiasm and went on:

"Yet when I lose my faith—and I am constantly losing and regaining it—do I fall back to innocence? No. Innocence is lost to me. I have never been innocent; I have always been this age." The waitress, nervously approaching them, placed another plate before Max—a plate of soft eggs, mixed with colorless strips of bacon and little sturdy-looking globules of fat. "Always—always to have been the same age! Can you understand that?" His gaze was tempted downward; he began to eat, slowly at first, then, as the food lured him, faster and faster, though he did not stop talking. He seemed to think that if he stopped he would lose Karen's attention. "How well I know that life is no imitation!—that it is absurd to have faith in anything except life. I won't come again to this—I will never sit here again. I will never eat this again." This was apparently a good point, for not only Karen but Jerry as well looked up. "Men make the error that things will turn out for the good— we religious people make that error, though our experience contradicts us. In literature, now, things are different; this long poem I've been rereading . . . temptation, sin, fall, and expiation, all around in a circle, into the garden and out of it, many angels, great blazes of rhetoric and light—an immense scheme of tautological relationships you need never believe in! As if it mattered that there was ever a paradise, or in what way it was lost to us—the only important thing is that we have no paradise; we have none. Yet a most beautiful poem! All an expression of something else—an imitation, a metaphor. These fragments that strain away from their center—they reel around,

182

they cannot penetrate through to the outer world; there is no outer world. But life is not like that, your life is not being created for you out of a mind. Your life is not a metaphor for anything beyond it. It ends when you do—and when your grave is lost, where are you? Where is my pretty Karen then?"

"My grave will never be lost," Karen said.

Apparently this was funny, for Max laughed luxuriously. He stopped eating for a moment to surrender himself to laughter. "She would be good for you," he said to Jerry, "if it were not for Shar—as you say, very shrewdly; if it were not for Shar. I would like to keep her with me always!"

Jerry looked at Karen. "Except for Shar and something that needs an operation," he said.

"An ugly topic to suggest at breakfast," Max said, wiping remnants of egg off his plate with a piece of toast.

"Shar is the one I'd like to give the operation to," said Jerry. He looked at Karen with an amused, sadly sympathetic look. "How much would he be worth then?"

Karen's face began to burn. She stared at Jerry's fingers as he tapped them patiently on the table.

"You know nothing—nothing," Max said angrily. His face was distorted with toast. He raised a finger and shook it at Jerry, as if Jerry were a child. "You degrade all things to your level."

"The hell with it," said Jerry. "She's going back home."

"That's it, of course, Karen," Max said, pointing the finger now at her. "We decided that, Shar and I, we talked of it for a long time. He understands that what he did is for the best. . . . Karen, I am prepared to help you, I hope you will allow me to help you—I will be very disappointed if you do not— Perhaps you would like to talk to me alone?"

Before Karen could reply, Jerry had already stood. "I'll be out in the lobby," he said.

Now Max clasped his hands before him and leaned toward Karen. Sunshine through the dusty window gave him a clean, eager look, though it seemed to trouble his eyes; they had narrowed until they were quite small, fringed by babyish lashes, and out of these he peeked earnestly at her as he spoke. "You wonder at me—you wonder what I am doing here with you, appealing to you. You wonder what kind of life I come from. I wonder at you too—I seriously wonder. I have never been able to understand you. I see you as innocent, and yet sometimes I am not so sure—not so sure of my own judgment— Perhaps I am the innocent one!" He smiled at her. His teeth were big and white. "My sister saw ghosts," he said suddenly. "Do you have a woman in your family who sees ghosts? Why is it ghosts appear to women? I didn't mind it but you do come to believe it—I mean, believe she sees them; I never did . . . myself, but perhaps it was only a matter of time— What could we say to her? I felt I should say something to her, since silence was, simply, a collaboration in ghosts! But you must be cautious with other people, people are so delicate, a word misspoken might never be amended, a look of the wrong sort never negated—no negations, only a slow piling up; try to get there and see what they want, to get it for them, you see how delicate it is—delicate and out of reach—dealing with the souls of others. Yourself you might negate, the conflicting wants, all, all the conflicts, you might negate one with another, heal yourself, but no one else—you only destroy—you only negate everything at once, a mistake. So it is with caution I approach you—with respect for you, for what you have endured. I will be happy to help you if—"

Here he stopped to take a breath. But it was at an awkward moment, since his last words hung between them. Karen stared coldly. Max, sensitive of an indiscretion, raised his hands as if to distract her and went on, smiling, "I have always enjoyed as much as we have said to each other, for I do feel, as I've told you, that we have something in common—something mysterious in common; I feel this. I—" He licked his lips. He was conscious of a rapidity of heartbeat that startled him, but he was so caught up in what he had to say that he had no time to worry. He was afraid Karen would rise suddenly in disgust and leave. "I would like to talk to you. Perhaps up in my room? I would like to ask you some things. Not only about Shar—but about your life before him, your childhood, your father, and family, your experiences— Your dreams— And, of course, of Shar—you have told me little of him, what you've felt with him— And the baby," he said. He was now leaning so hard against the table that his stomach bulged painfully against it. He and Karen looked at each other. "Will you come up with me?" he said.

Karen's eyes wandered behind him, behind his head. He felt for an instant that he had lost her. Perhaps she had heard little of what he said, perhaps she had been thinking all along of Shar. . . . Max waited, sweating, while she hesitated; then she said, "In what way will you help me?"

"Money," said Max.

"How much money?"

"I thought of a thousand."

"A thousand!" said Karen.

"I'll provide for the operation too, if you want it," Max said quickly, "that is—if you need it; I can arrange for you to have the best of care—"

Karen looked frightened. "I want to have the child," she said.

Max clasped his hands as if congratulating himself. "We'll talk about it. We'll decide about it."

Karen sat as if in a trance. Max could see tiny dots of perspiration on her forehead and upper lip. Her look of hauteur had changed and she seemed now surprisingly young—almost indecently young; but the incongruity of her youth and her situation delighted Max. Inspired by her helplessness, he began to shift himself about the cramping seat, crossing and uncrossing his hot legs at the ankles. "We'll decide about it. It's nine o'clock now. Nine o'clock," he said, wiping perspiration out of his eyes. His voice trembled with excitement. "At twelve o'clock we'll take you to the train station, we'll get you ready, get your ticket— I'll call from here to see when your train goes. Now . . . shall we—"

He pulled himself up out of the booth and waited for her. At the counter the doctor did not glance around; he sat stirring his coffee. A few other customers looked over their newspapers and white coffee cups to stare blankly at Max, and then with interest at Karen, as she got unsteadily to her feet.

In the hotel lobby Karen saw Jerry waiting for them. As they approached, Jerry stood up. For the first time since Karen had known him, he looked uneasy; he was licking his lips as he and Max conferred together. Though it must puzzle Jerry, Karen could not help staring at his face. She heard Max say something about Shar—"if he should come back." Karen wanted to run at him, pound his fat, perspiring back, wanted to cry, "He will never come back! You know that!"

When Max turned and took her arm, Karen pulled away. "No," she said. "I'm going home now. I've decided to go home now."

Through the buzzing sunlight Max wondered at her. For a moment they seemed to brace each other in their astonishment, their arms lifted; then Max released her. "Going home now?" he said slowly. "Why are you going home now?"

Karen tried to force him back by the bitter contempt she felt for him, by the power of her stare alone; but she could not.

186

He accepted and absorbed her hysteria and left her exhausted. "I want to," she said, backing away. "I've decided to. I've decided to."

"My dear child—"

"I don't want the things upstairs. I'll leave them. I'm going back now. I don't . . . I don't want anything. Please—"

"At twelve o'clock we will take you—"

"No," Karen said, shaking her head cautiously. "No. I've decided to go home now. I'm going home now."

She rushed past him just as he was about to reach out for her. She heard him say something to Jerry but she did not hear Jerry's reply. Outside, she turned and hurried along the sidewalk, as if she knew where she was going; she walked for some time, breathing through her open mouth, her heart pounding, without seeing anything. People loomed up before her, bright-faced, anonymous, and sidewalks gave way to streets that she crossed when others did, staring fixedly ahead of her. She was conscious of having avoided something, just as she avoided colliding with people on the sidewalk; but she had acted by instinct only. Where had her mind been? Her mind had been raveled out into the sunlight, giddy and unbalanced, she could not depend on it. Though Karen touched her hot face and saw her reflection in store windows and in the eyes of people who passed by, she thought that perhaps her humanity was being lost to her—her soul and her mind, all that had made her herself, were confused, weakened, and she had nothing left to show of herself but a face, a body, a set of emotions. A face and a body! She looked at her reflection in a store window as if she could not believe it. Yet there she stood —dressed in white, a skirt being caressed by the hot dusty wind, stark, pale legs, uplifted arms, hands about to reach out and touch their reflections. An incredulous face, incredulous that anything should be behind it—that anything should

187

stare out of those eyes. People passed her, amused reflections. Amused at her conceit, perhaps, or not noticing her at all. Karen felt a thrill of horror that she should deceive them— that they should assume, however briefly, that a human being stood where she was. All she could be sure of was a face and a body—her emotions came out as ordered. They were contrived. She could not believe in them any longer. She was sure she felt disgust for what had nearly happened, and yet, perhaps, she felt only regret for it, regret for having lost a thousand dollars; and the disgust was contrived to soothe her conscience.

She walked on. She murmured to herself, "I am lost. I am lost." The day was hot and windy with sunlight. It blew at her skirt and hair; sometimes raw bits of dust were flung up against her face. Scraps of sentences came to her, jumbled words. She found herself thinking, inexplicably, as she sometimes did when Shar made love to her, of scenes of her childhood—out-of-the-way barns, gullies, a bend in the creek she had not thought about for years. The proud pony one of the boys had ridden to school that time—why did she remember it now, and the big blue-black flies that worried it? The boy who owned it was forgotten; the day was forgotten; the child, Karen, who gaped at it was forgotten—only the pony remained, isolated out of time. How she had wanted a pony like that! How she had cried for it, crawling about her father's knees! "But why didn't he ever get it for me?" Karen wondered. She was struck by her father's queer injustice. She felt she could not forgive him for that.

She had prayed for the pony for months, and now these prayers returned to her. Mechanically her mind ran through them. Other prayers suggested themselves; she closed her eyes with the effort to remember them. Gradually her sense of horror lessened. She had left that behind, in the hotel. She had escaped him. The center of their lives! He drew them in to him, sucked them in, his appetite was insatiable. Perhaps Shar had not gone anywhere, but had been devoured by Max. . . . Her prayers redirected themselves, attached themselves to something else, more vague than the pony, more inaccessible; it had fled her. She could not quite reach it. The humiliation, the pain, the fear that possessed her! Karen felt that she had lost her mind. She could not even understand her emotions, or understand if they were truly hers—perhaps she took them from people who passed, that small boy crying and wiping his eyes with dirty fists, a man leering out at the street from an upstairs window—skinny in a white undershirt! In the middle of a confused "Our Father" she stopped and found herself staring at another of her many reflections. It was in a drug store window. The sight of herself staring at herself struck her as funny: murmuring to God, evoking Christ, she was in fact talking only to this reflection. The thought overwhelmed and disgusted her. The very presence of her image, the slight tilting of her head—was that coquettishness?—emphasized her isolation; she was indeed lost; she deserved to be lost. Like Shar, who could not hold together the fragments of his life, Karen could not hold together the snatches of herself that were revealed to her. She was incomplete, not quite human, a mockery of a person. Her beauty mocked the vacuity of her soul. She felt that the straggling people in the street, the people who lounged in doorways, could see through her disguise to the barrenness of her soul. Walking on, she became burdened by the pressure of their attention; she felt their curiosity turn into shame for her. . . .

After a while she found her way to the bus station. It was small and grimy, in the rear of a garage. She had no money, so she sat and watched the clock as if that might tell her something while the ticket seller whispered about her to one of

189

his customers. The morning went on: bus drivers sourly announced their buses, people milled in and out, a woman addressed her, asking anxiously if the newspaper on the floor belonged to her.

One of the mechanics from the garage, a young, foreign-looking man, swaggered through, wiping his hands on a rag; someone must have told him about Karen. She did not look up. The ticket seller, leaning forward on his elbows, stared in detail at her white dress, which had become soiled by ashes on the chair. He hummed loudly to himself as if he were very pleased with something, then very vexed. He cleared his throat finally and said, "Miss, there ain't no bus out of here till three o'clock now. You waiting for that one?"

Karen looked around slowly, but her eyes stopped before they reached the man's face. He stared at her a while, then scratched his head, muttered to himself, and arranged things before him on the counter. Another mechanic from the garage drifted in, smoking a cigarette, and put a coin in a soft-drink machine. He and the ticket seller talked together about the weather. Karen heard the ticket seller say something pettishly and end with: "—no bus out of here till three o'clock."

A while later Karen looked down from the clock—she was waiting for something, perhaps twelve o'clock—to see Jerry come in. He came right to her. He had gray eyes and small, sharp brows; he looked pleased with himself for finding her.

"That fat bastard back there is all in a sweat," he said, "but he sends you this anyhow." He took an envelope out of his pocket and gave it to Karen. She wondered at it: it was a wrinkled, used, manila envelope with farming equipment advertised on it. "He says good-by to you. He wishes you good luck."

When Jerry left, Karen looked inside the envelope. She took the bills out to count them: ten hundred-dollar bills. Her face went hot with blood. The bills and the envelope trembled in her hands. The murmuring prayers and doubts and self-accusations of the morning were hurled back at her: hypocrite, she thought, and liar! She felt that now, with this money, with even the dirty envelope it had come in—fished out of a wastebasket—her degradation was complete.

14

The history of the city of Cherry River covered a respectable amount of time. It had been a minor, prosperous port up until the Civil War, though its prime had really been in the late eighteenth century. A few homes and gardens from this era remained in spite of violence during the war and neglect afterward—Cherry River, belonging to a part of the country bordering the South, had been mobbed righteously by both sides. The neglect was more natural. After the days of the sailing fleets had passed and industry along the coast settled in other cities, the population ebbed, young people moved to find work in coal fields, liquor distilleries, and tobacco markets elsewhere, or penetrated the mountain wall to the west and dissociated themselves from the civilization, now thought aged, along the east coast. At the turn of the century the town consisted of a main street, unpaved, and a few stores and a post office serving the farms in the area. The old harbor still put out fishing boats, and sometimes wealthy people from the western part of the state—wealthy from coal—came there to sail or to fish from their luxurious boats. There was a small tobacco trade that seemed to operate in a vacuum, as if done by amateurs.

Because of its position on the ocean and its tendency to attract northerly winds, Cherry River remained mild until August and September. Its horseshoe-shaped, picturesque harbor, in some places visibly rotting, attracted boatmen and retired landowners from farther south, who were sick of long summers. It also attracted a businessman who had already started small amusement parks and commercial beaches in small cities along the coast and by palatable lakes, and who had built a boardwalk along as much of the harbor as he was able to buy, beginning out of nowhere and ending nowhere. The beach was improved by mountains of sand from mysterious sources— fine, pure, sparkling sand. The first dance hall was built, and then, annexed to it, the first tavern of a sophisticated nature. Prohibition made the prosperity of the town a certainty: so promising was its future, so forward-looking its new inhabitants, that the first Cherry River—cotton and tobacco port, an English-settled town with the reputation of gracious eighteenth-century living—no longer had any relationship to the new Cherry River at all. The present and the past were so incongruous that when a horde of boys from the beach, most of them of foreign descent, tipped over and defaced the Civil War cannon by the church—in Cherry River, it was called the

"War Between the States" cannon—nothing was done to repair the damage. The new people could not remember any such war and had no interest in it.

Decades later, when the huge auto-racing track was first opened, the city was a strange blend of old buildings and new, sleek creations, many of them adorned by intricate neon signs. The old boardwalk had been replaced by a wide, gigantic walk that ran almost the entire length of the inner harbor, and between it and the beach (admission to the beach was now fifty cents) were restaurants and night clubs and side shows and games and tents—at one end, near the new racing track, fairly expensive and modern; at the other end, called "Wop Side," cheap and noisy and dangerous after dark. The land to the north of Cherry River, bordering the ocean, had long since been sold to private, wealthy families, some of whom had made their fortunes during Prohibition and many of whom now owned interests in Cherry River. The commercial part of the city was operated by a congenial arrangement between two or three gambling syndicates to the north.

The population of the city was now vividly mixed—there may have been descendants of the original inhabitants, but no one knew about them. Tourists were surprised to discover a little New England-looking town behind the hotels and restaurants, with its own churches and a red brick high school and homes that were not beach houses. Many of the old-fashioned buildings on what had been Main Street were now turned into apartment houses to hold the Negroes and other workers, mainly of Italian descent, who had been attracted to the town to work on the beach or as waiters or janitors or kitchen help. The city's oldest inhabitants, who had boasted of never having seen a "Nigra" in their lives, were now accustomed to seeing Negro children running freely about on Main Street and seeing Negro families present themselves in church Sunday mornings, scrubbed and polished and dressed with a vengeance.

Though the population was sharply heterogeneous and the most recent section of it expanding rapidly, there had been little conflict until recent years. During Prohibition there had been violence and occasional murders, but these had to do with private quarrels begun in northern cities; the population was not hurt or even offended by them. In recent years, however, there had been a few instances of brutality without apparent motive —a carload of Negro teen-agers had been forced off a highway, a row of Negro huts in the old "Niggertown" section had been set on fire, and from time to time car windows had been smashed indiscriminately. On Hallowe'en the windows of the high school had been broken, but whether this had been done by the Negro children, who went by school bus to another school, or by the high school students themselves was never made clear. The first summer that Shar had come to Cherry River there had been some beatings of both Negroes and whites, and investigations, but nothing had come of them. Someone had had a shrewd idea and violated all precedent to appoint several Negroes to the police force—they would be assigned to their own neighborhoods—but no one could tell, of course, whether trouble had been averted by this. It was thought generally that it had been a good decision—it showed progressive thinking. Some of the oldest people, frightened by changing times, alternated between thinking of moving farther South and reflecting complacently that they did not have much longer to live.

Though some of the night clubs and hotels remained open all winter, summer was still the most prosperous season for Cherry River. The Fourth of July race was the most important event of the year, since it attracted people from remote parts of

195

the country. On the days before and after the race the streets would be crowded, the boardwalk milling with humanity, the night clubs and restaurants filled to capacity; on the sloping beach hordes of people would lie in the sun or swim or fend their way around, walking stiffly, as if walking itself had become a struggle. The sunny air would be filled with excitement and expectancy as well as with the tumultuous din of voices and music from transistor radios, held fondly up to ears and evoking in eyes a dreamy, narcotic peace.

Toward the end of June Shar and a few men had come to Cherry River to prepare themselves for the race. Shar had come immediately after leaving Synderdale, alone, and was joined before long by the mechanics and his alternate driver, Mitch. Following Shar's example, they declined Max's offer of rooms in a motel he partially owned—the offer included even the Negro Mitch—and rented rooms in an old boardinghouse not far from the garage they used when they were in Cherry River.

The days before the race passed calmly. Shar woke early in the morning and went down to the beach to swim, sometimes alone, sometimes with Mitch or one of the other men. In the early morning the beach, though littered with papers and refuse, had a pale, clean glare, and the water smelled hard and salty. Shar felt his strength returning. The air intoxicated him. Mornings at Cherry River had always been good; it was later, when the afternoon and night crowds dominated, that he hated the place. The look of the crowds with their sweating faces and bright clothes tightened his stomach so that only working out with the car relaxed him, or, if that did not work, he could begin drinking after supper until all tension dissolved into a hot stupor. One morning, a little groggy, Shar had explained to Mitch the secret of his life: "You got to keep going.

196

When you stop, it all catches up. Being a nigger, you'll understand that."

Mitch agreed with him. They were sitting at the edge of the beach, their feet waiting for the waves. "I been going for a long time," Mitch said, as if to help Shar with his argument.

"They can buy anything," Shar said, "as long as it stands still for them. They can buy anything, the best drivers, the best mechanics, the best races. They can buy me, I s'pose . . . I s'pose they have. But when I'm out there, there's no bastard that owns me, a fat millionaire or whoever it is. And they Jesus-well better remember that."

"He said anything about a circuit?"

"Hell! What is he waiting for?" Shar said angrily. "How much more money does he need? No, he puts it off; he puts me off. I got both arms broke once or twice, a leg broke—I forget which—collarbones a few times, lost count of it, ribs up and down and back again—and wrists and fingers and feet, off and on. What is he waiting for? That fifty-thousand-dollar policy he has on me? If I belonged to somebody else he'd have taken me over there a long time ago—I'd be a grand prix winner. How'd you like that last son of a bitch that won—foreign bastard!" But as he spoke, he felt odd—as if he were not telling the truth. As if Mitchie had said something, Shar snapped, "And I'm not old! I'm good for another ten years. Look at the South American bastard, how old is he? Forty-six?—What they're grooming you for, Mitch, isn't motor-racing. They fooled me with it. For them it's money and for me, waiting to die."

"The hell with that!" Mitch said. He looked at Shar with proper astonishment. "Who are you kidding?"

"But over there, driving a car, a thousand miles of a real road! How'd you like that, a real road for once? Not a goddam

197

horse track—a greyhound track! I been so many times around a circle I'm sick to death of it; how do you get out of a circle but carried out in parts? I'd like to stuff that fat bastard Max's money down his throat, stuff him up to his mouth. He won't let me go. . . ." Shar's argument, familiar to him and his friends, lost its enthusiasm. He could not help but feel that the American track, compressed and spectacular, answered his own hunger for brutality in a way that the European track would not. But that was not the only reason he no longer wanted to leave the country.

Later, swimming with Mitchie, lunging against the surf, Shar felt the strength of his body like electricity buoying him up. The sun was just above the horizon, streaking across the water. The staleness of his mind was freshened by the water and air; he felt young. The surf pounded behind him up to the empty shore, but before him there was nothing but water and light—nothing that was familiar. He yelled over to Mitchie, "Ain't this a goddam good thing!" Mitchie put his hand to his ear as if he were deaf; he grinned clownishly. "It does you good to have it like this! God, how I love this world!" Shar muttered fiercely. "A damn good world! I can't get close enough to it—"

Mitchie shrugged his shoulders; he could not hear. Shar did not look at him. He stared at the skyline and the hot sun. With the coarse water lunging about him he thought again that he could not get close enough to it, just as he could not get close enough to anything, finally—not even his racing, certainly not Karen. At the thought of her he felt his heart sink, as if he had succumbed to something forbidden. "A bitch!" he said. He trembled with anger at her. "Dressed like that, looking like a kid, to shame me! To shame me!"

In those days Shar was accustomed to leaving places suddenly, getting up and walking out, when he gave in to thoughts

198

about Karen. He seemed to think that in this way he would elude her. With a vague explanatory wave of his hand he left Mitchie looking after him and went back to his room.

Mitch came up a while later, his clothes changed, and he and Shar went to have breakfast at a diner. It was made of rusted tin and had tinfoil in its windows to keep out the sun. Mitchie noticed how some of the men inside—workingmen on their way to jobs—looked at him and Shar, but Shar, settling arrogantly into himself, noticed nothing. Mitchie said to Shar in a low voice, "You heard about that fight last night? It was after you left. Right out in the street in front of Max's place."

"No," said Shar. "Was it anything to do with us?"

"A nigger had too much to drink was being kicked around. They used their knees on him," Mitchie said.

"Anybody you know?" said Shar.

"No," said Mitchie, "but I—"

"But you for Christ sake had better keep your nose out of it," Shar said, as if reading off something that had no interest for him. "It's got nothing to do with you."

Shar spent his days at the garage or sitting in a bar nearby or driving south along the interstate highway that overlooked the ocean. He showered many times in one day, discovering himself sweat-stained and dirty—there was dirt under his fingernails he could not get out, though he spent half an hour one day digging at it with a toothpick. Night began after supper, and he would spend it in one of the cheap bars that the Cherry River workers frequented instead of the tourists. Sitting at his table, there would be an Italian-looking woman not much younger than Shar, with a big, healthy, smiling face, a large body, a loud, vulgar laugh; it had been the laugh that, for some reason, had attracted Shar to her. He would drive out with her along the highway and listen to her talk—she was full of anecdotes about things that happened to gamblers in the back rooms of the night clubs and children on the merry-go-rounds and Ferris wheels and misguided Negroes and friends of hers, girls, who took up with one man after another; all tales would be followed by her satisfied laughter. In Shar's room she would hold him, strong as a man, she would moan and rub her arms tightly about his body. Shar wanted to put his hand over her mouth. Her big, sweating body dazzled him, her opened red lips, her strength, and her response to him—they left him dazzled but oddly unmoved; he reacted by instinct most of the time. The first time they had met they spent the night together and did not get up until three the next afternoon. Shar had brought a bottle up with him and the woman had been sick off and on, but infatuated with him, and both had staggered downstairs with white, brutal faces, pleased with each other. In Shar's mind, whatever past he had had was obscured by a thick mist.

15

When Max arrived, Shar allowed himself to be persuaded to eat at Max's motel and to spend part of the night there, but he refused to move in. It was a gigantic building, made mostly of tinted glass. People with colorful clothes and straight, white teeth milled about in the doorway and in the lobby; they smiled tentatively at Shar, mistaking him because of his dark, surly look for the gunmen who were rumored to be around. In the lounge of the motel there was a cascade of water bubbling blue and red and green, falling in sparkling crashes onto rocks.

Max was particularly proud of this, which he had insisted upon himself, and he and Shar sat at the bar so they could see it better. "Now, outside the sun would get in your eyes. There would be mosquitoes or ticks or snakes—bears, anything. A herd of cows with horns, maybe, that would be enough for me. But in here—" Max sighed. The lounge was dark and spacious and voices were no more than murmurs in it because of the thick rug and the special ceiling. "In here there is no trouble—it is all under control. This is what civilization brings to us. I could exist nowhere but in civilization."

"You Jesus-well couldn't," Shar agreed.

At their first meeting Shar had cautioned Max about speaking of Karen, so that now, at times, Max had a blank, stopped look and his lips worked enviously; he looked at Shar as if pleading for the opportunity to say what he was thinking, but Shar ignored him. "A son of a bitch for not even asking," Jerry said to Shar's face. Shar, who had been drinking, did not think Jerry worth answering. "No, no," Max had said, upset, "you do not understand. You are sentimental—I am sentimental. Shar is different from us, we can't understand him. He is a brutal child. How I envy that! A brutal, clever child!"

Most of their conversations were about the impending race. Shar's only important rival, Max informed him, was a young Negro who had begun racing just this season. He was twenty-one, a slender, jet-black boy with a reputation for being wise as well as a skillful driver. He called himself Vanilla Jones. Max had pointed him out to Shar one day on the boardwalk: he had been standing in conversation with two white men and a white girl, waving his hands, throwing his head back with laughter. He had sideburns and wore sunglasses of the silver metallic kind that look like mirrors; Shar had despised him at once. "It isn't because he's a nigger," he had said, "but that might have something to do with it." He wondered if perhaps another accident like the one at Synderdale would happen.

"This time you must take care," Max had said seriously. "Not because of the car—what is the car to me? But because of you. Because you cannot be replaced. You must win the race straight."

"Mitch can always put in for me," said Shar, "if you don't like the way I do it."

"My dear God, Shar," sighed Max, "you misunderstand me . . . you weary me—and this weather . . . this weather is so hot. I am thinking of you yourself. I am worried about you."

"Worried about me?"

"Of course I am worried. You know how you are—"

"How am I?"

"You don't look well. You don't eat. How do I know? I watch you eat, I see what you leave. I ask Mitchie what it is you have for breakfast. And too much drinking—you drink too long, too much. You are with bad companions."

Shar laughed aloud, though he did not know why. He did not like Max's observations, which he felt to be true, but he did not know what to do about it. "I'm not taking any shots," he said peevishly. "You should be happy for that."

"I am happy for that," Max said, making a bowing gesture with his big head.

"I haven't had any since April. Since before I went up to that—" He stopped. A memory of that trip came to him at once, a startling picture: he saw his father burned alive, crawling out of bed just as the fire began and shouting curses at Shar, waving his bony fists at him. "At Eastertime. But this was no son that got laid out by his father," he said strangely. He felt feverish. He despised Max for Max's shrewdness, for the man's little piercing eyes, and he despised himself for his own weakness. He thought of asking about Karen but said nothing.

"Now, they tell me you started this out well," Max went on.

203

"They tell me you got up early—went swimming. They tell me you had a good breakfast and spent the day at the garage and the track. They said you looked well, you were—"

"What kind of bastards are they?" said Shar. "Who is this that tells you?"

"The men. The men like you—they worship you," Max said apologetically. "They want you to win the race. They want you to survive."

"But I don't give a good damn about them," Shar said. "I wouldn't care if I had to rip through them to get the car in. Like me? Do they like me? But how could anyone—like me!" Shar shouldered his way along the boardwalk to get a better look at Vanilla Jones. He stood against the railing and lit a cigarette, watching the Negro. But his anger was not directed at the young man, whose behavior was self-conscious and very foolish—he even wore a cotton shirt with leopard spots on it—but against the men who had professed liking for him, against Max, who loved him, and against himself. The purity of hatred appealed to him: how easy to hate a Negro, to spend no time with complexities but to jump right away to the righteous conclusion of hatred! How much that appealed to Shar, who discovered, with some surprise, that he could no longer love and hate immediately and distinctly: his life had become too complicated. He had left behind in the uncertain world of childhood such healthy, clear distinctions—a "brutal, clever child," Max had called him fondly, but that was not true. Shar, standing alone on the boardwalk, felt strangely old —aged—and he could not help but think it fitting that this young Negro would triumph over him, that youth would always triumph over age—and happily, too, and blindly, without even grinning back over his shoulder.

He looked back at Max. The fat, well-dressed man stood in the middle of the walk, peering anxiously at Shar while a stream of people passed before and around him; he looked like a gigantic rock protruding up in the center of a creek. Max had a dough-colored face and thinning hair; he looked awkward even while sitting, or standing still, as if life itself were a struggle for him. Strange man! Shar thought it queer he should have anything to do with such a creature. Separated by the crowd, they were strangers—how did it happen they knew each other? Better for Shar to approach the young Negro and to embrace him, to embrace his youth and vitality, than to return to Max—a bloated, insatiable spectator, a product of a refined civilization. Shar felt for an instant as if he were lost.

That afternoon Marian had another story to tell him. "Now, this girl used to be a friend of mine and I really did like her— I really did. I don't mean anything there. We went to school together and went around together—the same guys. So you can guess how surprised I was to hear about what happened! That was just this morning I heard. The man is down at the police station. Nobody knows about it, and we wouldn't yet, except for Hannie—he lives next door; I ever tell you about him?"

Shar was staring at the window. The shade was drawn and moved idly in the wind. "No," he said.

"Hannie works for the Dew Drop Inn, that big place. It ain't the biggest one any more, with those two new ones built last year, but it's pretty big, and nice inside. He worked in the back room to keep things quiet—you know—and seen some things in his time. He says he saw a man knocked out, beaten over the head with a shoe—they couldn't find anything else and didn't want to use a gun—and some other things too that I oughtn't to be telling about. I used to go around with him. . . . Well, he says this girl was all beat up so there was hardly a face there; one of the cops said that. The guy that was with her got found on the road, trying to flag cars down and none of them would have any of it except a cop car going by, and that was an hour or so afterward—after he woke up, anyhow, and seen what happened. They took his car and drove it in a ditch with water in it a few miles away, 'course he didn't know about that then—the cops found it later on. So they picked the guy up and couldn't make much sense out of him till they went back to see, and found that girl there. That was Veronica. Veronica herself, and her with a husband working down at the boardwalk! He was her second husband—she was married before, about sixteen then, to a kid her own age; but it didn't work out. He worked on a freighter and was gone all the time and finally went in the Navy—so they broke up. He was a good friend of my brother's. We all moved down here together, his family and mine, our fathers decided on it. . . ."

Marian's story was told calmly and with much interest, and she took it so seriously that she did not laugh at all. Shar watched her. At times, as she spoke, he wanted to put his hand over her mouth so there would be nothing to hear—there would be only her smeared face and perspiring, healthy body to see. Shar found himself wondering who the woman was and what he was doing with her, what he could have possibly wanted from her. He began to doubt his own sanity.

"So it was Veronica, all right. The guy told the cops all about it and Hannie heard from one of them—he's in good with them, from where he works. The guy says there were four niggers that did it. He says one of them was just a kid—maybe fourteen. He says the oldest one was maybe thirty, and had a familiar look; he seen him somewhere before, around the boardwalk probably, and thought he could remember him. But hell, no nigger that did that and had any brains would stay around here—he'd be on the first train out, hiding in a boxcar. Hannie told me that. He's sure as hell right, they'll never find them, they can take every nigger in the town and give them pills to make them tell the truth, or whatever they give them, and they won't find the right ones. But Jesus! Veronica herself! She got warned to be careful, but no, not her, one man after another—'course her husband liked to twist her arm around, some judo trick he learned somewhere, and even bragged about it and did it to her with people around—to make her squeal. So he wasn't an angel himself. But Hannie says he broke down when he heard about it and kept wanting to go see her, but they thought he shouldn't. Veronica herself! I can't get over it. It's a hell of a thing!"

"You stink," Shar said suddenly. "Don't you ever wash?"

When Marian turned to gape at him, Shar made himself smile. She hesitated a moment, then slapped his stomach with her hand. "Who the hell are you talking about?" she said. She leaned over him. Shar saw a look of fondness start out from the loose pursing of her mouth, move to her eyes, which were heavy-lidded and smeared with mascara, and to her arms and hands, as she caressed him. She forgot her story—it was to Shar strangely incomplete, since she had not laughed abruptly at the end. "What a bastard you are," she whispered, "you know what that smell is from. What a bastard, a bastard, a bastard. . . ."

She struggled tenderly with him; she took hold of his back with her fingers, knowing enough not to scratch him. She murmured to him hoarsely, and Shar, dizzy with excitement, thought of the first time—it had happened only twice—that he had been able to make Karen feel this way. He had made love to her slowly and patiently and had talked to her, bringing his eyes close to hers, until she had cried out in fear and astonishment, as if she had been betrayed . . . lying in his arms with her face hidden, she had whispered something to him, something about being afraid, and that her body would not stop throbbing, and Shar had thought that he loved her. He loved her! The memory seized and overpowered him and when he lay beside Marian again he was filled with a peculiar tenderness for her, as if she were a victim he had discovered—the faceless woman found in a ditch, attacked by four Negroes and beaten to death!—and one Negro not more than fourteen.

Shar and Marian were sitting at an outside café on the boardwalk when Mitch and a white girl and another man Shar remembered from Synderdale appeared. The three of them looked as if they had been drinking, and it was with a mysterious, awkward leer that the fat young man, holding hands with the girl, approached Shar. "So we meet again! Did you think you had lost me? You and your boss!" the young man cried happily. He had pulled the girl along with him. She protested weakly, touching her curly hair, and arranged a smile for Shar and Marian. "Did you think I would be left behind? Just because he had me fired! Did you think I had no presence of mind, or parents to write home to? They sent me money to keep me for a month! What do you think of that?"

Mitch put his arm around the sweating young man's shoulders and said quickly, pretending to be more drunk than he was, "Ponzi said how he wanted to see you again. He was in the pit for you at Synderdale—you know. Got in some trouble there and Max sent Jerry over to fire him, that was after you left town. He's all right, though. He's all right. He come down here to Cherry River to see you day after tomorrow. Just come down to see the race."

"I come down to see my old friends again," Ponzi said. "This is a friend. Him there, drives the car. What did I tell you, honey? I told you I knew the driver. That's him. He drives. He won the race last week—a man was killed in it. An accident." Here he laughed suddenly. "A goddam sad accident, with the car tilted up on end. He had his head sheared off."

Shar stared at him. He felt no emotion at all, not even disgust. Mitch, looking anxiously at Shar and trying to edge in front of Ponzi, gestured with his hands more than usual and even cracked his knuckles, trying to think of something to say. The girl whose hand Ponzi clutched against his stomach was young, with long, complicated hair tinted a pale red, curled in a loose crown around her head; she kept licking her lips and staring at Shar. Behind them on the boardwalk people passed in bathing suits and playsuits and straw hats, some of them carrying balloons.

"I never met them before," Marian said, leaning forward as if she meant to embrace them. "You just come down here?"

"I just arrived this morning," Ponzi said. His nose was sunburned and had started to peel. He had a frantic, young, earnest look, as if he were having difficulty with the language. "Now what am I stuck with? A goddam chaperon! A chaperon!" And all the time he stared at Marian and back to Shar, as if something mystified him. "A chaperon. . . . They got me to walk around with them and hold her hand so it don't look—it don't look bad. But no mistake about it! It's Mitchie she's got her eye on, not me!" Here the girl giggled and allowed her face to turn red. She and Marian exchanged a look. Ponzi straightened his broad shoulders and sucked in his breath so that his damp shirt suddenly went tight across his chest. "Why the hell she would prefer a dirty nigger to me I don't know. I don't know. Because of Mitchie's new suit? And that hat he's got, a straw hat with a chicken feather in it! He catches all the girls' eyes that way and I got to hold their hands and walk around with them—a hell of a thing. It's embarrassing." Mitch laughed with more enthusiasm than he felt. He had begun to look around at the other tables and at people passing behind him to see if anyone heard Ponzi.

"A girl don't hold it against a man on account of his color," Marian said seriously, "when he looks like him. If he was fat or real black it would be different. But a good-looking man is a good-looking man."

Ponzi roared with delight. "That's right! And I'm the fat one, aren't I? I don't have no straw hat with a chicken feather either. A hell of a poor slob of a bastard I am—got the same stinking clothes I had on at Synderdale, can't get them off, all grease and dirt got so stiff I can't get the pants down. What do you think of that?"

"They're going to hang looser on you before long," Shar said. He looked from Ponzi to Mitch and laughed. Ponzi, who had not heard or had not understood, lunged forward and brought his face close to Shar.

"Where is she?" he said. "What did you do with her? Is her head sheared off too? Where is she?"

Mitch pulled Ponzi back and, grinning tightly at Shar, said, "Ponzi been hitchhiking out in the sun. He been trying to get down here in time for the big race—never ate much, drank his supper instead—you know. He come down specially to watch you win."

"You come with him too, honey?" Marian said to the girl.

The girl brightened. Now, recognized, she cleared her throat and said softly, "No, I live nearby here. On a farm."

"What the hell, ain't I just explained how I'm their chaperon?" Ponzi said. "Are you thick-skulled? What happened to the other one?"

"This Ponzi just had too much to drink," Mitch said. "Maybe I better take him down to the beach—put his head in the water."

"No nigger is going to do that to me," Ponzi said angrily. Then he laughed and turned affectionately to Mitch. "Except Mitchie, who don't count. I explained to him how niggers are —how they come to be all brown, and white folks mostly white. Because the allotment of freckles on them was so numerous at childbirth that the freckles converged and went together and overlapped, sometimes making the area darker—you know—so it turned out all brown; one freckle."

The girl and Marian turned to stare at Mitch, as if seeing him differently. Shar said to Ponzi, "Maybe you better go back home."

"Why should I go back home? Why can't I stay here? Ain't this a free picnic up and down here? Girls in bathing suits—barefoot! And ladies of forty giving me the eye! The very dogs run along the boardwalk shaken with excitement, all a world of legs for them—brown legs, white legs, thin legs, fat legs, bare legs! Why should I go home?"

"You ain't going home till after the race, for sure," Marian said. "That's the big thing."

"How long you known him?" Ponzi said suddenly to Marian, indicating Shar with his chin as if Shar were not listening.

"Why, I knew him all my life," Marian said with a loud laugh, putting her hand on Shar's head. "Aren't you a nosy bastard?"

Everyone except Shar laughed, Ponzi loudly, Mitchie rather nervously. The girls were grateful for the moment.

"I'll tell you what," Marian said, standing, self-conscious of her body—she wore a red dress with heavy white beads—and smiling warmly at Ponzi, "since you ain't seen anything around here I'll show you through. They got a new show down at the other end I ain't seen yet—nor Shar neither—he ain't seen anything himself. The most he does is go down to the beach. Don't you? How come you don't care about the boardwalk?"

"He doesn't like the people there!" Ponzi said accusingly. His words came out so fast he must have been astonished at what they said. "He doesn't like the way they smell, maybe, or look—he likes them off a ways, sitting in a grandstand; he likes to hear them clap. He likes them set up for a target, ready to get spun off the track! But nobody to get too near, and girls to last him one—"

For some reason Shar looked at him in alarm. He felt an odd rush of pity, as he had felt pity for Marian earlier that day. "What did she say to you the other night?" Shar said. He stood and took hold of Ponzi's arm. "I heard her say something. What was it?"

Ponzi drew back. His face became mottled—white and red. His sunburned nose began to glow. Seeing their concern and feeling shame for his own obvious cowardice, he shrugged his shoulders. "A hell of a lot of difference it makes," he said. "This is Cherry River, ain't it? Synderdale is back there—a goddam hick town."

"What did she say?" said Shar.

"What did who say?" said Marian, pulling at Shar's arm.

"Tell him what she said," Mitchie murmured. "He ain't going to hurt you."

"I'm not afraid, for Christ's sake," Ponzi said. His face had begun to relax; the blood returned. "She said—she said—" He made an effort to straighten his shoulders and looked fiercely at them. "She said that I . . . I suffered."

For a moment no one spoke. The redheaded girl stared earnestly at Ponzi, waiting for him to continue. Mitch, who had heard this before—who had heard it many times—sucked at a tooth and stole a look up at Shar. Marian, her red dress tightening around her as she breathed, had a bright, vague, amused smile—she turned to Shar as if he might explain this. Shar, who had been lighting a cigarette, stood without moving and stared at Ponzi's wet face. It was the first time anyone had seen him look honestly puzzled.

Then Shar laughed. Easily, gratefully, the others laughed with him—Ponzi giggled hysterically. He poked his chest with his thumb. "Me! Me!" he said. "How the hell do you like that? I am bedazzled by such illumination! A martyr! I see myself— I see my destiny."

When they stopped laughing Marian said, "So now we'll go through the boardwalk. There's lots of things there. Honey, I didn't get your name— Kathie? Well, Kathie. I'm Marian. Funny I never saw you. Well, even if you seen it before it's all right, ain't it? I mean, I saw it a hundred times—a million times. I never get sick of it. Should we go through?"

"Maybe we ought to go over to the garage," Mitch said to Shar.

"The hell with the garage!" Ponzi said. "You like people, don't you? You like people?"

"I like anything to do with people," Shar said.

Walking in the sunlight, fending his way against the crowd, Shar felt that he had been drinking too much. He felt tired, and not even the effortless vitality of the others—especially Marian—could touch him. About them people pushed in a great sweat of excitement: there were young couples in bathing suits carrying wet, dirt-smeared towels, and groups of boys with hard round bellies wearing swimming trunks, and men in T-shirts and shorts, gaudily dressed, wearing sunglasses, and women of all ages—in sun suits and wearing earrings, in high heels, in low-cut dresses, in overalls. Many carried red balloons.

They stopped at a shooting gallery. Ponzi insisted on paying for everyone. The man inside the booth was fat, dark, Italian, and nodded a surly hello to Marian. Shar said to Mitchie, "Jerry ought to try this." Mitchie, glad to hear anything Shar might say, turned to him with a grin. "A little runt of a bastard," Mitchie said. Marian crowded them and wanted to know who they were talking about, and when they shrugged and looked away she seemed hurt. "You always do that," she said.

Someone shouted to the man in the booth, speaking Italian in a rapid, excited way. "This-here is America, you bastards," Marian said. She had been drinking too much; she stood swaying on the boardwalk and shaking her fists at the men. "They don't talk that here! You greaseballs!"

They got her away with some difficulty. Around on the boardwalk tourists stopped to stare with interest. A woman with blue-dyed hair approached Shar, who looked the most respectable, and said, "Is it trouble? I know a little Italian. Is there some trouble?"

Hot wind blew dust up against their faces. "That across the way is the best place," Marian was saying, pointing out a motel of beige and aqua. She spoke particularly to Ponzi and the girl, whose hand he still held. "That's a new one. There's s'post to be some gangsters own it."

"You're absolutely right," Ponzi said. "I believe you. This place is run by those bastardly gangsters."

"Well, I don't know," Marian said, "I mean, if they're so bad and all. . . . What would this place be without the boardwalk? A crummy hick town. What would it be? I wouldn't be living down here, you wouldn't of come, Shar wouldn't have no race—none of us would of met here! They ain't so bad."

"Max owns half of that place," Mitch could not help saying. Ponzi stared across the busy street as if fascinated. "He told us we could stay there if we wanted—me too. We decided not to, it was too fancy."

"Too fancy for me too," Marian agreed.

They went on. The day was hot and bright and windy. At times Shar could smell the ocean, past the odors of hot dogs and beer and tobacco. They passed taverns with crowded doorways and restaurants blaring with music; someone sang to a

214

guitar, sitting out on the boardwalk with his back against a wall, a young man with pale, curly hair:

"I know I ain't the only one of yours
But I'll be a man just as long as I can,
'Cause that's the way love is."

They bought beer in one of the little taverns, standing noisily at the bar. The bartender put it into paper cups for them and they trooped out. At the doorway they had to wait for a woman with a baby carriage who was coming in—slowly and with dignity. She met all eyes with a fierce, calm stare.

When Shar was outside again, squinting against the dusty wind, he felt enlivened; he felt almost excited. Ahead of him and Marian the other three walked quickly, looking around; Ponzi pointed and exclaimed at things. He had spilled some of his beer onto his shirt but did not seem to notice. They idled at a small shop. "Look here," Ponzi cried with pleasure, turning immediately to Shar. He pointed at some of the souvenirs on the counter. "What would you like but a plastic baby, a black baby like this? Hanging on a gold chain, with some feathers around its bottom! To put keys on." The young girl turned it about in her fingers. "It's a key chain," she said softly.

"All kinds of things here," Ponzi said. There were little felt hats in bright colors, red and blue and yellow, and giant pencils with feathers on them, and spiders with yellow eyes on little springs, and sunglasses with dark green lenses and frames of white plastic with great plume-like red feathers on the sides. There were neckties with naked women painted in coarse detail on them, and a dozen sets of false teeth, bright and pink, waiting to be rattled; there were pennants that said CHERRY RIVER with pictures of the ocean and of Ferris wheels and of auto racing on them; there were beads of gold and

215

silver, and friendship rings, and wigs of all colors, and post cards with cartoons. Ponzi bought one of the little felt hats, a yellow one with a long black feather, put it on his round head, and pulled the rubber strap under his chin. The young girl was given the little black baby, which she seemed to have become attached to.

Passing by an alleyway they were surprised by a gang of small boys who ran out onto the boardwalk waving sticks. The boys wore bathing trunks and had thin, insect-bitten chests. Ponzi made a drunken lunge at one of them, frightening him away, and as the boys ducked past, one of them—a boy with a large black head and a dirty neck—yelled to Marian, "Don't you bring no nigger home! Dirty bastard!"

Marian stood staring after him. Her big broad face showed a look of sorrow for an instant; then she said to Shar, "My kid Harry. Did I tell you about Harry?"

Shar finished the beer and threw away his paper cup. "He's a smart kid, he thinks up all kinds of things," Marian said. She took Shar's arm and pressed against him. He could smell her hot breath against his neck. "His father was a no-good son of a bitch. I mean, I don't want to give you the wrong idea. He was sweet as anything when we met. And took me out and treated me real nice, like they do. I wouldn't of married him if he didn't. I had a lot of them to choose from. I was only seventeen then—a while ago—" She thought of something and giggled suddenly. "I never wanted anybody like my old man, I made sure of that. He paraded around in his underwear and went to the bathroom—you know—right outside, where people could see him, and made noises when we had supper. He was the one got us to come down here, moved us down himself, and then never got used to it. He worked in a steel mill up north and couldn't get settled here—he said he missed where we used to live. A real sty, that was! And he said he missed it!"

Children sat at an outdoor counter, their flushed legs curled around the stools. They watched Shar and the others pass sulkily, sucking on straws. Shar thought it odd that there were no adults with them. Marian went on, pleased with what she felt to be Shar's interest. "You see that kid there? On the motorcycle?" A young man balanced himself on a motorcycle on the street below, talking to a group of teen-agers who hung down from the boardwalk. He had black sideburns and smoked a cigar. "He lives upstairs from us. And a sick bastard he is, too, only you wouldn't know it to look at him. They used to have battles up there you wouldn't believe—chairs throwing around, and things out the window, and things knocked rattling down the stairs. He started fights all the time. Only I heard the other day from a friend of mine—it was Veronica! Yes—Veronica—ain't that a surprise now, and Veronica dead like she is— Well, she told me he had this stomachache all the time and wouldn't do nothing about it, and finally went to a doctor or something—I don't know where—and found out it was real bad; something bad." They had passed the boy and Marian looked around, pursing her lips at him. "A kid like that! A kid his age! And all the while he's got that thing growing down there, down there in his gut! The little bastard!"

They stopped for a while at another tavern, then went down to the beach. Ponzi ran ahead, kicking up sand, waving his arms. He ran all the way down to the water, leaving Marian and the girl helpless with laughter. "He sure is funny, ain't he?" the girl said to Marian. "I don't know when I met anybody so funny before."

Late afternoon on the beach—bodies lay outstretched on

217

blankets, offering themselves to the sun, beneath a din of music and voices. There was an air of merriment that Shar could not ignore. "I wisht I had my bathing suit on," Marian said, gripping his arm. "You never seen me in a bathing suit, did you?"

Someone shouted behind them. A fat man in bathing trunks stood with his legs apart, shouting to someone in the crowded area behind Shar and the woman. His voice was bellowing and seemed to jerk and electrify his body—he shouted with rage in a foreign language. "Those bastards don't know how to speak English," Marian said. "I don't like to hear that, do you?"

"No," said Shar. The yelling in another language did disturb him somewhat.

They waited for Ponzi to return. He was cavorting in the surf, flapping his arms up and down. Though Marian and Kathie and even Mitch had to laugh at him, Shar stared at him with interest and did not smile. Suddenly Ponzi fell, sitting down in the water. He bellowed with surprise.

Shar looked around, shading his eyes. The sun and the constant hot wind, lifting dust up into his face, made him dizzy and uncertain. The heat made him feel excited, as if something were going to happen that he did not yet know about but his body sensed: a violence it craved and strained for. Nearby on a frayed olive-green blanket a woman in a flowered bathing suit sat plumply, rubbing lotion on her pinkened shoulders. She was perhaps thirty—young-looking, made-up, with red lips—and Shar thought about her. He wondered what it would be like to tear at her clothes, to attack her. . . . In the next instant his thoughts puzzled him; he felt nothing for the woman, he did not consider her attractive—not as attractive as Marian. Then he saw at the edge of her blanket two children, boys of six or seven, fighting viciously—sometimes with their fists, sometimes shifting their balances rapidly and somehow expertly, sitting down and slashing out with their feet at each other. They threw fistfuls of sand at each other's faces with terrible hatred. The woman looked around and began shouting at them. Her body was stiff and inert and cords in her neck stood out as she yelled.

Shar said suddenly to Marian: "I wonder if I have any children anywhere."

She thought this was funny and repeated it to Kathie, who pretended to be embarrassed, and to Mitchie—who looked at Shar with alarm. Then Ponzi came back, sputtering and kicking sand over people who glared up at him; he presented himself to Shar and the others as if he had accomplished something. "Sat down in the water," he said. "Got my pants wet. How the hell do I look?" He turned around for them. "I can't get the pants off to change them. I told you how stiff they got with dirt. Filthy, dirty things—I couldn't go home with them on. I had to telephone them at home. How could I go home? What if they looked at my face and saw something there? My mother has heart attacks, minor ones, all the time. She can't go upstairs. She stays downstairs—my father goes upstairs. I think they found me in a woodpile one morning. My father scratches himself—you know—but he's a good man, a goddam good man, and I—" He stared flatly at them. "I love him," he said. He adjusted the yellow felt hat on his head and made the girls giggle.

Shar saw, here and there on the beach, police squatting and looking around. "That's on account of the trouble last night," Marian said. "Those cops there." When the young girl asked what had happened Marian told her, swaying with excitement. Ponzi listened intently; Mitchie cracked his knuckles, glancing around nervously. "But they wouldn't be anywhere around here. Not now. Not after what *they* did," Marian said. She was satisfied by the look of fascination and horror she had evoked

219

in the girl's face. Both looked to Mitchie as if waiting for a confirmation of what Marian had said.

After leaving the beach they stopped at another bar for a while where Ponzi greedily ate a hot dog and the rest had beer. They then went over to the amusement park. They passed a roller rink and a number of squat, dingy hot-dog stands inside tents. There were rides for children—merry-go-rounds, boat rides, something called a caterpillar, a small roller coaster. Children screamed in ecstasy, lifted and hurled through the air. There was a bingo tent at which fat women sat, weary, with flabby arms, listening to the bright announcements of numbers. An array of prizes wrapped in cellophane had lured them in.

The air was filled with the harsh, urgent clash of music and voices and screams and the metallic clash of machinery—it enlivened people, even tired adults, who shared some of their children's excitement, allowing themselves to be pulled along. At a pony ride Shetland ponies trod miserably around a small track, their long, matted hair dirty; they looked down at their hoofs. Shar, dizzy with sunlight, found himself staring at one of the ponies—a skinny white and brown thing with a limp tail. Seeing the animal, Shar felt a wave of strong emotion course through him—but what it was, whether anger or excitement or joy, he could not tell.

Farther down the midway there were shows advertised. Dancing girls from exotic lands: the posters promised women with veils, with fans, with an array of feathers, with long cascading hair. Marian and the girl giggled as they passed. "You don't want to go in here," Marian said, tugging at Shar's arm. Shar ignored her.

They passed a wild man show and live animal shows that were crowded mostly with children; they passed a show of Negro dancers, men and women, who could be heard screaming and cavorting inside the tent. Strips of red, white, and blue crepe paper decorated this tent. "There's the new one. Just got in this week, to be in for the Fourth of July," Marian said, pointing to a tent. It was decorated gaily with many posters, some of them brand new—the freak show. "The freak show!" Ponzi cried. "A goddam good thing to go to! Why didn't I know about this before? I ought to of come here first off."

Advertised on the outside of the tent were mighty midgets, and a half-woman-half-gorilla, and crocodile people, and a vampire-like woman who was seen to be tearing flesh out of a man with her bare teeth. There was a great fat man and a fat woman, with several fat children dressed in baby clothes— blue and pink. There was a fire-eater, dressed conventionally with a Turkish hat and purple trousers, and armless and leg-less people, and people that were eating chickens alive. "I don't know if I much want to go in here," Mitch said as they started up the ramp. The girl pouted and looked significantly at Marian, who forced Mitch into going. "Why, she ain't seen this before," she said confidentially to Mitch. "She ain't been down here since it came."

The show was fairly crowded. At one end a man talked loudly through a megaphone; Shar heard a string of medical terms. The man was holding aloft a jar with something dark in it—embryos, probably. Ponzi and Marian went down to look, the girl followed hesitantly after. "Christ, it smells in here," Mitchie said. He glanced around at the stalls. "This is a hell of a place to go to."

Marian and the others came back, raving about the embryos. "It was Siamese twins, going to be," Marian said. "The man showed how they were joined. You could see the backbone there—it was white. Think if that happened to you!" She laughed and took Shar's arm.

Half the stalls were closed. "Where the hell is the fire-eater?" Ponzi said. "All my life I been wanting to see a fire-eater."

For an audience of small children the midgets went through a dance routine, then a sword-fighting routine. The fat man, who looked as if his gigantic flesh had begun to melt in the heat, sat on a creaking stool and watched them, clapping his hands. If he had a wife or children they were nowhere in sight.

The midgets had coarse, wrinkled faces, and seemed to be winking and leering down at the children and at Kathie. They raised and kicked their legs suggestively, arching their eyebrows. There was one woman with a white, painted face, elaborate eyes, and a frilly pink dress, and three men dressed in bright satin—green, blue, red—with high-buttoned shoes. An odor of stale unwashed flesh hung about them. Ponzi went up as close as he could get, cheering the midgets, stumbling and apologizing profusely to the children he stepped on.

"Aren't they cute?" Marian said. "They're so little. Why are they so little? That one of them—there—looks like an old man, his face is so wrinkled!"

They strolled past. Shar had begun to feel nauseous, but the sensation did not weaken him—it excited him, strangely; he was itching for violence. He gripped Marian's arm. They glanced at each other and a shock of understanding passed through each of them. Ponzi and the others stood gaping at the crocodile people, who were protected from their audience by thick wire. They had rough, greenish skin and odd Oriental eyes, and stared back sorrowfully at the spectators. "Holy Christ," Ponzi cried, "are those things real?" Mitchie dragged him on to the rest of the stalls. There was no vampire woman out just now—she must have been temperamental, for her stall was empty. But there was a creature of gigantic size that looked like an ape but was dressed like a woman and seemed to have, beneath its fur, a woman's face and body. Shar laughed aloud. The creature sat back in a corner, looking out, with its paws folded politely on its lap. "What a lot of crap this is," Mitchie said. "Do they think anybody believes this?"

They had neared the entrance again. The man up on the platform had put aside his embryos now and was announcing something else: a race. He had attracted a large crowd, and Shar and the others could not get very close. The smell of flesh was in the air, and food, and filth. The man shouted sensationally the names of the contestants in the race—"Bo-Bo, Terry, and Little Jo—here they are, just as they were born. They don't want your sympathy, folks, aren't interested in it, they take their fate as it is, they accept their condition. They don't question the ways of our Maker and so why should we? Look at them, folks, and let's have a little hand."

The contestants were without arms or legs, and lay on their sides, professionally, to show their faces. They were to race one another through sawdust to a red, white, and blue decorated finish line. The master of ceremonies was about to shoot his cap-gun pistol when the flare of excitement reached its peak in Shar and he pulled Marian toward the exit. "Let's get the hell out of here," he said.

"But the race! The race!" Marian cried. They struggled at the doorway; the cap gun went off. "Let me watch it, Shar. Shar—"

He waited outside until the race was over, smoking a cigarette. The desire for violence had grown so strong in him that tears of rage and lust had forced their way into his eyes.

When the others came out they looked a little subdued; even Ponzi looked quiet, and his wet lips were moving. But Marian laughed sharply and took hold of Shar's arm. "I knew you'd wait," she said. "I knew it!"

"We're going over to my room," Shar said to Mitch. "You come along."

As the afternoon had waned, the crowd had grown larger. Down on the street two automobiles had crashed, without much fuss, and a ring of spectators stood around. Horns blared. The smell of food was strong now, and the wind, rising at sundown, picked up dust and scraps of paper and flung it against faces. Shar looked at the young girl, Kathie, whom he had hardly noticed until now. She walked beside Ponzi as before and kept glancing back to him—she looked feverish. He saw her pale, smooth throat and the anxious movements of her jaw.

At Shar's room they had an argument with Ponzi. "You can go down by the beach," Mitch said. "Hell. What do you want? We been listening to you all day."

"What are you going to do?" Ponzi demanded. "You filthy bastards! Filthy! Four of you!"

"Get him out of here," said Shar.

"Now, you go on down," Mitch said, standing face to face with Ponzi and tapping his chest. "Why, ain't you said you was chaperoning for us? Ain't you? Now, why you want to go and spoil everything? You go on down now, and leave us be. Shar's been nice to you all day."

"You filthy bastards!" Ponzi cried in dismay.

There was a scuffle inside the room. Marian cried out; the girl answered her. "You go on! You go on! He likes me!" she said.

Ponzi pushed his way in to see Shar on his knees before the girl, moaning and rubbing his face against her loins. His fingers were outstretched on her back, closing into fists in her clothing. "He likes me! He does!" the girl cried, hiccuping in her proud hysteria. "He liked me best all along!"

Shar, his eyes wet, his face distorted, pulled the girl over to his unmade bed. "She was up in that son of a bitchen barn," he said, "but I had to go back after her. She was bleeding—she was ugly, dirt on her face, on her mouth—she was ugly, ugly, but I— I said, 'Am I too big for you? Am I?' and she didn't feel it—she was unconscious— Why didn't I leave her there?" He gave up on his tearing of the girl's clothes and collapsed onto her suddenly, burying his face against her throat. They could hear him sob. "A bitch—a filthy bitch, a whore— If I see her again I'll kill her—"

Mitch was able to get Shar away from the girl, though the girl, confused, wanted to hold Shar in her arms "until he makes sense again." Mitch knelt on the bed with his hands on Shar's back, as if trying to brace Shar's anguish. For a few minutes, sweating profusely, Mitch could not decide what to do. He looked around—Marian stood, crying pitifully, betrayed, back against the wall; Ponzi stood in the doorway with his hat askew and the black feather curled up tight with his astonishment. His face had gone pale except for his nose.

"Max will know what to do with him," Mitch said. Hearing Shar sob brought tears to his own eyes. He turned away and put his arms around Shar's wet, heaving back, as if he wanted to shield Shar from the others.

16

Because of the excitement, Max had his supper late that evening, around eight o'clock. He had been in a conversation with one of his business partners when interrupted by a fierce knocking at his door. He opened it to see, with great surprise, the clownish figure of that man he had had fired several days before—a grotesque young man with filthy clothes and an imbecile stare, who had reminded Max, uncomfortably, of a whimsical projection of himself. Jerry had begged for permission to do something to him, first luring him into the laundry room of the motel, out of the sight and hearing of the guests—but Max had rebuked him angrily. "For you it's a job—for us with responsibility it's a life! A man's life!" His defense of Ponzi irritated him, since it placed him on Ponzi's side and seemed to establish a peculiar relationship between them. "I am growing weary of this life," Max said. "There are few things that delight me. Shar—he is a delight. But what is happening to Shar?"

When they arrived at Shar's room everything was quiet. Inside Shar sat on the edge of the bed, smoking. The room looked as if a ferocious wind had tunneled through it briefly and disappeared. Mitchie came out of the bathroom with a wet towel, which Shar accepted and held against his forehead. "What the hell are you doing here?" said Shar. "Is something wrong?"

Max sat down shakily beside Shar. His heart was pounding, his breathing came with difficulty. He met Shar's cold stare with compassion. The flurry of his thoughts—his fears—was quieted by the admiration he felt for Shar's inhuman control of himself. Max could smell Shar's breath, and he could see the strain in his face. "You will never let me help you," Max said, putting a hand on Shar's arm. It was a curiously kind gesture.

"There's nothing to help," Shar said. He smoked his cigarette. "What the hell do you want, you runty bastard?" he said to Jerry. "Are you going to wave that pistol around here? Afraid to bring her along with you, weren't you? Bastardly little coward! I knew you wouldn't. You can't do everything with a pistol."

Jerry laughed shortly and went out into the hall.

"A man should never make enemies," Max said. "No man is protected from his enemies."

"What the hell do I want protection from?" Shar said. "What can hurt me? What can they do to me that I wouldn't want done? Enemies!" He put the towel to his eyes and sucked a long, shuddering breath. "I don't know what the hell you're worried about. I'll do the race for you. If you don't want me you can put Mitch in. Mitch is good—I'd stake my life on him. He's a good man. But I want to do the race. I can't stand it until the race. This is the worst waiting time I've had—the time won't move, it drags along, it's killing me. I'm itching to get in there."

"That's very good to hear," Max said happily.

"Vanilla Jones," Shar said. He looked at Max. They smiled together. "I'll run it straight this time. No accidents. I'd run it backwards if I could do it today—I've got a hell of a long time yet to wait."

"Tomorrow you can take it easy. Don't go out tomorrow and don't drink. Let me take care of you. You are not imprisoned in a body like mine, you don't feel the weight of your own guts pulling at your heart—you don't understand that I need you. You will take care of yourself?"

Shar stared at him. There was a clumsy silence, as if Shar did not want to answer. "Yes," he said finally.

Max leaned forward in his seriousness. "You will do it for me? You will live it for me? You won't leave me?"

"I won't leave you," Shar said.

Max sighed and got to his feet. He wiped his pale forehead with a handkerchief. "Shar, I know the price you pay for your self-control, I am sensitive of your skill. I am sensitive of your being. I understand you. You can rely on me to understand you." As if he had finished a prepared speech and was pleased with the response it got, his manner changed. He laughed, inviting Mitchie to join in with him. He said confidentially, "And here I was led to believe—I thought— A breakdown of some sort— But you have never broken down before a race,

228

never; sometimes after a hard race, and in the winter— But never before. I have faith in you."

Shar exhaled smoke slowly. He watched Max with a tight, perplexed smile. Except for his eyes, which were discolored by tiny threads of blood, his emotional breakdown of a short time before was adequately disguised and forgotten. "That's surely right," Mitchie said in an agreeable voice.

To show his concern for Shar, Max introduced him to a girl who had Max's approval. She was a tall, slender girl whose age was a mystery—she might have been anything between seventeen and twenty-seven. She had fine, clear, tanned skin, an elaborate, professional-looking beauty with detailed eyes shaded with silver and cheeks touched with pink, more becoming than a contrivance of natural health. The blended pink on her cheeks made her cheekbones prominent and gave her an artificial look that seemed to please her, since she glanced often in the mirror with a satisfied expression. Her hair was silver and glowed with cleanliness; she could not resist touching it occasionally and Shar, entranced by her beauty, wanted to touch it too. It lifted elaborately up away from her face, caught at the back of her head in a full twist that gave her a stately appearance. Walking about the room, she was mechanically self-conscious, a self-consciousness that had long ago lost concern for its object; Shar knew that she behaved like this when she was alone.

"Mr. Golyrod has talked often of you," she said. Golyrod was Max's partner in a number of businesses. "He is very pleased with you—he won quite a lot of money on some race of yours, just last week; I can't remember where. I am very happy to meet you."

She had a high, confident voice. She smiled at Shar. "I am very honored to meet you too and to be told that you are interested in me," she said. She lowered her eyes; the silvery film on her eyelids sparkled. Shar, who was lying with his hands behind his head, watched her with a fascination that had nothing to do with his own feelings. "You are a handsome man," she said. Her tone had no calculation or flattery in it; she spoke very politely. "My acquaintance with Mr. Golyrod and your friend began only a few months ago and so I have never seen you race—though I know people here at Cherry River who did see you last year. They are very interested in you."

"Is there much money put across?"

"A great deal of money," the girl said. She glanced in the mirror and touched her hair. "Mr. Golyrod is very interested in the race. He talks of it constantly."

She wore a summer dress of black cotton that revealed most of her smooth, carefully tanned back, and silver jewelry, and very high heels that seemed to stick slightly in the rug now and then. Shar could smell her perfume. "Of course, I have never been acquainted with an auto racer before," she said. If there was any snobbery here Shar could not detect it. "I have known quite a large number of people in various professions and trades, but I have never known anyone connected with racing. I hope you will excuse my ignorance."

Her facial expression belied her concern: she looked perfectly content, modestly pleased by her own beauty. The light from the partially shaded window behind her caught her silver hair and illuminated it, so that it looked like a halo about her face. "Mr. Golyrod became very interested in a person with ash-colored hair. Do you know what that is? A very light blond, almost with no color at all." She spoke slowly and clearly, gazing at herself in the mirror. "When I appeared to him the next day with this color of hair he forgot about her.

My hair before this was red, but a light red, not dark; a blond-red. I think it was too bright a color for me, because with my face I like to wear full hair, and red would make that too much—a distraction from me. I am very pleased with this."

She turned her gaze from the mirror and looked at Shar. Her eyes were dark brown, black. She waited for Shar to say something and when he did not she was not discomforted, but went on easily as if she were reciting dialogue already prepared: "What do you think of this motel? Do you think it compares with Mr. Golyrod's hotel in Jasper? Of course, this is much newer. We are very pleased with the response from the tourists—they seem to prefer the swimming pool to the ocean; I think they're absolutely right. There are strange things down on the beach, dead fish, little white fish like fingers, and jellyfish too—though I've never seen any. And crabs of all kinds. In the surf little pebbles are picked up and thrown against you, and of course the water can't be regulated, it can be very cold even when the sun is hot. I don't go swimming very much, though I have to sun-bathe for my skin; I prefer to do that. Have you seen their swimming pool? And the courtyard in the back? The pool is shaped like a four-leaf clover and has five sections to it; one of the sections, someone told me, is for the stem—the stem of the clover. The diving board is there. Your friend Max thought of a fountain in the middle, and of course lights are very common, beneath the water and above, for night swimming—it's very beautiful. You haven't seen it at night? This door opens out onto a little balcony and you can see the courtyard from there." She indicated a door with shaded Venetian blinds, but did not offer to open it. "We are very pleased with it. The patio tables are always crowded, even in the morning. My hours are from eleven to one and there are always a great many people there, and many of the same ones. I recognize them from day to day. Of course, the most ingenious idea is

231

the big glass dome so the whole courtyard can be air-conditioned. So far as we know no one else in the motel business has thought of this."

Shar sighed. The girl and her quiet, assured voice seemed to be presenting themselves in a dream. "I may have forgotten, but I don't think I have seen you out there," she said. "I know you have only been in Cherry River for a few days. My hours are from eleven to one, that's not a good time generally, but there is competition here and favoritism, of course, and since I'm new I can't expect to be put on at night; though at night there is more to do for me in town, and I am grateful to have the opportunity to go out. But the lights in the evening are more becoming than during the day—I mean than the sunlight; and so the older girls are probably better suited for that time. It's hard to hide anything from sunlight."

Since she stood in a crisscross of sunlight from the window, she evidently meant Shar to comment on this. Shar, staring at her flawless skin, her perfect lips, felt nothing but a sense of depression. Deep in his mind, in his bowels, the familiar itching for violence began, knotted and secret. He and the girl looked at each other. "Impossible to hide anything from sunlight, any kind of imperfection," she said. "I wear two-piece bathing suits down there and of course the light is very intense and I have trouble with my back sometimes—not right now, but sometimes, a horrible thing—and wear my hair down then, loose on my shoulders; though I can't do it with this color of hair and will have to have it changed back again if that should happen. It's nothing much—little outbreaks, pimples, and I have been told that no one can see them, but still—still— I would not want to cheat Mr. Golyrod."

Shar lit a cigarette. "What do you do down there?" he said.

"We walk by the pool, sometimes lie by the pool, and sit at the tables," the girl said.

232

"I heard that Golyrod was a bastard," said Shar. "And what else do you do for him?"

"I am waiting for you to tell me," she said.

Shar laughed, though he thought nothing was funny. The girl waited without giving the appearance of being patient, without even seeming aware of him, except that her gaze was directed toward him. In an instant—it electrified him—Shar felt that the girl was a parody of Karen, a sinister, bloodless mockery of her beauty. "Is something wrong?" the girl said. Shar shook his head. He smoked nervously, flicking ashes onto the thick white bedspread. "I'm afraid I have heard that some men in your profession are susceptible to narcotics," she said. "I think Mr. Golyrod told me. I hope that has not happened to you and that it has not troubled you in any way."

"A shot a week at the most," said Shar. "Sometimes in the winter. It never bothered me."

"You're very fortunate," she said. Shar thought she was about to continue—her expression darkened—but then she took a slow, careful breath and reassumed her polite half-smile. As if there were an understanding between them now, she came to Shar and sat beside him on the bed. "I am happy it has not troubled you in any way," she said.

At this close range her face was no less perfect: her skin looked poreless, smooth, a fine light gold. Shar could see that her eyes were outlined in black and shadowed with silver that was inclined to look a little greasy; but this took nothing away from her elegance. He understood her meaning and felt oddly shocked at it, puritanically shocked, and resentful. But he was not sure he would be able to make love to her, and he could not entice himself into it. He could not translate her beauty into physical terms or into anything personal—he was not able to feel anything for her. What dull, throbbing unrest he felt was not for her but for someone else.

"Sleep with me," said Shar. "For an hour or two. I want to sleep."

She did not look puzzled. Her smile remained the same. "I understand," she said. She began unbuttoning his shirt; her hands were slender, her nails long, oval, and painted silver. She wore a ring with a jade stone on her right hand. "As I said, you are the first auto racer I've ever met. But I am very pleased to meet you and very honored, and I hope that our acquaintance will last. You are an important man to us."

When they were both undressed they lay in bed with a blanket over them, since the room was chilled by air conditioning. Shar put out his cigarette and turned his head away from the girl. As he fell asleep thoughts of Karen were loosed in his mind. He moaned softly—he could hear himself, as if from a distance—then he could hear only the forced silence of the air conditioner and the girl's soft breathing. A gentle aura of perfume followed him into sleep.

When Shar woke, his head was throbbing. The girl was coming out of the bathroom; she wore a white robe made of many layers of thin material. Her face was not so golden as before— she looked younger—and she walked stealthily, though she saw Shar watching her. Her hair, still drawn up about her head, was loosened and lay on her forehead and neck in tiny damp tendrils. "I'll answer it," she said. She went to the door and opened it slightly. Shar had not heard anyone knock. She talked briefly and closed the door again; she smiled at Shar. "Your friend and Mr. Golyrod would like us to join them downstairs in a while. I said to tell them we would be there. I hope I said the right thing?"

Shar's eyes were sore from the short sleep he had had. He rubbed them viciously. "Sure," he said. Upon waking, he was assaulted by the same uneasiness and dismay that had bothered him before. He felt as if he had slept no more than a few minutes, but in this time had been drained of his energy. His tone did not discomfort the girl, who spoke in a high, polite voice: "I have had the pleasure of meeting your friend Max"—here she hesitated a little, not liking to use the man's first name, though she did not know his last name. "I met him several months ago but since then he has been away. He is a very pleasant man and is very fond of you. He spoke then of someone—one of his employees—and I have forgotten it now; but I suppose he meant you."

"One of his employees!" Shar laughed.

He went into the bathroom and took a shower. The bathroom was a marvel of white and pale, icy green: its cleanliness assaulted the eye. Shar could not see where the lighting came from; it seemed to glow out of the ceiling, hidden behind a metal strip of hard white lace. The cold water cleared his head and for the first time in days he had the sense of peering anxiously but sanely out of a dream—the sense of penetrating through the haze that surrounded him. But the vision lasted only a second and it had no object—he saw nothing. Then the uneasy fog resettled about him.

Shar heard the girl come into the bathroom and open the gigantic medicine cabinet door—it was a mirror that looked about nine feet square. She spoke in an even, interested voice, loud enough for him to hear: "I hope you feel rested. I think I heard from one of your friends that you were tired and anxious for the race; I can understand how that might be. I was in some theatrical productions"—she lingered over the syllables of these words "—in high school and found myself apprehensive about them." The effortless calm of her voice seemed to belie any apprehension, any emotion, she might claim. "I was going to be in a play in college but the role was small—I was only a freshman—and something happened about that; I don't exactly remember. You can use that white towel there if you want to."

She went out. Shar turned off the shower. When he had dried himself—the towel was inches thick, a dazzling, hard white—he looked at the steamy cabinet mirror and saw that the girl had drawn two large exotic eyes on it, complete with thick lashes, so that she could look through them at herself.

When he went out the girl was sitting before the bureau, a polished, pine bureau that had the neat and impersonal look that accompanies an expensive hotel, which she had converted into a dressing table with a profusion of bottles and tubes and boxes. Everything was arranged neatly: there were no startling colors, no grotesque shapes. The girl had let down her hair, which fell below her shoulders, and was brushing it gently. Her nails gleamed silver, the same color as her hair. "I hope you can excuse me," she said, not looking around, "but you understand the difficulty of . . . the difficulty . . . the trouble it is when something remains between people."

Shar did not understand, but said nothing. He looked with dislike on his clothes: they were not clean, they were soiled, he did not want to put them on. The girl brushed her hair as if she were counting the strokes. "I can never be comfortable with an acquaintance when something is unsettled between us," she went on, turning her face to one side so that she could peer critically at her throat. "You are still a stranger to me. You and I have not been close. When I was young I was warned a great deal about taking care with boys, about not being too close to them. I went to a girls' school: the Holy Angels. Before our confirmation my class was instructed about these things—about boys—but it was only lately, I mean only in the last two or three years, that I understood this had anything to do with what I had been doing. I can't remember the first boy I knew that way, but I am sure we came together to get rid of the feeling that we weren't close—the way it is with you and me."

She had finished brushing her hair now and put down the brush. She lifted her hair from her shoulders and began to arrange it, slowly and carefully. Shar saw how lovingly her fingers worked the thick gleaming mass. "I can never be at ease with a man when there is something unsettled between us," she said. "Afterward everything is all right—we can forget each other, or be friends, or continue that way; what relief that is— It was the same when I was young. There are some people who don't feel that way. Did you know that?"

Shar had been staring at her image in the mirror. Something about her depressed him, pricked at the secret dark swelling of his outrage. He felt no danger that she would see him suddenly through the mirror, and take offense at his impertinent concern; he understood that the mirror was opaque for her, that her sight could not go past herself in it. "There are some people who don't want to be close to everyone. They want just the opposite. I can't understand that. I think it would bother me to be that way." She fastened her hair with silver pins. It ballooned up over her head in a swelling gleam, as if her head were distorted at the back; it gave her a brittle, regal appearance. The splendor of her hair obviously pleased her, for she sat attentively at the mirror for a while with her hands in her lap. "Do you agree with me?" she said politely. She did not look around at him.

"Yes," said Shar. "I know what you mean." He said after a moment, "Did you ever see a man without arms or legs?"

The girl did not reply at first. When she did, she said thoughtfully, "I don't think so." Her expression was frank and a little apologetic. She had taken up a white jar with a gold top and was opening it. Shar, half dressed, sat on the edge of the bed and lit a cigarette. The girl went on: "I had a dream once that a great crowd of people came to me, not only men but

237

women too. I was told that it was the whole world, but they looked like Americans only—I mean, no foreign people or Negroes. They were all crying to me and waving their hands and I cried because I couldn't get close to them; I would never know them. Did you ever feel that way?"

"Yes," said Shar.

"Even if you do know them, one by one, you might forget some of them at the end—you couldn't have them all at once. My best friend in high school—I don't know where he is now, he got married and went in with his brother-in-law, a shoe store, I think—made love to me the most that I can remember, I mean any one person, and I remember him the best, though that was a while ago. Then I got pregnant and had a very wonderful baby, but it was thought best for me to give it away and I agreed; though it was a beautiful baby, a girl like myself. I worried at first that I would think about it, since I read in a pamphlet the organization gave me that that sometimes happened, but I didn't worry about it and it was all right. Then I thought I would get married—I was in college then, just a freshman, I was doing well in most of my classes but I didn't like them very much. I mean, I liked the professors," she said, almost quickly, "they were very nice men. They were intelligent. I got married and we went to live where he was in the army and I was there for two or three months. Then I thought I would go somewhere else and we broke up, though he didn't want to and had some trouble with the army—some kind of trouble. I had been living in Jasper about a year when I met Mr. Golyrod through a mutual acquaintance of ours. Do you know Allen Norwood in Jasper? The Norwood Real Estate Agency?"

When Shar said no the girl did not go on, as if she had exhausted her conversation. Shar finished dressing, sucking at his cigarette. The drone of the air conditioner was getting on his nerves. The girl suddenly got up, her white robe billowing around her, and went to a television set in the corner. She turned it on and went back to the dressing table. While the girl finished with her make-up and got dressed they listened to a static-marred program at which neither of them glanced. Shar lay back on the rumpled bed, smoking, while the harsh, urgent voices from the television set mingled together, separated, were joined by music, interrupted by other voices, by bells and chimes, by flurries of static. When the girl was dressed and ready to leave she had apparently forgotten about it, and they left without turning it off.

They walked together down a long, carpeted hall. The girl took Shar's arm and smiled at him. She wore a black cocktail dress that fitted her tightly about the waist and breasts, though not vulgarly, and eased out to a short, full skirt. She wore very high black heels and stockings that were tinted black, and heavy gold jewelry, several bracelets on each arm, and gold earrings that climbed up in an elaborate pattern about her ear, like tiny cobwebs. Her eyelids were tinted gold, her lashes were thick and black; a beauty mark Shar had not noticed, near her eye, was accentuated. Her lips were outlined carefully and sharply and were full, orange-tinted, and set in a companionable smile. Catching sight of the girl and himself in a mirror, Shar was startled to see himself with a stranger—he would have been perplexed to say what he was doing with her.

They had dinner with Max, who was filled with enthusiasm, continually smiling and patting Shar's arm, and with Mr. Golyrod, a small man with gold-framed glasses and a quick, nervous smile, who was evidently pleased with the girl and with Shar, for he turned often to them and nodded. Mr. Golyrod had white hair. Also at the table were Jerry and another man, probably Mr. Golyrod's parallel of Jerry, a fair-skinned young man with sensitive manners and very short pale-red hair. Shar

239

saw that his nails were polished. Perhaps out of consideration for Shar, the talk was about motor racing: about the newest cars, about Max's plans for a new car that winter, about Shar's record, about the young Negro's record, about the attendance at the new stadium, about some newspaper stories—Max turned to Shar and said he would show him the stories later. There was a familiar argument about the relative merits of good motors and good drivers, the conservative arguing for the driver and his experience, the liberal for the quality of the motor, both sides giving in to each other at the end. Shar chewed his food without tasting it. A dull, hateful pounding had begun in his head and he wanted to upset the table, to smash at the faces that surrounded him. Mr. Golyrod was in the middle of a long sentimental speech about the motel and the room they were in —a low-ceilinged, amber-lighted, thick-carpeted lounge in the center of which a gigantic oak tree grew unimpeded up through the glass ceiling—when Shar said suddenly: "If I smash up in the race and get my legs and arms amputated, I can still do racing of another kind."

They looked at him politely. Max laughed a short, wheezing laugh, patting Shar's arm. "He is apprehensive about his work. He shows no nerves—you see?" He took hold of Shar's hand and lifted it into the air and let go of it. "He is perfectly calm—a miracle. A magician, to keep himself so!—when any of us would turn cold with fear. A man is a magician to have such control of his heart."

Mr. Golyrod agreed. He looked at Shar with respect. A slight, paternal man with kindly eyes behind his glasses. He wore a heavy gold ring on one finger, probably connected with a secret fraternal order to which he belonged. Shar could see, as Mr. Golyrod lifted his arms and his cuffs were revealed, that he wore cuff links of small, opaque eyes, mock human eyes,

240

made out of glass. Shar felt the hard knot in his bowels tighten. Max was talking on, something about "magic," about Shar's skill, Max's enthusiasm and pride making him charming—making him seem loving, and refined by his love. Shar got to his feet. "I'm going after some cigarettes," he said.

"Jerry will get them for you," said Max.

"Jerry knows what he can do to himself," said Shar, and walked away.

He went through to the foyer and out to the plate-glass lobby. It was early evening outside: lights were on, playing gaudily on the boardwalk. Shar clenched his fists. He felt tears coming into his eyes. When he went outside he was startled at the difference in temperature. It was still warm outside, and humid; he felt betrayed. Crowds passed idly, looking at the motel. Some people still wore sunglasses. Music from the boardwalk rose giddily into the air and mixed with the hot dusty wind and the smell of food and beer and salt and perspiration. Shar stared into the crowd. A few days before he had thought he had seen Karen in the crowd—a girl with blond hair, walking away from him; but he had had enough sense not to go after her. His insides had burned, watching the girl. Now the crowd passed along, some turning into the motel, moving slowly, easily, sun-tanned, and evidently pleased with themselves. A few children carried red balloons that had been given away that day: they advertised one of the night clubs. An Italian-looking young man, dressed in a white outfit, appeared out of nowhere and began picking up scraps of paper and refuse that had been blown against the front of the motel.

Shar saw her coming as soon as she appeared. His face went hot with blood, his ears pounded. She was half a block away—now hidden by some people, now in sight again—coming right toward him. She looked at the gigantic building as if deliberating about it; then she seemed to decide that she was in the right place. She came up the broad stone steps and was about to go into the lobby when Shar said angrily: "Karen!"

She looked around at him. Her hair was wind-blown and loose, a pale, soft gold. Her eyes took him in and absorbed him, her jaw tightened, her lips parted as if she were going to speak; but she said nothing. They stared at each other. Shar was blinded by a wave of emotion—he could not tell what it was, he did not know if it was anger or lust or joy. He took hold of her arm and pulled her, clattering in her high heels, down to the walk. "I've been waiting for you," he said, "I've been waiting for you, I've been wanting this— I've planned this— I'll show you— I'll finish it for you this time—this is the last time!"

17

As soon as they were inside the front door of the rooming house, Shar could no longer control himself and seized Karen. They struggled together going up the steps, Shar with his arms around her and jerking her from side to side, Karen with her neck arched back, her lips tightly closed. They fell heavily against the railing and Shar heard it splinter. He was shouting at Karen: "Why did you follow me! What do you want!" A door opened at the foot of the steps but no one called after them.

Inside the room, Shar pushed her before him. His jaws had begun to clench convulsively; he could hardly speak. Karen did not back away but faced him quietly, calmly; his bitter rage seemed absorbed and defeated by her, mocked by her. "Do you want me?" Shar said. "Is that why you followed me?" Down on the street a horn began to blare. Shar and Karen stared at each other. Their faces were wet with perspiration: in the dim light Shar could see Karen's eyes freeze in their serenity, as if she felt a terror too deep to acknowledge. "Karen—" Shar said.

"Karen!" she said. "Do you think that's my name? Do you think you know me?"

It was the look with which she said this, Shar remembered later, that pushed him past the brink of sanity. Her child's face seemed to him to mock his anguish, his rage, his pride in himself, his humanity—his soul—and he understood that they were locked together, hopelessly entangled, and lost—and in that instant he acknowledged everything. They would never be free of each other. Never be free! He heard his voice shout this at her as he took hold of her.

When Shar woke it was dark in the room. He got to his feet and stumbled backward against something. There was something on the floor—an overturned chair. Shar went to the wall and snapped on the light. "Karen?" he said. She was lying on the floor near the window and seemed to be looking at him; her eyes were thin blue crescents, almost coyly turned toward him. Shar, rubbing his eyes, squatted beside her. He touched her forehead. Leaning to her, he could see that she was not looking at him. For a while Shar squatted by her, his elbows on his knees. Everything was quiet except for sounds from the boardwalk and the midway, and Shar found the silence restful and strengthening; his body was quieted, it sensed

244

a completeness it had not known before. Shar thought back over his life—the odd moments here and there that had protruded out of the usual passage of time, claiming significance—and could not remember ever having felt like this. It was as if he had finished now with action—his life, never anything more than an accumulation of actions, was now fulfilled. But he could not understand why he felt this way.

Shar caressed her shoulders and arms. Pale flesh—such weak flesh—the hint of white bones beneath it, delicate as ivory. The first time he had seen her, Shar thought, standing stiffly poised out in the road, self-conscious, petulant, spoiled, he had felt something for her, and his peace had been worried by anger. But he thought with surprise that that had not been the first time: he had known her as a child, pale-haired, with fat cheeks and dirty fingers, something to pick up and swing idly through the air. Yet her soul had peered out at him, dimpled, sly, it had calculated the distance between them—it had conquered him. Shar saw himself at sixteen again, with his long bony arms, a nose that was always damp, running out to the road one night with the money his father had hidden under the pump floor boards—laughing at the night air, at the smell of the creek, at the stagnant world he was leaving. He had dreamed of lighting a gigantic torch and turning it upon those people—burning them down, burning all civilization down, all faces, eyes, upraised hands, souls of babies waiting to grow into womanhood and devour him. It was not a life dominated by fathers Shar had fled, but a life of order, of meticulous, heart-straining order!—in imitation of man, Shar's father had arranged a chaos of junk into selections of junk, cardboard in one pile, metal in another, wood in still another— The great torch of Shar's rage would have flared up all careful piles of junk, blended them in a single holocaust of flame. Burn down everything! Fire everything, as the Herzes fired their fields each year, preparing for new growth. Shar had been drunk with the idea of destruction as a child, until the night he ran away; then, leaving that world of a father's insanity and long, bone-freezing winters and mornings in school and a life of prepared poverty, he had gradually lost his rage. He had grown out of it. As an adult he was proud of his self-control: he prided himself on his lack of emotions, his failure to involve himself seriously with anyone, his refusal to accept anything as permanent. Karen had ruined him; she had destroyed his faith in himself. With her descent from the cold world of their childhood had come Shar's old anger, his old desire for destruction—but he had felt, once alone with Karen in this room, that his passion would be ended. The insane fragments of his life would be made whole—cleansed through violence, a communion of pain.

Under his hands Karen began to shiver. Shar went to the bed and straightened the mattress, which had slipped halfway onto the floor. When he came back to her he saw her eyes open; for an instant she seemed to see nothing, though she was looking straight at him; then her eyes narrowed as if in fear. Shar picked her up—she cried out sharply, surprised with pain—and carried her over to the bed. "What's wrong?" he said. He looked at her face: it was white and a little distorted, very subtly distorted. "Are you hurt?" He looked back to where they had been lying with a pang of guilt. He saw blood there—yet it was impossible that it should be blood. He went back and looked; he bent and touched it. Wet. It was blood. "Did I hurt you?" Shar said. He felt angry and betrayed.

Karen lay very carefully on her back. She had begun to claw at the mattress covering. Shar leaned over her. "Where are you bleeding?" he said. He saw a pitiless absorption of pain in her eyes—blank and pitiless as the cold suffering of a statue, a muted ecstasy of pain. In Karen's look there was confusion, shame, fear. As he watched, she began to turn into a child again, features softening with fear, eyes filled with tears—a tear on her cheek, a child's trick! Shar wanted to seize her and shake her violently. There had always been something between them, a secrecy that kept them from each other—when Shar surrendered, Karen would have withdrawn; when Karen surrendered, the nature of her surrender, mindless and even without pain, would have ruined Shar's delight in her. They had moved through their months together in an elaborate dance, always avoiding each other, at the same time luring and entrapping each other, and it was with disgust that Shar realized this mockery of love had not yet come to an end. He had not yet violated Karen's secrecy; she had eluded him. The communion of pain to which he had forced her brutally had given Shar to her but it had not given Karen to Shar.

"Where are you bleeding?" said Shar.

No more than forty minutes later, when Max's doctor came out to where Shar was sitting on the stairs, Shar had figured out the trouble. "A miscarriage," said Max's doctor, whispering; he bent to Shar with his hands clasped together. Shar, smoking, sucked on his stub of a cigarette.

Max's doctor had been enlivened by the occasion. He had been easily available, propped up in bed in the room next to Max's, drinking and apparently staring at the wall. When they came in Shar had noticed his toes twitching inside his brown socks, but nothing else—hardly a change of expression. "Not me this time," Max had said, waving his flabby arms in a parody of despair. "You must come. Shar says—there is some trouble, the girl that I—that Shar— Some complications," Max had said. "Get up, get up! What am I paying you for? What have I bought you for? Will you lie there drinking while someone is dying?"

Max, white-faced, had remained at his motel. He awaited a telephone call that the doctor now went to give him. Shar flicked what was left of his cigarette down the dark stairway. "Son of a bitch," he said. Speaking to Max, the doctor was concerned and urgent, professional, clean—human— Just as Max was refined by his love for Shar, so was the doctor refined by involvement with pain, involvement with suffering. Shar, too, was refined by love and suffering, and he understood now the strange sense of fulfillment he had felt earlier. Fulfilled! He had been betrayed. A warning from Karen would have avoided this, but Karen had not wanted it avoided. She had demanded it; probably it had been her own death she wanted—she would have pulled Shar into death with her. "Do you think you know me?" she had said. What contempt, what scorn for him in that—he had never known her, he would never know her.

"Max wants to talk to you," the doctor said quietly. He stood by the pay telephone, waiting for Shar. When Shar went to take the phone from him, he saw the man's intelligent, nervous sympathy—his dark eyes, his forehead crossed with tiny wrinkles, his sagging flesh. Until now Shar had never really looked at him. "A miscarriage is not dangerous," he said, touching Shar's arm. Shar turned away.

18

The day before the Fourth of July was bright and clear and the influx of visitors to Cherry River was so great that business was predicted to be more successful than anyone had yet imagined. Though most of the crowd would not arrive until the next day, many of the motels and boardinghouses were already filling up—by noon the roominghouses on a side street by the shabby part of the boardwalk were crowded, with carloads of young men and boys and occasionally high school girls and other young women who had two days off from work, and whose gold-tanned faces and pleased eyes showed they were ready to enjoy themselves. There was some trouble early in the afternoon when a group of boys battered down a wall in one of the roominghouses, stomping through to a big, disorderly room that five or six girls were sharing: in the good-natured scuffle, furniture was thrown through windows, smashing the glass and bounding to the sidewalk, someone was trapped up on the roof, and the entire length of the stairway railing was knocked down. Police intervened and established order. Another incident took place on the beach, which was very crowded, involving some six or eight young men vacationing from factory jobs and some Negro beach attendants, but the cause of this scuffle was a mystery. Police, who had been alerted to look for racial trouble, were able to stop the fist fights before they involved too many people.

The more luxurious side of the boardwalk was preparing itself for the national holiday. A team of workers struggled to put up a large crepe-paper flag, accurate down to the last five-pointed star, across the front of the largest hotel. It stretched from one side of the building to the other. Banners were strung across the busy street, flags appeared out of nowhere to decorate plate-glass windows and doors. The front of the gigantic racing stadium was a marvel of crisscrossed red, white, and blue banners that waved gaily in the breeze. On the big marquee before the central entrance a Negro was as far as the last word in INDEPENDENCE DAY RACE.

Shar spent the day in his room with Karen. He had gone over to the track for a while in the morning, but had taken no interest in the car and had stared at people who spoke to him as if he did not understand their language. The mechanics muttered of his breaking down, but only to one another; everyone except Mitch avoided Shar. "Don't you listen to none of that talk they're going to put me in instead of you," Mitch said. "That's crazy talk. I ain't ready for it yet and ain't good enough anyway, not when they got you to do it. You still want to take it around, don't you?" Shar had been staring at the young man's smooth, polite face, but he did not seem to have heard Mitch's question. Mitch took out a folded tissue and wiped his forehead. "I ain't slept the last two nights for thinking of it," he confessed. "It ain't the car that scares me, nor the track, it's something else—I ain't so sure what it is. I got to talking to Vanilla—you know—was down at a nigger tavern last night, and he says he ain't scairt at all; he's all in a sweat to get going. The last man they had at their garage got in a crash-up and lost his nerve—why they let Vanilla drive it, and him that young. 'Course he's been in the pit with them for four-five years. I told him you was the same—I told him you knew the car front-wards and back, better than your own body, and could take it apart and put it together better than the guys that built it. I told him—"

"I'm going back now," Shar said. He touched Mitch on the shoulder and turned away. Mitch, his breath ready for a long, appeasing talk, an effort to draw Shar out of his silence, stared after him. He thought secretly that Shar looked sick or shocked, that something had happened to change him inside; but no one knew about it yet and had better not know. The difference between the Shar who had driven so skillfully a few days before in the qualifying heat and the Shar who now walked away, unaware of eyes following him, was so great that Mitch did not like to think about it. "Love always gets a man into trouble sooner or later," one of the mechanics told him.

Shar sat in an old straight-backed chair by the open window, smoking as if in a trance; Karen lay in bed with a blanket over her, though the air was warm. The doctor had given her something to make her sleep and she had been sleeping for some time. One arm lay outside the cover; loose about her wrist was Shar's wristwatch. She had awakened and in a petulant delirium had demanded something of Shar's to hold so that she could sleep, and they had given her the watch, though the crystal was already cracked and the doctor was afraid she might hurt herself with it. Sometimes Karen murmured, "God, my God," or "Shar—," but she did not seem to be in pain.

While Shar sat by the window and watched her, Karen was having a dream. She was running through grass, up the slope before her home to join her father; his face when he embraced her was always rough, sometimes his arms hurt her. She was going to cry to him that it was done, everything was finished, clean, she had come home, but when he gripped her she shrank suddenly in size and the air turned hot and humid, and she was running in the air and waving her short arms and only after a minute was she given, still running in terror, to her father. She was seized by him—how young he was!—and she realized then that someone else had held her, had lifted her through the air—Shar—it must have been Shar—and she turned at once to see him, to see Shar as a child again. But when she turned, the dream ended; she saw nothing. She grated her teeth in anger and dismay. "Shar!" she whispered.

She woke. She saw him sitting a few feet away. They looked at each other. Shar took his cigarette from his mouth; his face was clean, clear in the vivid sunlight, his dark, secretive eyes were clear, turned directly upon her.

He did not say anything for a while. They could hear the roaring of motors from the stadium and the clamor of sounds from the boardwalk. Finally Shar cleared his throat and said: "If you want a baby you can have a baby. We'll have one."

He looked at Karen, but she did not reply. They fell into silence again. Shar lit another cigarette and turned to stare out the window into the street.

Some time later, when the doctor knocked and entered the room, they still had not spoken. Karen fingered the crack on the watch face, and Shar sat and smoked. The room was flooded with sunlight. The doctor's face was freshly shaven; he looked younger than Karen had supposed him. He smelled of soap. Shar only looked around when the doctor was closing the door behind him.

He got up and stretched his legs. A lean, hard-looking man: if Karen had seen him in a crowd her instinct would have protected her against him, turned her eyes safely away. "A hell of a world," Shar said suddenly and self-consciously, "but at least it's my own fault." He laughed and looked at Karen, who stared at him without expression. His smile turned sour, his eyes showed knowledge of betrayal. He went back to the corner and sat heavily in his chair.

They did not speak again for hours. Karen slept a little, but her sleep was transparent; in the corner of her mind Shar kept his forlorn vigil. He got up and went out once, and Karen heard voices in the hall. He talked there with someone for a while, then he came back, and footsteps—it sounded as if there were two people—sounded on the stairway. He went to the window and leaned out, sniffing at the wind. Karen saw how his fine black hair was touched and burned by sunlight.

When the doctor brought food for Karen to eat she withdrew into herself and did not answer. The man's face bobbed before her, he spoke earnestly, he touched her limp arm. Karen shrank away. When she opened her eyes he had left. Shar wandered around the room, still smoking, eating a candy bar. The wrapper was a waxy blue and curled back over his fist.

Karen watched him secretly through her lashes. She saw

253

him with wonder. Her heart went out to him, she felt shame for her emotion. I can't help it if I have fallen in love, she thought defensively. But the warm dark wall of sleep protected her from Shar's eyes, and he could not know what she felt. The afternoon sun shrank away from them; shadows touched the wall. Karen saw at the top of the old-fashioned window behind Shar a row of flowerlike designs, delicate and crystalline, tinted pink. There were thin petals, lined with veins, and tiny stems and leaves. In the waning light they were rigid, cold, as though frozen in astonishment, in regret, at never having lived.

She woke when the door opened and someone came into the room. One of the men was Shar, she thought, and the other —maybe—Max; but she did not look up. She feigned sleep. After a few minutes of whispering, the other man went away and Shar remained, looking down at her. Karen heard the stairs sag and creak and supposed that it had been Max. It was dark now, and the only light came from the window: the sky was a vivid, glaring blue. Shar walked restlessly around the room for a while, then he went to sit again in the chair. Karen could hear him breathe. He looked toward her. "Are you awake?" he said.

When she did not answer, he settled back again and lit another cigarette. He tossed the match out the window. "I want to marry you," he said. His voice was cold and angry. "I don't want you to go back there. You're not going back there. You're staying with me."

He did not move for a while. Karen must have slept again, for when she woke—her body was throbbing with pain now—Shar had come to the bed and was kicking off his shoes. He lay down beside her, his arms behind his head, his legs crossed. "It's all right," Shar said. "Go back to sleep."

When she woke again, it was close to sunrise. The window was glaring with a cold, restrained light; the tiny flowers etched in the glass bordering the top were frigid. Against the white sky their pinkness seemed touched by blood.

Beside her, Shar slept with his head turned toward her, his mouth open. He had not shaven for some time and his face looked rough. He was still dressed and had taken off only his shoes—he had on white, soiled socks. His toes twitched now and then as he slept. Near his left eye was a small white scar she had noticed many times before. "A stone one of your goddam brothers threw," Shar had said, touching the mark and rubbing it. His forehead was touched by faint lines. His nose was straight and slender. His eyes, beneath the thin lids, seemed trembling, blinking. Once he moaned softly and seemed about to wake, but did not. His long fingers moved hesitantly against nothing.

When he did wake, hours later, he got up and went into the bathroom. Karen heard the shower. He came out and squatted to take something out of his suitcase, which was set on the floor. Straightening, he got dressed. The room was still cold from the night before; Karen, watching Shar, began to shiver. He turned as if she had called him. "Are you awake already?" he said. "How do you feel?" He did not seem to expect any answer. His fingers slowed and fumbled with the buttons of his shirt.

While the doctor was with Karen for an hour or so that morning, Shar went out. He and the doctor did not speak, nor did he speak to Karen. Karen drank something the doctor gave her and accepted some pills. "I don't have any pain," she said. "It's all over." "It's all over, yes," said the doctor, smiling.

Karen could hear traffic outside. Horns sounded from a distance, and there were voices, music, firecrackers. The boardinghouse must have been emptied and rented by Max, because there were no sounds in it anywhere. When Shar came back, he found Karen sitting up in bed against the pillows Max's doctor had arranged for her. "How do you feel?" Shar said. Karen nodded slightly. "He wanted to send a girl over here to stay with you while the race was on, but I told him no. I said you'd be all right. The house is taken care of and he's got a guy downstairs watching it— You'll be all right. Or would you rather have someone to stay with you?"

"No," said Karen.

He was encouraged by her answer. He sat on the bed beside her. "It was a hell of a long day," he said. He touched her shoulder but seemed to forget what he was going to say. She saw a patient, waiting perplexity in his expression. Pretending to yawn, he stretched his arms, made his arms go hard with muscle, and said suddenly: "After the race we'll pull out of here. You'll be all right if we drive slow. I'll take care of you. Then when you get strong we can—we can—"

Karen's silence slowed his words. She saw his mind racing behind his eyes, racing to rearrange itself, to understand what was happening to him. "I want you with me," Shar said. He fumbled for a cigarette and matches. "I don't want you to go back. You aren't going to go back?"

He lit his cigarette and shook out the match. Karen saw that his face was clean, savagely pale about his nose, and that he had nicked himself shaving by his ear. Tiny ridges of blood had hardened there. "You aren't going to go back," he said. "What do you want me to do?"

Karen stared up at the frozen etchings above the window. Behind them the sky glared, vivid with heat, but they were poised in the same brittle tense designs: staring at them Karen felt her heart begin to pound, slowly and gravely and yet with a pleasant nervous anticipation, as if her entire life had led her irreparably to this moment.

"What do you want me to do?" Shar said.

With the knowledge of his love, she faced him as if in that

256

instant she had somehow forgotten about him—Shar with his suspicious narrowing eyes, the tiny lines on his forehead that would soon turn to creases if he lived to be as old as her father. He had been a stranger and now he was familiar to her; she could not have said precisely when this had happened. The finicking nervous strength suggested in his fingers had been transmitted to her. She felt, gazing at him with the mild unhurried look of the possessor, that her tingling fingers would have been capable of touching him, fumbling against his chest, reaching inside his chest to stroke his sweating, pumping heart. Yet she wanted at the same time to embrace him, simply and utterly, as she had imagined she would someday. . . . But she said in the calm, ordinary voice she had despised so in her sister, "You make me sick."

Shar's eyes narrowed. Perhaps he did not believe what he had heard. He exhaled smoke and cleared his throat; for an instant he looked very young. Karen saw his boy's face in that moment —a face within this face, something summoned up out of her own shadowy childhood to appeal to her. Shar's gaze dropped. "Then what do you want me to do?" he said. For a minute at least he seemed not to know. His mind must have flinched before the idea—his lips curled up suddenly in a grimace, showing his teeth, as they had from time to time when the knife he carried inside him lurched against his delicate organs. Then he relaxed. His shoulders slumped. That was the look, Karen thought suddenly, that he hid against the side of her head, the exhausted, betrayed look he had always kept from her. He was old and yet he was a face from her childhood—strange, fragile man, who had disguised for so long his secret wound! She leaned forward, as if to penetrate his flesh, to see the stubborn hard skull beneath it. But if he dies, she thought, then I will die too. If he dies, everyone will die. No one will survive. As if prodded by her thoughts, embarrassed by them, Shar began to speak. His words seemed to come from nowhere. He might have felt the necessity of violating their silence without knowing how to do it. "Well," he said, "I've done a lot of driving. I've been at it a long time." He turned away and picked tobacco off his tongue. "I've been a lot of places. . . . There were other ones I wanted to see, but I've seen most of them. I measure out how old I am on the beginning of each year," he said with the slow, modest air of one admitting a secret, "since he never told me when my birthday was. Each January there's one more. And here I am, almost thirty-one, a half year from thirty-one, and I always said I would never live to be thirty, even; I would never want to. And I knew I would never live to be thirty-one."

After he had left the room and was on the stairs, Karen put her hands to her burning face. She heard his footsteps. Without him there to keep her still she felt suddenly wild, lost, terrified —she did not know what she would do. She started to get out of bed, then stopped. "Shar," she said. Was it possible that he would really leave her here, sick as she was, so far from home? She wanted him back, she did not care what he had done— She struggled out of bed, swaying, and went to the door. He was at the bottom of the stairs. She opened the door, her blood pounding so furiously that she could not see, and listened to his footsteps as if fascinated by them. Her vision cleared. She was staring across the corridor at something—it drew her gaze to it like a magnet. A fat cockroach crawling precariously up the wall, its delicate little legs visible at even that distance. Karen's lips parted as if in awe. Her mind was emptied, her thoughts were sucked out from her. She did nothing. She did not call after Shar, nor did she look down the stairway after him. After a moment she realized that she was listening to nothing, that he had left.

19

Before the race, Shar chewed on a stale, melting candy bar. He stood dressed in his fireproof clothing, feeling himself beginning to sweat with an odd, satisfied pleasure. Men ran around him. He watched the stadium: a beautiful curved structure that looked big enough to hold a small city, filled with heads and hands and flashes of bright clothing. Firecrackers were being set off and the start of the race had been set back a few minutes until the offenders had been found or intimidated by the presence of police to put away what firecrackers they had left. ". . . A matter of gravest urgency," the voice over the loud-speaker declared with righteous passion, ". . . human lives many be endangered by the setting off of firecrackers during the race. You can see why we must insist. . . ."

"A man would have to be damn stupid to mistake a fire-cracker for one of his tires," Shar said to someone.

The minutes before the race passed as if in a dream. But Shar saw everything clearly. He liked the look of the day—it was clear and a little windy and, though no rain had fallen for some time, sprinkling trucks had dampened the track to perfection; the track looked good. Fine, hard, black dirt. The infield here was a bright, vivid green; it looked as if it were carefully tended. Shar liked the look of green against the dark brown of the track and the white retaining walls. Everything was clear, everything defined itself with precision. The stadium, nearly filled, bobbed dizzily with humanity, yet this too defined itself clearly. Shar felt none of his usual bitter antagonism for the crowd, but felt instead a peculiar tenderness toward them. From time to time he had toyed with the idea that the spectators did not really come to see drivers be killed, as most people thought, nor did they come—as Max told him—because they wanted to share in the skill and triumph of such speed and such courage. Shar thought that perhaps they came to share the speed, the danger, and the occasional deaths —with exultation, maybe, but with something more than that —and to force themselves into the men who represented them down on the track: they thirsted for death, they were fascinated by it, and envious of it; they gave up their identities to risk violence, but were always cheated because the violence, when it came, could not touch them. Races left some people pale and hysterical. They had surrendered to the insane danger, they had entrusted themselves to one of the drivers—but nothing had happened. If the driver lived they were cheated, and if he died they were cheated. It was a mock communion and Shar understood that only the driver could get any satisfaction out of it—and he was a driver, he would be experiencing it again today, he would urge himself to the traction limit and speed poised on the invisible point at which control turned into chaos —beautiful feeling! The anticipation of the race turned his mouth dry, tripped his heart. He finished the candy bar and threw away the wrapper.

The head mechanic came to instruct him. Shar was putting on his helmet. Wearing the helmet, looking out through the green plastic, he had always seen that the eyes of others were different toward him, as if he were not a part of their humanity. He had made himself different from them. And with the helmet on, the smells of the garage—oil, rubber, dust—would be intensified; he could enjoy them. A slow, hot wind: good. Rubber burning somewhere: good. The sound of engines, shuffling crowds, screams, applause, screeching of tires, angry shouts—all these were good; Shar remembered them with sudden urgency. He went to Mitchie and embraced him. "Wish me luck," Shar said, to the astonishment of everyone around him. Mitchie stared with a vague blinking smile. Shar wondered at their surprise; hadn't he ever done this before? He tried to remember himself, but could think of nothing. Had he wasted his life? All life before he had fallen in love was empty, a mockery, a half-world; he could not really remember it as his own. It was love that endeared the crowd to him, that endeared the men to him—men at whom he had hardly glanced for months. He gripped Mitchie's arm; he thought suddenly that he liked Mitchie, that he had never got to know him. "Good luck, good luck," Mitchie gulped. "But you ain't the one to need luck. You never was—was you, Shar?"

"No," said Shar. "I make my own luck."

At the car Shar felt the urgency, the familiar excitement,

overtake him. His heart pounded joyously. "A damn good car," he murmured. He ran his hands along its side with obvious pleasure. Yet in spite of the clarity of everything, in spite of the familiarity with which all things presented themselves to him—this race was, after all, no different than any other—Shar felt that he saw the day through a dream, slightly distorting it, withdrawing it from his touch. At the limit of his speed, when he understood that to urge the car farther would mean destruction, Shar had never been able to penetrate through the fine invisible barrier that separated him from other people, from the world, from reality. He had never understood it to be impossible until today. But now, adjusting himself in the car, adjusting his mind mechanically to what awaited him, Shar knew that nothing could help him. He would never penetrate through that film—he would never escape himself. On the other side of his limit there was nothing except violence, mutilation, death; but there was no communion. It was no different from his passion for Karen, which was always blocked, confused, by the girl's soul. At the very height of love, when Shar reached the limit of his body's control, there had been no communion—they were two people. Sleeping, they were remote from each other, wandering in separate dreams. Only today, for a minute, had Shar looked into her mind—had they understood each other. He felt that his life had been a preparation for this instant, his education in the narrow part of the world he knew no more than a preparation for this instant; and there was nothing possible beyond it.

There were nine other cars on the track. Shar knew most of the other drivers; there were two new ones, Vanilla Jones and another man, a white man, whose driving he did not know. Rumors had circulated, as usual, about better engines, secret improvements, but Shar knew that the betting was on him, and he accepted this knowledge with gratitude. Shar had been placed at the head of the cars, at the inside, because of his time in the qualifying heat, and he felt a certain pleasure in the position; he was happy to see a driver he knew, in a green car, beside him, and, on the man's right, the Negro Jones, who looked tense and frightened. Shar saw that he was chewing something, probably gum, and showed his big white teeth in flashes. Shar gripped the wheel and shuddered as the enormity of the situation struck him: a beautiful day, a goddam beautiful day! Above the glinting stadium the blue sky was flecked with clouds, hardening with clouds; it had been hardening like that for thirty years. What was there beneath it that had charmed him? Long roads, new towns, glimpses of the sea—new tracks, new people, anonymity! In such a vast world a man could never be himself for long, for a simple journey through time dissociated one identity from the other: not even the expensive new highways he traveled could link the two times, like towns on a map, together. Shar's heart pounded with the excitement that he had finally transcended the fragments of his anonymity. He wanted to get out and run back to Mitchie, or to Max, and explain to him: he knew who he was, he knew exactly what he was doing, and why; he was guilty—completely guilty—and his guilt, like his love, had pulled him together. The limit! Shar grated his teeth in impatience. He hated the gloves that kept him from the wheel, he hated the helmet and the goggles that disguised him, denied him humanity; he hated the shock absorbers, the fireproof clothing, the devices invented for safety's sake—as if there were any protection possible against mortality.

The race began. Shar's car shot forward. He grinned at the release of power, and the roar of the motor ripped through him. He could feel the other cars behind him as if he were watching the track from a distance, and he looked over to see the drivers beside him—clenched and sweating with the exertions of their magnificent automobiles. Sunlight glared off the hood of the car, mixed with dust and the fleeting white wall and a smell of oil—Shar gripped the wheel, leaning forward in the seat, as if the straining of the wheels at his back worried him. As he covered the stretch and prepared himself mechanically for the turn, he remembered visions he had had at the starts of other races—visions of brake failure, of a tire giving out, the steering column breaking, a sudden spinning, shuddering, a somersault off the track and against the wall: one, two, three seconds, and the crowd would jump roaring to its feet. But this time he felt nothing.

Shar urged the car faster. Speeding into the turn with the other cars whipping along with him, Shar felt the wheels slide a little—he had boasted once he could calculate the number of inches the wheels on any car he knew would slide. The cars seemed grouped together around the turn, roaring and screeching faintly as if in terror at the precision that separated them from death, but once out of the turn, Shar pulled away again and the green car behind him followed.

The wind was no longer warm but a little chilly. Shar squinted past the glaring hood. He sat low in this car—the center of gravity in this model was lower than in any he had driven before—and the sensation of skimming just above the ground was fascinating. The dirt track with its terrific clarity roared beneath him; Shar wanted to reach out and touch the ground. He took off one of his gloves and dropped it beside him. The wheel felt good to his grip, a little hot from resting in the sunlight. To Shar's right the driver in the green car, sucking his lower lip, began to fall back. Shar watched out of the corner of his eye as the front wheels disappeared. He felt disappointed. In the stretch before the grandstand he took time to look around—as if in search for faces he knew. A mob of faces jarred his vision: men, women, children, men with hats, men without hats, bald men, fat men, women with fancy hair, women staring at him, children waving flags. All leaped to his eye and were drawn away.

He passed his men. They stood waving locked hands, their teeth grinning at him as he passed. When he came out of the next turn, his nose clogged with dust and his lips grimacing against the wind, he saw that the young Negro was moving up on him. For an instant Shar's heart expanded with rage. "Bastard!" he shouted across. The Negro, white-helmeted, crouched forward in his car and did not look at Shar.

They stayed together for a while, Shar ahead, the Negro a little behind. Again the turn, the stadium, racing through a tunnel lined with officials and ambulances and platforms with loud-speaker mechanisms attached to them. The crowd screamed, furious at the Negro for inching ahead, impatient with Shar: a vast, drumlike roar. Shar took off his other glove and threw it toward the infield. He could imagine the gaping, fishlike looks on his mechanics' faces. Shar! Shar! Max would begin to murmur. What are you doing?

Shar urged the car up. He felt the wheels hold in the dirt, hang on as if they were trying to help him. At the turn he did not decrease his speed enough and the back wheels spun out, though not very far, and as if he had been touched, the Negro moved away with discreet skill. Shar squinted over at him: they looked at each other, Shar's face distorted into a grin, the Negro's face set rigid in a mask of wrinkles and lines, like that of an old man. In the straightway they raced almost side by side, glancing across at each other. The Negro cupped his hand to his mouth and shouted something; Shar could not hear. His heart had begun to pound so tightly that it hurt him and interfered with his breathing. He breathed through his mouth, sucking in dirt and dust; he spat toward the side of the car, coughing. The sunlight and wind pounded on the front of the car, thumped inside him, jerked the steering wheel and shot with fresh, energetic pain through Shar's head. He urged the car ahead. He felt it respond to him at once, inching faster, faster than he had ever taken it around a turn—but at the last moment his foot relented, slowed it a little—then he prodded it up again, reeling out of the turn. He looked across to see if the Negro had followed him; he had not; he was a few feet behind. The pounding of Shar's heart mixed with the pounding roar of the car, both being pushed toward their limits, strained mercilessly, unable to understand what was being done to them. The car protested, beginning to shake. It seemed weightless, as if a sudden wind could send it flying off the track. When Shar looked around again he saw the Negro inching up on him and he thought, while fumbling with the buckle on his helmet, of taking Vanilla Jones with him.

The retaining wall ahead had been whitewashed and glared in the sunlight. Smooth long wall, protecting spectators from sudden death. Shar's head pounded, filled with sunlight and pain, and he waited for the instant when the onrushing air would be so powerful as to suck his breath away from him, stun him, empty his mind so that he was no more than an animal, a mechanism—but this did not happen. The car went faster, faster, Shar pushed it toward the limit, again he thought of taking Vanilla with him—and, indeed, the Negro seemed to have this in mind, for he would not let Shar go—and he felt with triumph the skill and strength of his body, he remembered the look of his face, his eyes—how proud he had been of himself! How proud of his manhood! How proud of being loved! He could not get the helmet off and so, sheering past the Negro and heading out, off the track, Shar enjoyed one or two more heartbeats before the car smashed headlong into the retaining wall.

266

20

When Jerry ran up the stairs and into the room Karen was staying in, he saw the bed empty, with sheets and blankets twisted together as if someone in a desperate rage had attacked them. The bed was stained with blood, most of it hardened and dark. "Karen!" Jerry said. He heard a noise in the bathroom and went around the bed. Behind him, toiling up the stairs, Max hung onto the doctor's arm and was saying something to Jerry in a thick, whining voice.

Jerry opened the door and for some reason kicked it in. The room was filled with steam. "What the hell are you doing?" Jerry said. "Are you in there?"

Max struggled, panting, into the room. "My God, my God," he murmured, clutching the doctor's arm. His eyes, stung with sweat, bulged out at the rumpled bed with its bloodstains. "She is dead too. The girl is dead. They are both dead." Panting, he approached the bathroom door, where Jerry was craning his neck and sucking at one of his teeth. "Is she in there? Karen? What are you doing, Karen?"

Max pushed Jerry aside and let go of his doctor. He went into the steamy room where Karen stood under the shower. "What are you doing? What is this? My God, Karen, do you know what has happened? Do you know where we have been all this time? What I have been seeing? Do you know what has happened?"

Karen stood naked beneath the hot, furious shower. Her hair lay wild against her head and body. "Get out of here!" she screamed.

"What are you doing? Why are you out of bed?" Max cried. "Do you want to bleed to death?" And he clutched at his heart. His face was getting wet, splattered from the shower. He waved at the steam as if he were trying to get rid of it. "Do you know what has happened? Shar is dead—Shar is dead! Shar was killed today on the track! Can you understand me?"

"Get out of here," Karen screamed. Her voice lifted higher and higher until she could no longer bear it, and she began to sob insanely. "Get out of here! Leave me alone!"

Max backed up suddenly. He took hold of the door and leaned, gasping, against it. He stared at Karen. Behind him the other men, without glancing at each other, began to back up too. "Come out of there," Max said. "Come out here. We'll talk to you out here."

He closed the door. His heavy face was labored, pale, and stricken; when excited, he breathed through his mouth in fast, choking gasps, as if he were a great fish suddenly dragged up out of the sea. He turned to Jerry and his doctor. "What is happening?" he said. "They are rioting out there. What is that noise? What is happening? My God, I am weary of this life—I am sick to death of this life!"

Jerry was leaning out the window. "A bunch of kids, looks like," he said. "White guys. One of them has a fishing spear—or something."

"Madness! Everything is madness!" Max murmured. "Where are they going?"

"There's some men in front of a bar down by the corner, I think they're going to them. A big mob. Bastards," said Jerry.

"I have come to Cherry River every year of my life," Max said angrily. "What is happening this year? What is this? The world is insane! Shar's death—that Negro finishing— They have a right to be angry over it, a man like Shar! I would be angry over it myself! But it is madness to do what they are doing!"

"We better get the hell out of here," Jerry said.

The bathroom door opened. Karen stood in the doorway with a soiled white robe wrapped around her. She was still wet—her face streamed with water and her hair lay against her in savage, dripping clots. "Karen," said Max, putting out his arms to her, "I have something to tell you. You must prepare yourself. I have some bad news for you—like the last time, though you disobeyed my instructions—some bad news. I—"

"I know Shar's dead," Karen said angrily.

Max blinked. "Yes—yes—" he murmured, with his arms still outheld, wavering, "but you—you are not well— So much has happened— Do you understand what has happened?" He had gained control of himself and stood with his big legs outspread, balancing himself; behind him Jerry turned from the window to stare narrowly at Karen, and the doctor, haggard and shaken, with pinched, bloodshot eyes, looked at her as if he could not remember her. "I can hardly understand it myself. There was trouble somehow—on the straightway, not a turn, and he lost control of the car and smashed it into a wall —dead at once, immediately—" He stopped, panting. Again his hand crept to his chest, grasped tightly at the soiled shirt. "They think the Negro driver did it but it didn't look that way —I'm sure he didn't do it, didn't prod Shar or sideswipe him— no—there was an announcement, but— The people blame the Negro and his men. There were some fights in the grandstand, whites and Negroes. Just beer bottles, but— But Shar dead like that! I can't make myself understand it. . . . But I knew that when it came for him it would be like that; it would be an ac- cident, a child's death, something done to him suddenly—a broken steering column, brakes locked, whatever it was—they don't know yet— But so soon, so young a man—"

"That isn't true," Karen said.

"My dear Karen," Max said, "I'm sorry to tell you, I can hardly make myself tell you, but it is true—it is true."

"No," said Karen. She shook her wet, heavy hair. "It wasn't an accident."

They looked at her. She stood swaying in the doorway, the bathroom behind her choked with steam. Her face was wet and distorted, as if she were tightening a muscle somewhere in- side her cheek. "And he wasn't a child! A child!" she cried. "He was a man!"

"Yes, he was a man," Max said, nodding anxiously. "Of

course he was a man. —But we must get out of here, we have to leave. This town is headed for trouble. Karen? Why do you look at me like that? Are you in pain?"

"He was a man!" Karen cried senselessly.

"Yes, yes," said Max. Then he said oddly, "What do you mean by that?"

"I mean, you have misjudged him," she said. "You never knew him. You never knew him."

"What do you mean?"

"You never knew him!" She pushed past Max and went to the bureau. She left damp footprints on the floor. "You can't even understand what he did! His life was an accident, without plan—I know that, I am part of it—I know it—look at that, there," she said in a shrill, angry voice, pointing accusingly at herself in the mirror, "an accident! My face is an accident! Shar was trapped by it, by an accident—his life was an accident but his death wasn't—he made his death for himself! He was a man!"

Max stared at her. He saw that she wore a man's wristwatch. His expression remained rigid as his mind raced. "Karen—" he said.

"I mean it, yes, yes, I mean it," she cried.

"We better get out of here," Jerry said. "We better—"

"Shut up," said Max viciously. He turned back to Karen. "What are you trying to say?"

"You know what I'm saying," said Karen.

They faced each other. Karen stared at him with her fists clenched at her sides, her expression nearing hysteria. Her face was feverish and part of her robe had fallen open to show her reddened, raw-looking body. Max, as if by magic, turned calmer, heavier, breathing deeply through his mouth: he might have been strengthened by Karen's loss of control. Outside, down on the street, automobile horns began to blare suddenly

271

and shouts erupted, and there was a sound of men running on the sidewalk below. When Max finally spoke, his voice was cold and incredulous. "You are telling me that you knew about this? That you knew what would happen to Shar?"

Jerry looked away from the window to blink at Karen, impatient and perplexed. If he had ever had any desire for her it was gone now, not because of whatever she and Max were saying—Jerry, accustomed to ignoring Max, did not understand it—but because of Karen's feverish eyes, her strained, reddened face, and the ugly, smelling blood in the bed. The doctor, licking his lips, watched in a nervous alcoholic stupor.

"Is that what you are saying?" Max demanded. "That you knew about this?"

Karen angrily brushed a wet strand of hair back from her face.

Max said slowly, "Murderer." He pointed his fat finger at her as if it were a weapon. "There is the murderer."

"Let's get the hell out of here," Jerry said. He looked frightened. "Do you want to take her or not?"

"I'm not going with you!" Karen screamed.

"There is the murderer!" Max said. "No accident! No mistake! There she is!"

"Goddam it, let's get out of here!" Jerry said.

"Shar is better gone out of such a world!" Max went on, staring at Karen. "Why, he loved you—he loved you more than he ever did me, all those years, he thought of you more often than he ever did me!—in spite of all I did for him, giving my life to him, anything he wanted!" He turned to draw in Jerry and the doctor, spreading his arms wide. "And no one believed Shar when he said he didn't know you were pregnant. We all thought he was lying—of course. But he wasn't lying; he never knew about it. You never told him. All done on purpose —done on purpose!"

"I couldn't help it!" Karen cried.

"All a trap—yes, I see, very slowly, finally—a trap, an elaborate trap—an insane trap— For what reason? Surely you are insane! And look at you there, look at what it's done to you! Your insides drained out on a dirty bed, a mattress soaked with blood! Two people dead! Murderer!"

Karen put her hands to her face. "I couldn't help it," she said.

"What? What are you saying? Only look at yourself! What could be worth this? How could you do it? And to yourself too and to that child—that you said you wanted! Insanity! Do you think you'll survive this? You'll live past this? You'll ever be the same again? Do you? Impossible! I can see that you're going to die. I can smell it in this room." And he took a great passionate breath, his nostrils widening and flattening. "Can't you smell it in here? Smell it from her? I don't know what to think—I am sick to death. My God, what a thing! What a thing! The fruit of your love is blood, the fruit of your womb —blood! all that blood! all you want of it! a mattress soaked with blood, your own blood, and Shar out alone on the track— his skull smashed, everything black, burned, all that blood—"

"Leave me alone!" Karen screamed. "Leave me alone!"

"Insane!" Max stared at her with righteous, passionate anger. The taint of deformity that usually qualified his talk was now replaced by a swelling, confident force; he seemed, in the last several minutes, to have become younger. "Insane! You were insane when he left you—I thought so—or you have been all along, to throw yourself at him so! To crawl after him! What have I done to let him go to you? What have I done to him? And he swore at me sometimes when he was drunk, saying that I was ruining him, that I was pushing him too far, asking too much from him, wanting him too much—that I loved him too much— And now he is dead! My good God—"

273

He backed away. His face was taut with rage and a queer, satisfied disgust. "Leave me alone!" Karen cried.

He followed Jerry and the doctor out of the room and closed the door on Karen's mad, hopeless screaming. "Now let's get the hell out of here!" Jerry said, already halfway down the stairs.

Before the race was officially over fist fights had already begun to break out in scattered parts of the grandstand, beneath it, in front of the stadium, and in the parking lot. Cars raced up and down the street, horns honking, the young people inside wild with elated rage. As the crowd left the stadium, milling around in the street, police drove up in two cars, sirens wailing. The sirens seemed to excite the crowd. No one wanted to leave in spite of the policemen's shouting, and some men shouted back, hidden in the crowd. The sun was burning. Suddenly the crowd began moving, swaying, in one direction; they stampeded out into the street, then stopped. Then something had happened in the parking lot: some automobiles overturned and set on fire. The sirens on the police cars continued to whine.

A fire was discovered down in the row of Negro tenement buildings and it took some time for fire trucks, inching through the crowded streets, to get to it. A great mob of people watched the fire, which was disappointingly small, and shouted encouragement to firemen who struggled with hoses, smashing in windows and doors with great columns of water. High-school students in parked cars cleverly turned their radios to the same station so that the firemen were accompanied by shrill enthusiastic music, turned on as loud as possible.

A while later, down at the boardwalk, a group of Negro youths marching to the beach entrance were stopped by some white men, but were apparently prepared for the occasion, since they took out of their beach bags and rolled towels such weapons as bicycle chains, greasy and flecked with dust, and jackknives and hammers and ice picks. People on either side of the fight drew back, some of them fleeing beneath the boardwalk railing and leaping down to the street. Automobiles drove up, horns blaring, radios set loud, and out of them more boys jumped and scrambled up onto the boardwalk. Everyone cried, Fight! Fight! Fight! Blocks away, the message was heard, as if communicated through the blood, and everyone ran to watch. In newspaper articles this particular fight, in front of the big gingerbread archway—like that of a castle—leading to the beach, was named as the beginning of the Cherry River race riot; but the riot had really begun before this, some insisted, as soon as that white auto driver was forced off the track by that Negro. More philosophical observers claimed the riot had begun even before this, with the assault and murder of a woman earlier that week—and perhaps before this, even; but such observations became abstract and lost the flavor of particularity, and so were not worth much.

By the time Jerry had driven Max and the doctor around to the back of Max's motel the riot was well under way. The plate-glass windows of the motel, stained green, had been cracked and even smashed in some places by rocks. Women ran about screaming, tables in the lounge were upset, and Max screamed: "But I am not Negro! I am not Negro! What is the meaning of this?"

Before the motel the crowd converged in the street, spilling off the boardwalk. At first most were white, but then the number of Negroes, counting women and children, began to increase mysteriously, as if they were coming out of the ground. At one corner a few policemen stood watching. To the aid of the white race a horde of men stampeded down the street, running with their knees lifting proudly and their arms swinging: some carried weapons of an improvised sort, chair legs or

275

broken bottles, and one young boy brandished a fishing spear. With a great medley of roars and screams, the groups came together.

The railing between the boardwalk and the street was smashed in. Windows in the big hotel were smashed, people appeared on the roof and threw things down—hotel chairs and lamps and wastebaskets. The crowd rushed up onto the grass of the new motel and kept going, the people at the outside pushed screaming into the plate-glass window and on through. A great section of glass shattered—the air seemed to rock with the violence. Max, standing at the back entrance, stared up the spacious carpeted hallway to the lobby and cried out in a rage: "We are not Negro here! We are not Negro here!" The people who had been pushed through the window lay screaming in the bloody glass, and others appeared, surging through the broken window. Some teen-aged boys, no more than dazed by the accident, slowly got to their feet, began to move, their eyes falling hungrily upon the luxury of waxen rubber plants and golden chandeliers and long, narrow, stark black and white paintings. Max saw several of them seize a fleeing woman and begin tearing off her clothes, and he turned suddenly to go. "What if this is an act of God?" he cried to Jerry as he scrambled to the car. "What if the insurance company calls it an act of God? What will I do? I will be ruined! I will be ruined!"

"Close that goddam door!" Jerry said. He backed the car around, pressing angrily on the horn. A man with a shocked, paralyzed expression had tried to inch in front of Jerry, driving a fin-tailed red convertible filled with children and two other adults. "Out of the way! Out of the way!" Jerry said. "Let me get through!" The man tried not to hear and was about to drive out to the street when Jerry took out his long-barreled revolver and shot over the man's balding head. "Get out of the

276

way!" he yelled, and the red car screeched, rocking, to a stop. Jerry eased past its fender and out to the street. "A hell of a thing to happen," he said. He honked angrily and inched out into the crowd, driving with black revolver in his hand. Beside him Max sat in a sweating daze, clutching his wrinkled shirt, and the doctor, in the back seat, lay down as if he were trying to hide.

Firemen were trying to calm the mob by shooting water from hoses into the street, but as Jerry watched, some men took the hoses away from the firemen. At first the furious water rushed up straight in the air, then it was under control and redirected back at the mob. The air was filled with screams and shouts of exultation. Jerry, his mouth dry, kept inching the car out into the mob—mostly women at this end, though there were some younger boys who might make trouble. The women jumped up and down in their summer dresses and summer playclothes, bright-colored, with shining hair and jewelry. One woman of about thirty, in a red sun dress that revealed much of her ruddy chest, pounded with her fists, hand over hand, on the hood of the black car. In a rage Jerry pressed down on the accelerator and drove out into the street. There were shouts and a vicious thudding at the back of the car. "My God, my God," Max moaned, clutching his heart, "what is happening? Is the world gone mad?" Jerry, twisting around, turning back and forth in the seat, now exhibited the skill he was reputed to have by driving with one hand and threatening with the other, waving the revolver at the surging crowd and shouting at them in a high, steady, unrelenting rage.

The mob was thinner at this end; it had begun to surge down the street. There a young boy had crawled up onto a first-floor window ledge of the big hotel and, to the great satisfaction of those who watched, grabbed hold of the bottom of the gigantic American flag and, kicking his feet out into space, fell straight down to probable injury and brought the whole flag, stripes first and then stars, sailing down on top of him. Jerry was nearly in the open—there were only a few children milling around, but they seemed to sense no danger from the big car or from Jerry's gun, which they probably thought to be a toy. He waved and shouted at them, "Out of the way! Out of the way!" A little boy stood picking his nose thoughtfully, staring over at the crowd; he glanced up at Jerry and, as if he had just thought of it, got out of the way. "What if it is called an act of God?" Max demanded. He turned around to appeal to the doctor, who lay on his stomach, his head cradled in his arms. "What will I do?" Max cried. "Who will make this up to me? An act of God!"

Jerry looked around to see Mitch, the young Negro who was Shar's second, racing straight at them. He was about to drive off when Mitch grabbed hold of the door and yelled into his face: "Let me in! Let me in! There's some bastards after me!"

"Get away!" Jerry said, slashing at Mitch's face with the gun. "Let go! Get out of here!"

"They're coming! There they are!" Mitch cried. He tried to reach in the window and grab Jerry. He thrust his sweating face at him. "There's too many of them for me— Mr. Max! Mr. Max! You let me in with you!"

"You f——g nigger!" Jerry screamed. He struck Mitch on the side of the face and, while Mitch stumbled back, Jerry stepped on the accelerator and drove away. "Goddam him! Goddam them! Goddam them all!" Jerry shouted out the window.

He drove skidding through the traffic-crowded town, pressing on the horn with the grip of the revolver. At a traffic signal he eased around a line of cars and went through the red light, blaring on his horn as if he were on a special mission. Beside him Max gasped for air, rolling his window halfway down and then, thinking better of it, rolling it back up. His huge bulk heaved and pulsed with the indignation of his fury. "What of the insurance company! What lawyers they have! With Shar it is all right—who could guess that was a suicide today? But with our motel— They will call it an act of God!" he wept bitterly. "There is no escape from injustice!"

In the back of a restaurant near the boardwalk, squatting on his plump thighs in the grimy women's rest room, the ex-college student Ponzi was trying to hush a little girl's screaming by putting his fingers to his lips and blowing out his cheeks. "No, no!" he cried. "Do you want them to hear you? Do you want them to break in here?" The girl's mother, a well-dressed, trim, impersonal woman of about thirty-five, held the screaming girl against her stomach. "Stop her! Please stop her!" Ponzi begged.

There were screams in the street. The windows in the restaurant had been smashed long ago, but occasionally sounds of destruction—tables being tipped over, china broken—tripped Ponzi's heart and set him sweating twice as much as usual. He had his back to the door, which began to open slowly, pushing him forward. He cried, "Who is it? Keep out of here! Keep out!"

He put his feet against a sink and pushed back, but the door, after a momentary relapse, continued coming in. Someone was pleading on the other side. Ponzi stood suddenly and opened the door. "Who is it? Get in here, then, and keep quiet! Keep quiet!" He looked down to see a man crawling in. The man was thin and nervous, wearing a bright plaid sport shirt and sunglasses. "They're killing someone," he said. "I saw them. I can't get out. They're killing someone out there."

The little girl began to scream convulsively. Her mouth

279

opened until Ponzi thought it would envelop her whole face, draining all her features into it, swallowing them. "No, no!" Ponzi cried. He leaped forward and put his hand over the girl's mouth. "Don't let her do that—make her be quiet!" The little girl kicked him viciously in the leg, whipped her face aside, and began a series of short, breathless screams that rose higher and higher. Ponzi, white-faced, staggered back to the wall and sat down heavily.

He had run into the restaurant to hide from the crowd, which had formed out of nowhere in only a few minutes. One minute the boardwalk had been filled with people as usual, perhaps not so many as usual, and the next minute something had happened and people were coming from all directions, running, riding bicycles, screeching to stops in cars. Ponzi, gaping, had been shoved from place to place. Someone had struck him in the stomach and he had nearly been sick, doubled over with pain and astonishment. Then, when he had straightened, when he could breathe again, he found himself looking at a group of young men his own age who were methodically beating to a pulp the face of a Negro man—the Negro's screams, like the little girl's, had risen higher and higher until Ponzi joined them, screaming himself, and staggering backward. A woman with sunglasses pushed him on the chest and laughed, showing bright, even teeth. Ponzi had fled into the nearest doorway.

The little man with the sunglasses breathed rapidly, like a rabbit. "I can't get out," he murmured to himself. "My car is out there. My car is out there." The little girl, a pretty child with long red hair, a little tangled now, gasped and wheezed for breath. Her mother did not seem to know how to express fear or horror, but looked only bewildered, as if she were trying to remember the names of Ponzi and the little man but could not. She stood smartly in white high heels, back against the damp, defaced wall, as if she were waiting under shelter for the rain to stop. "The police will be here," she said, petting her child's hair. "They're here now. I saw some coming."

Another crash came from the front of the restaurant. An automobile horn sounded, as if someone were trying to drive a car into the building. There were shouts and scufflings and, from a distance, a siren. Ponzi's hands were trembling and his knees were shaking so that he could see them, in spite of the thick dirty trousers he wore. He tried to cover them with his hands before anyone saw. "Did you see the race?" he cried. "A beautiful race! Beautiful day! That was a killer that got killed there today—his soul goes straight to hell! Down there in the frozen mud!" Only the little girl, blinking suspiciously, looked at Ponzi. "What am I doing here? Why did I come here?" Ponzi said, his big hands over his knees. "The sea is such a beautiful sight, and—and there was someone I wanted to see too— She's out there somewhere." Babbling, he took something out of his trouser pockets: his wallet, a dirty comb, loose change and dollar bills, and some crumpled color postcards. He picked up the postcards and stared at them, trying to read the small print. "Cherry River! Where the scenic Cherry River empties into the Ocean! A resort area! Amusements—a midway—nightclubs! An annual motor-racing event!"

He dropped one of the cards and picked it up again, trembling. He muttered to himself: "I've got to send these home. Or call home. They're waiting for me." Then, louder, he said: "The sea is such a beautiful sight! Beautiful to behold, beautiful to submerge yourself in! I could spend my life overlooking the sea! Miles and miles of waves, and they never stop—it wouldn't freeze, I don't think. What would happen to the fish then? A beautiful sight in summer! But you wouldn't want to go too far out in it. Because of the fish." The little man with the sunglasses was staring in terror at Ponzi. Ponzi absorbed his fright and began trembling all the more. His pants were

281

wet with perspiration. He went on quickly, while he still had the attention of the man, and of the woman and her child, "Because of the fish! Certainly! Farther out, miles out where it's truly deep, and all the way out—all so deep—there are these fish swimming all the time, sharks and all; and smaller fish made for them to eat, and smaller ones those eat, and other things—long things—like worms, all kinds of worms, thirty feet long! What do you think of that, little girl! Thirty feet long! Would you have thought so from looking at the top? But it's fine to look at from shore. We live on shore. In the hallway between our living room and kitchen at home there's an old painting of the ocean done by my grandfather himself— seventy years old when he did it, what do you think of that! White caps and blue waves and blue sky and white clouds! What do you think of that!"

Unaccountably, Ponzi began crying. The postcards slipped through his fingers and with them he felt his mind slip, falling to the dirty floor, lost with the crumpled-up hand towels of brown paper and bobby pins and used Kleenex and strands and balls of hair, most of it brown. He thought of the girl and saw her mobbed and torn apart, golden hair, fair, pale skin, innocence, beauty—all—and sympathy, moreover, and perhaps the beginning of love for him: "You have suffered," she had told him. "No one saw that before!" Ponzi cried angrily, shaking his fists at the frightened people. "No one understood! I'm going to go out and save her—save her—I'll go out and—" He muttered righteously, distorting his mouth to mimic the little girl's widening, lengthening mouth. But he did not move. His plump body shoved up tight against the wall, his legs in the filthy trousers outspread, he looked as if he were ready to sit there for some time. "I'll go out and save her from them!" he cried, angrily and helplessly.

•

Hearing the noise, Karen had left the room and crept slowly down the stairs, holding the railing. Her legs were weak and a buzzing had begun in her head. She was barefoot and held the robe tightly around her, as if she were cold; she stared straight before her at the high old-fashioned door, which had been left slightly ajar in Max's haste at leaving. The rest of the boardinghouse seemed to be empty.

Karen opened the door and stepped out onto the porch. Men were running down the middle of the street: two Negro men. Karen thought she saw something flash about them, perhaps the blade of a knife. A pick-up truck turned the corner and raced down the street, but now the Negroes were gone, hidden behind buildings, and the men in the pick-up truck roared past. The horn was blowing steadily. In the back of the truck a small horde of people, young boys and men and a few girls, stood shouting at nothing. There were bricks on the floor of the truck. The horn blew until they were out of sight.

Karen came barefoot down to the sidewalk. Her mind was so empty and so hollow with buzzing that she thought the sun would burn right through it. She seemed to be on fire: her body stung, burned from the hot water, her feet stung on the hot pavement, the slow seeping of blood in her loins stung, red-hot, creeping down her legs. Karen went out to the street and stood looking around, as if she believed she might see something. Her hair was wild and matted about her face. She thought her body probably jerked and flinched with the beating of her heart, and yet she could not have said why she was frightened, or if she was frightened—she did not know what was wrong with her at all. She could not remember where she was. She could not remember who she was, to whom she belonged. Looking up at the hot white sun, she felt its light go through her, shine right through her brain.

Firecrackers were exploded somewhere. Karen jumped,

frightened. Footsteps clattered up the street. Shamed into an awareness of herself, her brain still throbbing and confused, Karen sank to her knees in the street. Cracked pavement, lined with mud. She put her hands to it and pressed against it. The sun burned around her and for an instant she felt terror that she might be pulled off, away from the street, sucked up into the sun. She clasped her hands before her face in a child-ish gesture of prayer. "My God," she said softly. Her legs were wet with blood. But instead of praying, she was tempted at once to think of something else: she thought of Shar. On that day he had given himself to her. She thought of the silver car and Shar's face above it, his goggles, his tense grimace; she thought of his personal hatred for her beyond his impersonal infatuation. She thought of him driving— How the grand-stand of people would dissolve before him, before the speed at which he moved, how the sky would melt out of its rigidity— its surface look—as he sped beneath it, and around, around, and he would think of her: he knew that she clung to him across whatever space separated them. And slowly, deliber-ately, she felt herself penetrating through to Shar, she felt herself calculating what he must have felt—he would have driven faster and faster, he would have prodded the speed up —she knew—and he would have thought, perhaps in the in-stant before he knew he could go no faster, he would have thought of—

Karen cried aloud. "I can't do it," she murmured. "I can't do it." She thought she heard something behind her, but she did not look around. Her own sobs confused her. She held her hands against her face. "My God, forgive me," she said, "for-give me. Forgive me for what I did." Then she turned sud-denly—she saw some men behind her. There were three of them, in their early twenties, with cheap new clothes and wrist watches and sunglasses. They looked as if they were in a hurry, yet they had stopped to stare, one of them not even grinning, at Karen. She saw they carried knives and that all the knives looked alike. "And you too," she said, turning to them, blinking, "because you are just like me, I am just like you. We are all killers. We have the same hearts. We did the same thing. We need help, we need forgiveness, we—"

One of the young men, a pimply-faced youth with black sideburns and the beginning of a mustache, laughed shortly and scratched his head. "Well, now, honey," he said, scratching his head furiously and not knowing whether he should grin or not, "I mean, honey— What are you doing out here?"

"God forgive us," Karen said, closing her eyes, "God help us—help us—"

"For Christ sake," he said. They shuffled their feet as if they were about to break into a dance. "Honey, I mean, do you want some niggers to drag you off? I mean, is that what you want?" Their laughter was cut off at once, as if with the stroke of a knife, and they stood, scratching, on the sidewalk, staring at Karen. "For Christ sake," someone said. "It's a nut. A real nut. And she ain't no more'n a kid either—that's just a kid."

Karen opened her eyes and looked at them. They wavered in and out of her vision, in and out of focus, as if she were staring at them through rippling water. One of the men, who wore a farmer's straw hat, looked angry with her for some reason. He was chewing his lower lip as if he wanted to bite it off. Then the black-haired young man said again, scratching his scalp with five fingernails at once, "That's a real nut. A real nut. Honey—"

"Let's go," the angry man said.

"But, Howie, this here is a—"

"Hell with it!" he said violently. "I don't like it! Gives me creeps to see that— Let's go! We got some bus'ness to do!"

"But what if some niggers come by and—"

"Hell with it!" the angry man said, shouting at Karen as if he were arguing with her. The others shrugged their shoulders and turned to leave, the man with the straw hat turned to follow them, and, at the last instant, turned back to Karen and said with an embarrassed, hateful snarl: "Oughtn't to be out here dressed like that!" and, raising his black-booted foot thigh level, drawing his knee far back, he kicked out and struck her on the side of the head with a final, grunting, "Hell!" Then he ran to catch up with the other men as they walked fast down the street.

FALL

21

Before the massive, clay-colored building five miles north of Craig was appropriated into the state system of mental hospitals (there were twelve others, all, like this, in small towns or in the country), it had belonged to the widow of a railroad millionaire, and before this it had been one of the first convents in the country. The millionaire's widow had bought it after a long search for an old, abandoned, expensive home; she had apparently retained from her childhood dreams of castles, for she had the old convent remodeled with certain towers and points of battlement that suggested the Middle Ages. The ruined little gardens with their statues of saints and the chapel in the very center of the convent were kept untouched. The widow, whose sons had moved to distant parts of the country, lived there alone with an aunt related by marriage and some maids, and waited for the sons to come and visit, bringing their wives (they never came), and for tourists to come, only a very few, refined tourists, who would be shown graciously through the house (they never came either).

After the building was bought by the state, expanded and divided into hundreds of rooms, the statues of the saints were removed and the gardens leveled. In place of the gardens there was one large lumpy park with a few shade trees at one end and many benches, arranged in spots as if in an auditorium. A long, narrow sun porch overlooking this park was only emptied of its damp, infested furniture and rugs and otherwise kept untouched, for it was thought that patients who were not seriously ill would enjoy sitting there. For some reason the chairs on the sun porch were canvas lawn chairs, in striped colors of lemon and green and red and orange, and suggested sunlight and gaiety; a few persons would sit on the porch, staring out in warm weather on the small groups of patients watched over in the park by attendants, sitting on benches or looking for four-leaf clovers or playing quiet games or exploring the grass with bare feet, and in rainy or cold weather staring at the dismal uneven lawn and the warped wooden benches and the gray streaming of rain or cloudy light on the new brick wing opposite—a wing inhabited by people never seen, secret people, whose screams sometimes carried across the park.

The building was a mixture of old-fashioned rooms and hallways with high ceilings and new, remodeled, or added rooms with smooth white walls not yet water-stained. The foyer floor was made of cracked marble that could never be

290

washed clean, and the foyer itself was immense: it reached up two stories to an intricate ceiling, and in several places on the walls there were the indications of filled-in doorways to which ghostly staircases led. The towers at each corner of the roof had been taken down, and there were dull, erased-looking marks where they had been, as if horns had been cut off or were preparing to emerge. The front "grounds" of the hospital, in which patients sometimes strolled, consisted of a long rocky decline to the road, decorated in spots by patches of flourishing grass or weed flowers in season. There had been no wire fence between the road and the grounds until recently, when pressure was put on the state officials by the small town of Craig, or by a small group of its citizens, and a high twisted wire fence of bright metal was erected to protect motorists from the wandering old women or nervous-handed men who were allowed to spend sunny afternoons out front. Behind the hospital, stretching back for several acres, were the hospital gardens, where men were put to work with tractors or on foot; the gardens, property of the more aggressive, had always been securely fenced off.

The first time Celine and her husband—they had been married in May, as soon as possible after the trouble—came to the hospital to see Karen, they had been ushered along a hallway and into a small, cell-like room, no doubt once the room of a nun, where Karen sat up in bed. She had been pale and remote, smiling and unsmiling, and kept pulling the covers up about her shoulders though they would not stay there. A nurse who accompanied Celine and Albert, and to whom they were grateful for not leaving, remarked that Karen believed she was not well that morning, but that perhaps she would decide she was better and would take them for a walk in the park. But Karen had protested, saying she was sick, and with childlike self-pity had begun to cry. "We drove two hundred miles to see her," Albert had said hesitantly when the nurse ushered them out again. "Is this all? Is this all there is to it?"

The next time they came, about a month later, they met Karen on the sun porch. She awaited them, dressed in a dark wool suit and conspicuous high heels, with her hair pulled back from her face and twisted into a thick roll at the back and top of her head. They had noted her easy familiarity with the nurses and the other patients and the doctor himself. She was polite, smiling, charming. No mention was made of her father—she had written to him in the beginning, but he had not answered, a series of hysterical letters in a large childish scrawl that Celine had told the doctor had never been Karen's, not even when she was a child. The doctor had seemed proud of Karen, whom he called, in a low voice so the other sun-porch patients could not hear, his prettiest patient; Karen had flushed with pleasure, and there was something in her renewed vitality, something feverish about her smile, that made Celine think she was being introduced to a stranger. Later, in her room, Karen had told her in a whisper that she thought she was pregnant. While Celine stared in shock and dismay, Karen went on to talk about the friends she had made, the nurses, the doctor, the church she was taken to on Sundays, she and a young college student, a boy who had had a nervous breakdown. She talked back and forth to Celine and Albert and sometimes to the woman attendant, who smiled fixedly, as if on display. Then, suddenly, she had become tired; her face sagged, she could not keep her eyes open, she felt nervous and faint. After leaving Karen, Celine and Albert talked with the doctor, who discussed Karen in vague, abstract terms, dissatis-fying them. They had been shocked to hear that Karen had begged him and some of the other men, patients and attendants, to make love to her, and more shocked to hear that the doctor did not consider this strange at all. "No, no," the doctor had

292

said confidently, "her lover was killed. You know about that. We only gradually found out what had happened—the man killed, the miscarriage because of the shock, the involvement in that riot down in Cherry River. A very clear and external case, so far as I know—the most logical case I have had for some time." And he had smiled at them as if he were thankful for the phenomenon of logic in an insane world.

The third visit was spent in Craig, where Celine and Albert took Karen to dinner to celebrate, belatedly, her eighteenth birthday. Karen had lost weight and the clothes that Celine had sent her fit loosely; Celine saw that Karen had drawn in the waist of her dress and fastened it from beneath with a pin, so that it fitted tightly about her. Karen had a fierce consciousness of her appearance as they walked through town and as they entered the restaurant, looking icily about her, meeting eyes, seeking out her reflection in mirrors and store windows. But as they talked she lost her polite, poised arrogance and began to smile more often and to inquire sweetly about the wedding she had missed. "And Father, too," Karen had said, staring into her water glass. "I realize he is ashamed of me. I understand his not writing to me, or coming down to see me."

"He had a stroke after the . . . the trouble," Celine said hurriedly. "He doesn't get around very much now."

Karen had stared fixedly at the glass, or at her hands, and did not speak for some time. Albert, grown a little softer and plumper since his marriage and given confidence by Celine's usual smile upon him, tried to draw her back into conversation. "Doctor Trantam tells me you've been reading a lot. What have you been reading?"

"Oh . . . books," Karen had said vaguely. The sweet, purposeful evasion of her eyes was familiar: Celine recognized it and felt relief. Karen smiled at them. "He has mystery books in his office. I began with them. Then some medical books, the simpler kind, and books on psychology—favorite reading for the insane." She smiled but, seeing they were alarmed, she went on quickly: "But they are interesting. You know, in a morbid way. Most of them have case studies about people, other people. Then Mr. Harlan, who was going to college—he's a short, thin boy, about my age or older, with glasses—has some of his textbooks that I've borrowed, and other books about history. Mr. Broussard—that old man with the hearing aid—has some books on philology, but I don't know enough to read them; they don't make any sense." Albert and Celine, who did not know what philology meant, gravely approved this. "I'm getting better, I suppose," Karen said, shrugging her shoulders. She caught sight of herself in a mirror somewhere and stared across the crowded room with an embarrassed, guilty look, as if she had encountered someone she did not want to meet. "The doctor will tell you about that. Being allowed to come down here for church has made a difference to me," she said with weak enthusiasm.

On the next visit Celine brought along two of Karen's suitcases, and on the next—and final—visit Karen was ready to come home.

Karen packed her clothes and stripped her bed early in the morning, evicting herself from the narrow, colorless room so that she spent most of the time waiting on the sun porch or talking with the nurses in the halls. The building was damp and dark and everyone shivered. The doctor, back from his serious cases, strolled with Karen through the sun porch and talked of his student days—for some reason he had taken to associating Karen with his youth. He was a short, soft, serious man, of an age lost somewhere between forty and sixty. He wore plaid wool hunting shirts around the hospital and was given to taking deep, profound breaths, expanding his narrow chest, sucking in his prominent little stomach. There were many attendants in the hospital, a dozen or so actual nurses, but only one doctor—for some two hundred patients. Many of the attendants were local people, married women with grown children or sensitive young men who seemed incapable of doing anything else, and some of the attendants were even patients—older people who were not mentally disturbed but who could not, for various reasons, return to their former lives or to any lives in the real world. As the center of the hospital, the final authority on local emergencies, the doctor had seized his role with despair and humor. "I will miss you!" he said frankly. "So very few people we send out of here—rarely anyone like you, self-cured. A magnificent will power you have. Beautiful. The others—they are imprisoned, waiting to die. You saw the psychiatrists the other day?" He lit a cigar, grinning bitterly. Karen nodded. At regular intervals a group of private psychiatrists, hired by the state, came to the hospital for amazing fees, but spent most of their time playing cards in one corner of the sun porch and drinking discreetly. "They say it is hopeless, everything is hopeless, the only cure is death. I wish I could think they were wrong."

Karen thought it best to change the subject. The doctor complained about this to everyone who would listen, ending all his objections with a cynical, mock affirmation of what the psychiatrists did. "We may see each other again," she said.

The doctor laughed. "Certainly not! I don't want you to come back." They sat in lawn chairs and looked out into the park and at the sky. "May be the first snow of the year today," the doctor said.

The sky above the red brick wing was a hard, brittle gray, like chopped ice. Karen looked at it politely. "Yes," she said.

When the doctor excused himself and left, Karen remained, staring out at the empty park. She had noticed in herself a

peculiar susceptibility to the feelings of others, to their moods
—so, in the company of the doctor, she felt herself weary and
disillusioned, and she took care not to jar the doctor's senti-
ments. With the nurses on their coffee breaks she was an interested, smiling listener who had earned their liking by pretending interest in their boy friends and husbands. With several
of the other patients she was sorrowfully optimistic about herself—a pose they appreciated, since all at this stage of recovery
were jealous of their own advancements and liked to use their
wits to build up confidence in Karen. The sick, nervous boy
who lent her books and stared at her secretly, whose mental
trouble had been partially the result of a strict religious childhood, talked liberally of Catholicism to Karen, who expressed
fear of communion and confession and shame because of her
fear. "There's nothing to be afraid of," he had urged. "I know
how you feel, that you're not worthy. But it's wrong to feel
that way. I was taught that—it was a heresy in the Church,
actually. It's wrong to feel that way." But neither he nor Karen
went to communion, nor did they go to confession at the
church in town. By a silent mutual agreement they did not even
sit together.

Her early days in the hospital, in a locked room, Karen had
spent in a delirium of prayer and sexual excitement, murmuring prayer after prayer until her frenzy turned to thoughts
about Shar—she would cry aloud at the memory of his body,
his muscles and sweating back, his clenched teeth, his strong
thighs. She could talk of nothing else to the nurses, who pretended professional disapproval. During the first month—
which she remembered, now, as strangely dark, sunless, and
stifling with stale air—Karen had refused to go outside, refused
to leave her room except when forced (when she would turn
sweetly and viciously abject), refused to talk coherently to the
doctor in the hopes that he would decide she was hopelessly

insane. Somehow she knew about the ward in the other wing and had begged to be taken there. "I'm insane, completely insane," she had screamed at the doctor, "why don't you believe me? What do I have to do? What do I have to do?" Later, allowed to come shyly onto the sun porch in the company of an attendant, a girl her own age, Karen had pretended fear and excitement and had rattled the pages of a newspaper so that everyone looked up at her. She had smiled naively at them. In the days that followed, dissatisfied with them, angry because they did not stare at her continuously, Karen had squirmed to show off her body, had talked softly to one of the men—a harried-looking salesman about to be released—and had ended by upsetting him so that he fled. She had gone to another man, pushing the attendant away, and told him she wanted him— she wanted him to make love to her. Before she could be persuaded to leave she had cried hysterically, "You don't want me! None of you want me! You won't let me make you happy!"

Karen remembered these incidents with discomfort, but not really with shame; they seemed to have happened in a dream. She understood, too, that as soon as she forgot them, or seemed to forget them, everyone else forgot too. The boy looked at her sometimes with hard, unmistakable, and unconscious lust, but even he did not seem to remember what she had said. On her eighteenth birthday the dining hall had sung to her, and Karen, laughing in surprise and embarrassment, began to feel, for the first time, that the recognition of a birthday, the conclusion of a year of one's life, did have a meaningful and real function.

When Celine and Albert arrived Karen went to them and allowed herself to be embraced by Celine. She felt tears coming to her eyes—she brushed them away, trying to laugh. Albert stood a little apart, in a new overcoat buttoned importantly across his chest, carrying a hat. Karen's heart went out to him: his serious expression, his slightly nervous fingers, his tentative smile. But most of all she felt love for him because he had married her sister. "You look so nice!" Karen said to Celine. They smiled at each other, they laughed; Celine said, "But you're the one—you're the one to say it to." "You do look nice, very wonderful," Karen said. Her sister did look younger. Her hair was shining and soft about her face, her eyes were bright in a way Karen had never before seen them. She wanted to rush to Albert and embrace him and whisper thanks to him for what he had done; yet at the same time she realized that Albert, too, must be grateful—that he too had become a different person, nourished by the discovery of love. "I'm so happy for you," Karen stammered. She felt older than either of them —older even than Albert. The strange space that separated them from her did not diminish her happiness for them.

Riding back home on the long, frozen roads, Karen's enthusiasm waned; thoughts of home were sobering to her, and she understood the nervousness of Celine and Albert. She wondered what people thought of her in Pools Brook. She wondered how her father awaited her—what had happened to him. Most of all she wondered how the home of her childhood would jar her, unsettle in her the strict, precarious equilibrium between contentment and despair she had disciplined in herself. To reward herself for a day of sanity Karen allowed her thoughts to return sometimes to Shar, and most of the trip home was passed with her dreaming about him, recalling words he had said to her, actions he had done. She was able now to think of him calmly, though often at night her dreams would frighten her awake: violent, ghostly dreams, haunted by accusations of betrayal, that left her stunned and ashamed. But as they climbed through the foothills to the town of Pools Brook, as the ragged fields of old corn gave way to woods and rocky slopes, Karen had the strange feeling that it was into a dream she was moving, or returning, and that the nightmares that so vexed her, claiming her guilt, and the daydreams about Shar, were very real compared to this snow-locked land. How much more real the memory of Shar's breath than the look of that icy sky, a sea of ice! A hint of the Eden River, frosted even and white, rocks bare and cold in the colorless light, trees shorn of leaves, twigs and branches shocked into rigidity: an unreal land. As they turned onto the road leading home the sensation of unreality deepened. Karen felt intoxicated with the cold brittle look of things. Impossible that she was returning! Impossible she could return to it as herself, see it as she had once seen it—for in spite of what she had endured, this land had not changed, even to her vision. There was the ruin of the water mill on the old shallow creek; and the Harnacks' farmhouse with an old wreck of an automobile under an apple tree in the yard—the rope swing, limp and rotten, the Harnack children played with in summer; there was the beginning of her father's land, a big spread of woods with NO TRESPASSING signs like slaps across the mouth. Empty woods, black trees, no hint of life. There were pastures with stiffened grass, and old creek beds gone dry, meandered away from water; there were lonely, abandoned shanties back in fields, and now the big old bridge up ahead with the board floor that would seem to jump up at cars that passed, rattling and grumbling. Karen stared in fascination at the bridge as it loomed up above them. From that high rusted beam Shar and her brothers had jumped, holding their noses, falling straight as stones, afraid even to kick their skinny white legs. And there was the scarred grass beside the road and the twisted guard rails—still not fixed—where Shar's fancy automobile had skidded off the road while Karen screamed in hysteria. The car was gone; grass had recovered, grown up straight again and now frozen with the cold, as if nothing had ever happened.

"Now I am home," Karen said. They got out of the car. Albert, grateful for Karen's suitcases, busied himself with them. "Now I am back." The big house looked exactly like something in a dream. Yet it could not have been a dream, for Karen knew every room inside it, the look of every ceiling, every corner, and especially the look of her own room with its windows facing east. "We've done a little something to your room," Celine said. "I hope you'll like it. Albert did the painting and I thought that something bright—your old curtains were a little faded—"

"Thank you," Karen murmured. They climbed the steps to the house. Behind, the big trees listened, stiff as if frozen out of their life, limbs outspread in caution. The sky was hard and white. Because it was nearly winter Karen could see far, through leafless trees and skeletal bushes, to the abrupt horizon a few miles away; and to her right, rearing out of the quiet ground, was the cemetery with its secluded gravestones. The unreality of the land perplexed Karen. Was it a betrayal? No ground is holy, no land divine, but that we make it so by an exhausting, a deadly straining of our hearts.

At the top of the steps they paused, as if needing rest. Karen's heart had begun to pound hard. Absurd to be frightened of her own home, her own childhood—absurd to be cold with terror when it was only her father who awaited her, whose command she had so well fulfilled. But Karen gripped Celine's arm and cried, with such anguish that Albert had to look away, "Help me. Please help me. Please don't leave me."

22

The first day was spent by Karen in her room, unpacking her suitcases, putting away clothes, while Celine talked to her cheerfully. Nothing was said of her father; Karen supposed she would see him at dinner. She listened for him in the house, but had heard nothing. "And what about Jack?" Karen said. "Jack?" Celine said hurriedly. "He's down at the capitol. He's in the legislature." "I'm glad to hear he's done well," said Karen. "He was married," Celine said hesitantly, "after the election, I think. . . . It's no one we know."

She waited for Karen to reply, or to indicate something by her expression, but Karen felt nothing. She had not thought of Jack until that moment—their long good-byes, their walks, their staring at each other meant nothing; Karen did not think she could even recall his face. "He was over around Easter-time, to talk to Pa," Celine said, as if leading Karen on.

But Karen's mind skipped past. "Tell me everything about the family," she said. Celine looked up in surprise, for Karen had never cared anything about the family—it had been one of her cute, unforgivable tricks to pretend not to know the names of her little nephews and nieces. "I want to know every-thing," she said. She sat on the edge of her bed and clasped her arms around her legs. A thin, mild-featured girl, Celine thought, and in the abrupt light from the window it was only from time to time—a certain slanting of her eyes, a turn of her head—that Karen's supposed beauty showed itself. "I want to know it all, as if I had never been gone," she said.

Karen did not see her father that day—it turned out that he had dinner in his room. Karen was astonished, and Celine and Albert embarrassed. They ate in the old-fashioned dining room and from time to time Karen stared up at herself in the mirror of an old cabinet facing her. She remembered when her image had peeped up at itself over the top of the cabinet shelf, a child's face peering with great interest at its chewing mouth. The cabinet was made of dark, rich mahogany, with many small windows of glass in it protecting the frail white glass-ware inside. Karen saw the cabinet for the first time: in the years she had sat at the table, in this exact position, she had never really seen it. A sudden wave of fear engulfed her, as if she had missed many things—she gripped the edge of the table, as she had gripped the hot dirty pavement of a street some-where—she could not remember when—afraid of falling away, being sucked away. Celine and Albert talked cheerfully; Albert was describing a dance they had chaperoned at the high school only the week before. "Yes, yes, I'm going back to school," Karen interrupted, as if this was what they were talking about. They looked at her in solemn perplexity. "I'll go back to school next year," Karen said. "That's very fine," Celine said without enthusiasm—thinking, no doubt, of rumors and whispers and Karen losing her mind, screaming, tearing off her clothes. "You can take my courses then," Albert said. He went on to describe his method of teaching geometry, and Karen's mind wandered. She felt a sly, grateful pleasure at having brought herself back so easily—merely talking to them, claiming her humanity, her kinship to these strangers: with their stares they reinstated her.

As if to aid in Karen's redemption—her consciousness of herself as a human being—many eyes and mouths and gesturing hands appeared in the next several days. First the closer brothers and sisters. They happened over after dinner one night, as if by accident: Ed and his wife Penny and their baby Billy Ray and their two older boys, and Ed's best friend among his brothers, Stewart, with his big-boned wife Sarah (as pregnant as she might be) and their five children—nameless, look-alike children. The next day there was the oldest sister, alone, and cousins from the neighborhood, and aunts and uncles; which were blood relations and which were not Karen could not recall. Their efforts to avoid hurting Karen and yet—yet—to insist upon her separateness, her oddity, were obvious to Karen, and though she responded at first with polite enthusiasm, she found herself as time went by reassuming her old role, staring at windows while they talked, dreaming of the land outside or of nothing at all. "You always were the queerest one of them," someone had told her years ago. Now Karen remembered the remark with interest. Perhaps she had always been unbalanced, always weak mentally and emotionally. Certainly her stubborn strength might be no more than an indication of an underlying weakness: the fear of change, of losing faith, of losing herself. Karen had always thought that the lives of her sisters and brothers and cousins and aunts and uncles were unraveled and raveled back up, neatly, without fuss, whenever they got together—no secrets there, no shameful corners. When their lives lay on the old parlor rug like strands of yarn in danger of being entangled Karen had felt almost with terror that if she were to give herself to them, to release herself, she would be lost within them; when it came time to retrieve her life, identify herself, she would grope and come back with someone else's life—that of her ever-pregnant sister-in-law, who was marveling now at how healthy she felt, "strong as a horse," and how the baby would turn around in her, she was certain of it in spite of what the doctor said. "He turns around like you do in bed. Turns over and around, trying to get comfortable. Oh, he'll be a devil!" she cried.

On the third day Karen's father came down to dinner. Karen, who had thought him seriously ill, was surprised to hear his footsteps on the stairs—almost the same as before, heavy and arrogant. She was sitting by the fireplace being attended by some sisters and brothers, who talked mostly to one another, and when she heard her father coming, she turned cold. She looked around for Celine, but Celine was in the kitchen. "Father is coming," Karen said. She had interrupted conversations. Since some of the talk had been about the farm —speculations about how it would be divided at Herz's death —her brothers were grateful to her, and smiled and lit pipes and cigars and crossed their long legs.

Herz came into the room rubbing his stomach—before-dinner buffoonery that Karen remembered with a shock. But the real shock of the moment was her father himself. He had aged, he was old—an old man, like any old man; his clothes hung a little loose on him, particularly his trousers. He wore clothes that needed cleaning, heavy winter overalls and a wool jacket of bright red and tan plaid that he called his hunting jacket. His face was thinner: cheeks hollowed as if his teeth had disappeared, eyes blinking suspiciously and cheerfully at them, heavy crease lines on his forehead. Karen stared at him. So this is what Shar has done to him, she thought; and she saw them again, facing each other in murderous anger, two killers who had killed each other. The bitter justice of it appealed to her! "But what have I done? What is my place here? What have I become?" Karen wanted to cry at him. She wanted to run to him—to seize him, embrace him, to beg forgiveness from him or to scream hysterically into his face.

But nothing happened. Herz's appearance was apparently the signal for dinner, or would be; he would demand it. Karen followed the others to the dining room. Surely at dinner her father could not avoid her, since she sat at his right hand. But nothing happened at dinner either—it was filled with outbursts of merriment, witticisms, advice from Herz to his sons on farming, accepted in dutiful silence. Karen saw that her father did not eat what the rest of them did, but had a special plate of something with gravy poured over it: soft pieces of meat that looked as if they had already been chewed. With his eyes frozen in concentration, he ate it. Dribbles of gravy appeared on his chin but no one, not even Celine, seemed to notice; Karen understood that her father, for the moment, was happy.

After the others had left that night Celine helped him to his chair by the fireplace. Once at the chair he jerked his arm away from her and made a face. "Fussing over nothing!" he grumbled. Karen sat on the sofa and stared into the fire. Her mind was hollow and she remembered with dull surprise that she had ever been capable of feeling. "How was the ride up here?" Herz said to her. He lit his pipe and sucked viciously at it. "It was fine," Karen said. "Albert drives very well, very slowly," Celine said. Albert, who sat off to one side with his hands in his lap, was visibly flattered.

And that was the end of that day.

23

Sunday morning in church: Karen knelt on the hard kneeling bench, hands clasped up before her mouth, eyes lowered. When the Herzes had come into church—some of Karen's brothers and sisters had come to late Mass just to be with them —Karen had felt eyes turning discreetly upon them as they marched up the aisle to the Herz pew. There were gangling men and red-faced, smiling women, a dozen children of all sizes, Celine walking proudly with Albert (who was not Catholic but hinted at becoming one), old Herz himself with a new winter overcoat on top of which his thin neck and head were balanced precariously, turning to nod at acquaintances. Most interesting of all this clan was Karen, who walked beside her father without looking at either side. She wore her black coat with the high, proud black fur, and the same black hat she had worn for several years—a familiar sight that disappointed many women who watched. Once seated, taking up a whole pew, they scrambled to kneel with a flurry of rosaries and prayer books and children's mittens. One of the smallest boys stood immediately on the kneeling bench and had to be forced to sit down. There was a sudden scuffle; a furious look; children were urged to change places and adults or older children placed between them. Then they fell to prayer.

Because it was nearing Christmas there were greens at the front of the church, decorating the little side altars. The scent of fir branches and the heavy, luxurious odor of incense mixed, a pleasant smell, faintly hypnotic. The church was a little cold. Somewhere a baby began to gasp, preparing to cry. People hurried in out of the snow, stamping their feet. A murmur of voices came from the vestibule. Children sniffed hard; people coughed expectantly. The priest—an old man with shocked white hair—appeared at the side entrance to the altar, craning his neck around to look for something. He made a signal: a boy on the other side of the church got up, scrambled out of the pew, genuflected, and with hands tightly clasped and eyes lowered, hurried up to the altar. Karen remembered when her brothers had helped serve Mass. It seemed a long time ago. She remembered the pained apprehension with which she had stared at them, as if by the strength of her hope alone they could be protected from error. . . . How strange it was, Karen thought, that her brother Ed had once been before the congregation, when now he sat so comfortably back in the pew, his heavy fingers holding a prayer book at which he would not glance—a grown man, a man with children, to whom the transformation from a white-surpliced altar boy to a grumbling, big-stomached farmer was no surprise. Beside Karen her father sat, fumbling with a rosary. The black beads were worn smooth and looked like flat, oval seeds. His nose had started to run because of the sharp cold and he wiped it, sometimes with a crumpled handkerchief, sometimes with the back of his hand. Clearing his throat, he made the loud, important, gargling sound Karen had heard other old men make in church.

Upstairs in the choir loft the organ suffered a fast, tentative run. Notes fled past one another up the scale and disappeared. There was a scuffling sound of people arranging themselves, then silence. Karen sat back and with her empty hands folded on her lap watched the backs of heads before her, a small sea of nodding, alert heads, bescarfed and behatted and bare, all the way up to the white gleaming altar banked by fir branches. The church began to fill.

From above, music. From behind, the sudden scrambling to feet that meant the beginning of Mass. The priest and the altar boys walked up the aisle, blessing the people. They stood, and as the priest passed, solemnly murmuring, his white hair vivid as if with rage, they crossed themselves and genuflected with humility. As if from heaven, the straining voices of the choir penetrated the rich, chilly air, and beneath them the old organ trembled with a dignity so profound it threatened to lose control of itself. Somewhere downstairs, a lone elderly woman began to sing along with the choir in a high, sharp, discordant voice, as if she were with malice parodying the music. As the priest and the boys passed to the front of the church there were final coughs, a hurrying to seats. Everyone was standing.

Karen was submerged in the thin splendor of the ceremony

as if in a dream. The priest sang the Mass, though he had nearly no voice, and the sound of the persistent, cracked Latin somehow reassured Karen. Now I am home, she thought. Now I recognize what I have come back to.

The church grew steadily warmer. As the altar light shone richly upon the priest's vestments the purple turned lighter, deeper, commanding all eyes to it. Karen stared at the priest's back as he bowed his head. Purple: the color of penance and expiation. Humility before oncoming mysteries. There was no fear there, nor was there hesitation or doubt: the priest's words, as smooth as an eye in a socket, would never stop. The Latin pressed through the old man's wavering voice, demolished and transformed his voice, as if it were an unleashing of sound stored up for centuries. Before its brittle splendor everyone must bow, kneel, forget himself. Impossible to remember an individual past when the Mass, with a blast of music and a whining, wrestling interplay of voices and the merciless Latin itself, cut through all pasts, erased all pasts. Karen awaited, trembling, the moment at which her individuality would die. She saw the long torturous nights and the days filled with self-pity and guilt sucked away, absolved of their reality—just as Ed was absolved of his childhood and need no longer think of it. The voices swelled with grandeur and love and pride in themselves. The organ, operated by an old woman, pedaled skimpily after them. Karen touched her father's sleeve and he turned to glance at her, surprised. She saw that his face was sallow and flecked with small black dots of dirt, but that streaks of tan still remained from the summer and from his past. His eyes were shrewd and calculating and oddly kind, for they smiled at her first, and then his lips allowed themselves to smile. Then he looked away and rubbed the beads of his rosary between his fingers. That rosary is as old as he is, Karen thought clearly.

310

The congregation limped through prayers, murmuring the unfamiliar Latin in waves of clarity and incoherence, like breathing. The priest's voice rose sharper, signaling his anger. On Karen's left her pregnant sister-in-law, squinting in her prayer book, tried to follow the Mass with moving lips, sometimes running her forefinger slowly under the lines. She held struggling secretly on her lap her youngest boy, who reached up to the shadowy ceiling of the old church with clenched white fists. Beyond her the other relatives knelt, heads turned this way and that, eyes scanning the pews before them or fixed stonily on the priest and his hands. Karen saw them with a peculiar flash of warmth. Their feelings toward her had at first puzzled Karen, but now she saw—suddenly—that their polite, easy discretion, their hints of reproach, expressed only through looks or finger tapping or impatient scoldings of nearby innocent children, simply disguised their love for her. That was it: they felt love for her. Not for Karen herself, she knew, for they had never had much patience with Herz's youngest, spoiled daughter, but for the Karen who had suffered to prove to them the justice of their universe. They could not but love her, who had strengthened their faith in the vague beliefs they mouthed and heard mouthed to them in the ceremony of the Mass: the sacrifice of the Mass was a distant, calculated ritual, and the perfunctory humility of the priest was for their eyes alone, but Karen's sin and penance and expiation had been real enough, and showed, probably in her eyes or somewhere in her face, the crushing justice of a moral universe. For this they loved her, though their love was nothing personal; for this her father would begin—if he had not begun already—to cherish her as before. Karen saw it with excitement. That was true! That was true! She understood them, she was with them and at the same time a little apart from them, and had not lost herself in the experience. About her the

311

music kept on in its appointed path, straining upward. The priest cried, *Kyrie eleison!*

Karen put her hands to her face and begged silently for mercy. She knew she was in danger of losing control of herself, of crying—for did not glimpses of Shar's face flick on and off in the corners of her mind?—did not glimpses of her father's bloody face, jaws grinding with delicious hatred, rush at her, call her to herself? "What have they done to me!" she thought. But then, as the congregation kneeled and was swept along to new prayers, Karen knelt slowly with them and forced her mind to stay clear. She would not lose control of herself. Wasn't her family, and perhaps even a sick, perverse part of herself, waiting for this?

She stared at the short old priest and thought, as if she were talking to him, whispering in his ear: "I will not give in to it. I know who I am. I have always known who I am." As if she were already at confession, already whispering to the strange old man—she had discovered that she hardly remembered him, though he had been in the parish for years—she tensed herself, felt her lips curl upward in the usual disdain and half-mockery with which she listened to her own confessions. "You must remember me, Father. Karen Herz. The youngest girl. I have done enough to end my life at eighteen, or spend the rest of it thinking; nothing in the future will mean as much to me as what is behind. Or I can go on with what they have taught me—they have initiated me into the communion of killers, murderers, who are staring right now at your back." Here she hesitated; was there not betrayal here? Did the skill of murder have to be learned?

"I can continue with it, with what I have become," she thought, staring at the old man angrily, "and begin this afternoon, when the dishes are cleared away, with the closest man

312

—that will be Albert. I can wear twenty pounds off him and make his eyes swim behind his glasses and I can make him and Celine tear each other apart if I want. And after Albert, one of the hired men. There are men enough for me to feed on until I lose my youth." As if he heard her, the priest turned suddenly and raised his hands to heaven. A bell sounded. The priest had heavy white eyebrows, like brushes. Watching his face, Karen went on, "And I can hurry my father to death, who richly deserves it, for I see now that he is a cruel, ignorant old man who has always disguised himself with strength; and now that his strength is gone, all his failings rush out, expose themselves with pleasure! Somewhat like a shell you find by a swamp, turned over on its back and wriggling in the mud, trying by the ferocious charm of its eyes to avoid the stroke of death—which no one cares enough to give it. Father! I can accuse him of my own crime and guilt and with enough hysteria I can convince myself that I had no part in what I did— that the filthy way that strange man made love to me the first time did not have anything to do with that man's death. . . ."

The altar boys prepared the communion rail. Uneven white cloth, oddly clean; it looked starched. The boys did not have the stately dignity of the priest or the gravity of his old bones, and so hurried with mincing steps, genuflecting hastily, crossing themselves as if chasing away invisible flies. Karen's sister-in-law hid a big yawn and her dull eyes brushed past Karen's face. But most of the congregation, including Karen and her father, waited very seriously. They bowed their heads at the ringing of the bell, they knelt, they touched their breasts with their fingers. Again Karen's mind begged mercy. She felt herself drawn along with the people, teased away from herself—even from the tiny germ of nausea that had accompanied her, secret in her stomach, for months. The past is done, her

313

father might be trying to whisper, and what is the past at such a time? What is the past when we are approaching the transformation of Christ before our eyes? "My Lord and my God!" No one could help exclaiming this, even silently. Here is a real sacrifice, her father might say, pointing up to the altar. You think you have given yourself, you think you have been fed upon—and so in a way you have—but still you are alive, you have health and youth and beauty. Be as bitter as you like, mind your dead lover every night in detail and wrap yourself around him in sleep, and later, when you are married—of course you will be married—deceive your husband each time you give yourself to him! But still you are alive and that is a miracle. You were not crucified and changed into flat pieces of bread—and if Christ were not God, but only Christ, only a man, is His suffering any less? It is more, certainly more; we men do not have resurrections. But you are still alive. Consume yourself with bitterness, destroy your life—but remember that all that you have done is your own doing.

Karen touched her feverish skin. Her father, his beads dangling forgotten, his eyes transfixed upon the altar, did not glance at her. "But he is an ignorant old man!" Karen thought. "Never even finished school! He is ignorant and brutal, a killer, he has no right to my life, and no right to judge it. . . . But he is my father," she thought, "and I love him." As the others passed out to communion she remained kneeling in the pew. Everyone in the row but the youngest children shuffled up, following the wavering lines to the communion rail. Karen watched them jealously and fondly. Were these her people? With what did they commune? When she went to communion next week, she would be giving herself to them; she would commune with them, share with them whatever experience they shared—whatever mystery it was. She recognized her home, her place. She knew where she was. "I can accept them but they will never accept me," she thought. "They know that something is wrong with me, that my mind is wrong, put together wrong. Am I to blame for that? Can I help my mind? It is insane to look for meaning in life, and it is insane not to; what am I to do?"

After Mass there was benediction, and after benediction, while the church emptied, Karen and her father remained kneeling. The old man muttered his rosary, moving his lips: he felt guilty because he had not finished it. His mind, like Karen's, must have wandered. Karen knelt silently beside him. At the altar the boys put out the back row of high, white, gold-tipped candles. The magic of the Mass had left, quite suddenly, but its odor still remained; incense weighed heavily on the air. In the sharp smell of the incense, in the low muffle of voices and footsteps at the back of the church, and in the vision of her father's unbowed, aged profile, Karen saw her future.

Her father put away the beads with a last contrite rattle; they stood. Karen found a child's grimy mitten left on the bench and picked it up.

They were the last to leave the church. Out in the vestibule several old women awaited cars, their necks thick and clumsy with wool scarves. Karen took her father's arm. He looked at her with gratitude—he was old, he did not walk so surely as he had once. And he said suddenly, embarrassed and impatient, "Karen, you are my girl, my good girl! In spite of what they say about you— You are my girl, my only girl, I forgive you anything you did, I love you."

His words stopped. He was breathing hard, his heart must have been racing. A slow angry flush came over his face, beginning at his ears. Karen stared at the swirling snow as they stepped outside: it turned, white and cold and innocent, like the disorder of her brain. "I love you too, Father," she whispered. He might have heard. He pulled at her arm. "Over there—there—" he grunted, pointing at a crowded car. "There they are." As they approached, a familiar face—one of Karen's brothers—opened the door to receive them.